White Out

Tom Sawyer

White Out
A Black Bed Sheet/Diverse Media E-Book
April 2017

Cover and art design, and layout by Nicholas Grabowsky and

Library of Congress Control Number: 2017939485

ISBN 10: 1-94687400-0
ISBN 13: 978-1-9468740-0-9

White Out

A Black Bed Sheet/Diverse Media Book
Antelope, CA

Also by Tom Sawyer

The Lighthouse

Fire Sale

The Sisigwad Papers

The Last Big Hit

Shadows in the Dark

Dark Harbors

From Paradise to Hell

White Out

Tom Sawyer

Storm Warnings

It was the dead of winter and a horrific storm was approaching. Coming with it was something even more terrible than the weather:

The Wendigo.

Once again and for centuries, it was on the prowl and searching for prey.

This time it was on the hunt for Man.

An eerie stillness hung over the Northern Lower Peninsula American countryside as a thick quilt of snow blanketed the landscape. A herd of deer waded through the deep snow that covered the clearing, scrounging for food. As they searched, the snow began to fall.

Being creatures of habit, they were on alert for any predator, with Man being the foremost.

They sensed Man was in the area, but knew that the closest were a very fair distance away and no immediate threat.

The deer could sense something *else* was approaching as well…something extremely unfamiliar and wretched. And yet while similar to the presence of Man, it was much more dangerous and sinister.

As the wind picked up, they caught its scent in the approaching storm.

The oncoming stench of death and decay forced all the deer to recoil and bolt for the security of the *deep* woods, just as the front edge of the blizzard began its assault upon the countryside.

As the last deer exited into the deep forest and the storm had worsened, an Ojibway hunting party reached the far edge of the clearing.

Waemetik, his brothers Nawautin and Waubegun, as well as their friend Needjee, had departed before sunrise to hunt for food and for plenty of it. They didn't care if they were able to get more than they needed, and that was a problem for the rest of their kin.

If gathering more than was necessary angered the Manitous, Waemetik and the others didn't care. They had left the village of their birth in a dispute with the elders over the very same thing. They felt it was better to have too much than too little. Waemetik would see to it that his family would not go without, even if that meant others had to.

According to the elders, Waemetik and his brothers had become selfish, and while gathering bounties, they had become wasteful and took more from nature than they should, and by the time they'd consumed their fill from the forest, the remainder of their bounties they could not consume in time had spoiled.

Now they were exiled to their own village where they now thrived regardless, and beyond expectations.

Yet with the harsh winter storm, there was no longer such a thing as abundance….

As the blizzard worsened, the hunting party stopped to rest. The ordeal of pushing the sled with their animal carcasses had exhausted them. They were so close to home and yet they were so far.

***

Beewun was worried. She knew the storm was on its way and Waemetik and his brothers were out in it. Even before they left that morning, she had been filled with a sense of dread, a dread like never before. She continuously checked the sky and the weather throughout the day.

As the wind picked up, she checked outside from her lodge with increased frequency. Her sister-in-law,

Waubigun's wife Meemee, had come to keep her company. She had brought their children over. Together they kept a vigil, waiting for their husbands' return.

As they prepared their evening meal, they listened to their grandfather tell stories to their children about the Manitous of the Anishinaubae peoples. He had just finished telling the legend of Pawguk, who mistakenly thought his sister-in-law loved him and killed his own brother to have her for himself. Yet in her grief, she took her own life. Pawguk then overturned his canoe out of guilt and drowned beneath it, his spirit only to be cast out of the Underworld and into the Land of the Souls for his terrible crime.

Upon completion of the story, Beewun once again rose and went up to the lodge's door. She looked outside to see no signs of her husband and his brothers…and the snow was getting worse.

Meemee approached Beewun and placed her hand on her shoulder gently, trying to reassure her. "They will be fine," she said softly.

"I am concerned," Beewun replied. "There is something else. I can feel it. Something bad is coming. I cannot describe it."

Meemee hugged Beewun. "Try not to be afraid in front of the children," she said.

Beewun somberly nodded.

Suddenly, an icy blast of wind violently forced the door open, causing both women to jump back, startled, before finally closing the door against the cold.

"Now let me tell you of the Wendigo," the grandfather said as the two women looked outside to see a blinding snow storm descend upon their settlement. Now Meemee was just as concerned as Beewun. "Of all of the beings that dwell in the world of our people, none are more terrifying than the Weendigo. And now it is his time. The time of the Wendigo."

***

After much effort, the hunting party had managed to push the sled a short distance away from the path that led to their village.

Once again, they had to rest.

Waubegun stopped. He thought he heard something large stepping across the snow nearby. His eyes searched the through the foggy haze, seeing nothing.

Then he heard it again.

A step. Followed by another.

He listened intently.

Waemetik listened again, then looked at his brother. "We should go," he finally said.

He turned to look at Nawautin, who was nearby and also listening. When he returned his gaze towards Needjee.....Needjee was gone, and then suddenly they all heard him struggling somewhere out in the snow and fog as a very bad odor of rot and decay filled the air.

"Needjee?" Needjee?" they all called out, recoiling from the smell.

"Needjee?" Waubegun cried. "Needj..."

Needjee let out a blood-curdling scream from somewhere above them in the fog and snow. His screams stopped abruptly as they heard ripping and tearing followed by terrifying and boisterous chewing sounds.

For a moment, they stood in stunned silence before hurriedly gathering their weapons from the sled.

Once again, they heard something large prowling around in the snow.

"What *is* that?" Nawautin asked softly.

"A Manitou?" Waubegun answered with uncertainty.

Fear filled the brothers as they watched and waited. They had heard stories of great manitous and legends from the elders, but never really expected to actually come to face one.

If it was a Manitou, which one was it? they asked themselves.

"What should we do?" Mawautin asked.

"Kill it," Waemetik replied. "For we could be legends. Then we push our kill home."

They stood ready to fight whatever beast or Manitou was coming towards them. They continued to hear it lurking around in the fog as it came closer.

Each one felt fear like they never had before. Being brothers and loyal to one another, they would not abandon each other to flee to their settlement.

The large mysterious creature let out a loud, shrill scream that caused Waemetik to drop his spear in sheer terror.

Waubegun looked over at him. "Are you all right?" he asked.

Waemetik nodded and quietly picked up his spear.

Waubegun turned back and felt something close pass by him. He looked over only to see that Nawautin was now gone, his spear broken upon the ground.

Before either one could react, they heard Nawautin's agonizing screams somewhere out in the fog and snow. The screams ended abruptly.

"I am coming, brother!" Waubegun exclaimed, trudging desperately into the dense fog to save him. "I am com…"

Waubegun was cut off in mid-sentence, followed by a loud, guttural and painful groan, then nothing.

Waemetik was now alone. He backpeddled towards the sled as he realized that the others were all dead. He held his spear tightly as he trembled with fear as much as he did the cold.

The dead silence was overwhelming and terrifying.

He could hear the large creature moving around and eating something.

Waemetik turned one way and then another to try and determine from which the direction the creature would attack. Finally, he decided to attempt an escape by running for the woods.

Waemetik heard the creature behind him. As he turned to look up, he was seized by what his people considered the most terrifying thing dwelling in their world.

All he could do was gasp "*Wendigo*" before his screams of agonizing death echoed throughout the forest and upon the ever-attentive ears of the deer herd, miles from the slaughtered tribesmen by now, all too aware of the abominable carnage they avoided by simply being attentive and escaping while they still could….

***

Beewun thought she heard a scream in the distance. She ran to the door of her lodge and looked outside. The storm was at its peak. Then she heard one last scream. Her heart sank. She knew it was Waemetik and the others. She ran out into the storm.

Meemee followed her to the door and implored her to return back inside, but to no avail.

"Come back, Beewun!" she pleaded. "Come back!"

She heard her baby cry and withdrew inside.

Beewun was joined by Winonah and Waubizee-Qaue, Needjee and Nawautin's wives. They too heard the screams.

"You heard them too?" Winonah asked.

"Yes," Beewun replied solemnly.

All three women stood together against the storm, silently listening for more screams.

The smell of death and decay filled their village. Winonah fell to her knees and became violently ill from the smell. Waubizee-Quay checked to see if Winonah was all right. When she looked back upon Beewun, she shrieked. Before she could take another step, her heart ceased beating, no warning required. She perished right then and there from sheer terror.

Beewun bellowed out from the top of her lungs as well, as something monstrous erupted from out of the dense fog that had descended upon the village and enveloped it, something alive, something colossal and ravenous. She was lifted upwards by this unseen beast, and found herself pleading aloud for her soul's salvation in her ancestral tongue. The pleas were to no avail and were silenced as the unseen thing lifted her high and tore her apart.

Winonah struggled to her feet, but stumbled. The creature outside began to shriek as the wind howled. Fortunately for her, her heart seized from desperation and fright just as was Waubizee-Quay's fate, not long before the beast discovered her also and continued its flesh and blood feast.

Hours later, when the storm had passed, Meemee ventured out of the lodge. She stood in the center of the village. The silence was eerie and unsettling. She noticed three large blood stains on the snow-covered ground. The smell of death and decay still lingered in the air.

Meemee bent over and a wretched sickness erupted from her gut, from out her mouth, and dissolving into the snow.

Today's Weather Forecast

Rachel Torrey felt nauseous.

Her stomach was in knots. She leaned over the toilet, wanting to throw up but not wanting to at the same time.

She stood back up in her fluffy blue bathrobe and took a deep breath. "Oh, God," she muttered, softly, as she held her belly.

She winced in pain from another strong cramp.

She could not be sick. Not today. Not on *Friday*, one of her busiest days. Her schedule could not be changed. At least not now and not for this.

She had a full day ahead of her. As a personal trainer, she had well-paying clients to put through their workouts. Besides, she'd labored too hard building up her clientele. That was the benefit of being what she was. She made her own hours and got sweet compensation for it.

She'd started doing this when they were first married. Later she went to college for exercise physiology.

At forty-three, Rachel was in excellent shape. Her light brown honey-colored hair and slender, yet model-athlete-like physique made her look a good ten to fifteen years younger than she was. Her athleticism could put many of the younger women to shame.

It had helped that she always stayed active. She'd lettered in swimming, volleyball and softball in high school. Even through four pregnancies, she'd stayed reasonably active. She had also fallen in love with and married an athlete from and right out of high school. She attributed her condition to good genes, a competitive nature, and a healthy active lifestyle she shared with her now-husband Matt.

But right now, she had a tough time standing up, let alone freestyle across an Olympic pool. Just limping to the bathroom had been a chore.

Once again, she doubled over from a severe cramp. She took a deep breath, then clutched her belly.

Flu, she thought as tears welled up in her eyes. *That damned flu.*

Matt Torrey was awake in bed. He knew it was still early, but not sure exactly of the time. He had heard Rachel pull up the covers and race to the bathroom. When she didn't return after a lengthy absence, he knew something was wrong.

Like Rachel, Matt was in great shape. Then again at six-foot-three, he was still built like a linebacker. He barely looked like he was in his late thirties, let alone forty-four. Like her, he had lettered in sports in high school. He had made all area teams in football, wrestling and baseball. His time in the U.S. Army Rangers after high school had pretty much seen to that. He was pretty solid, not only for a man approaching middle age, but a community college history instructor.

Matt sat up and listened intently. He thought he heard Rachel moan again. He decided that he'd better see if he could help.

"Are you okay, honey?" he asked.

Rachel let out a sigh. "I've got cramps real bad," she replied. "I feel really sick…It really hurts. I think it's the flu."

Matt knew that she had a high pain tolerance and for her to be complaining meant that something was truly wrong. He walked over behind her and gently held her belly with both hands in the area she indicated where the pain felt the worst. His warm hands helped. He knew the routine. Whenever she felt like this, he knew this was what helped to make her feel a little more comfortable.

"Thanks," she said softly, and placed her hands over his, loving him for his consideration. After a few moments, the pain and nausea passed. "Help me back to bed."

"Maybe you should cancel your appointments and rest up today," he suggested.

"I'll be fine in a little while," she said. "Just hold me. I'll be fine in a bit."

Matt dutifully helped across the bedroom. Once in bed, he continued to hold her. He remembered the first time he held her like this. It was when she was pregnant with their son Mathew and how it temporarily helped her morning sickness. She had also been that way when pregnant with their other kids; Mark, John and Danielle. He was proud of the fact of how she was as beautiful then as she was in her twenties.

Rachel took a deep breath and held Matt's hand in place. She loved him more now than she ever did. His comforting hand and warm body were at least helping her psychologically. She moved his hand and kissed it before putting it back in place.

'Thanks old man," she said, softly trying to joke around. "I love you."

"Anytime, old girl," he joked back. "Anytime. And I love you too."

Both laid there in a semi-sleep for a couple more hours to follow.

***

Brandon and Marlene Markway just finished making love and were lying in bed in each other's arms. Their eyes were closed, but they were not really asleep. They were just enjoying the intimate moment together. They had some time to rest before getting ready for work. Brandon wished that it was Saturday so they could just spend the day in bed. Right now, it didn't get any better than this.

After only a couple of years of marriage, they only had themselves to think about. A nice house, new vehicles and good careers. They were reasonably happy. He was a fireman and paramedic for Waterford Township and she was a kindergarten teacher in one of the Waterford elementary schools. They were reasonably comfortable when it came to finances.

The only thing they didn't have was children. While they both wanted kids, Brandon was more willing to accept what life threw at them and roll with the punches. Marlene was more desirous of children, especially since she dealt with them every day. She loved kids and was very good with them. To add to her disappointment, she had suffered two miscarriages in their short marriage, one just a year prior and the other only three months ago.

As bad as Brandon felt about it, Marlene felt much worse.

Brandon tried very hard to get her to forget the pain of the children she'd lost. He knew his actions helped a little, but the sorrow was still there in the back of her head. He knew that Marlene felt her biological clock was ticking, since she wanted to have children by the time she was thirty.

They had met when Brandon's station answered a call to help a child who was having an epileptic seizure. What had impressed Marlene most was how good he was with the boy, and how he explained to her class what exactly epilepsy was on his day off afterwards. It also didn't hurt that he was built like a linebacker. He was attracted to her warm and friendly smile and nice body.

He asked her out and almost one year later they were married. It had all been so fast, and yet it all had been so right.

As they were about to doze off again, the alarm clock went off. So much for spending any more time in bed.

"Shit," he muttered.

***

Another hour in bed had been enough for Rachel. While she still felt a touch of nausea now and then, the cramps had subsided and enabled her to get out of bed, shower, get dressed and start her day. She was feeling better than she had earlier, but that wasn't saying much. She nibbled on some buttered toast and some Coca Cola for breakfast. Rachel figured she could survive the day with only three clients to put through their work-outs.

"How are you feeling?" Matt asked, dressed in tan slacks, shirt, tie and brown sport jacket.

"I'm okay," she answered. "I'll make it. By the looks of the main bathroom, I see Danielle already left for school. I won't be home for our usual lunch date though. I figured it will just be easier to stay at the gym instead of coming home. What classes do you have today?"

"Michigan History from ten to twelve and Twentieth Century History from two to four," he replied. "Do you want to get dinner out? If you're not feeling well, why not make it easy on yourself?"

Rachel nodded. "Sorry about lunch," she said, leaning up to kiss him. "I'll make it up to you later."

"I'll hold you to it," Matt said, as Rachel smiled coyly, knowing what he meant.

"Have a good day," she said, twisting into her coat and grabbing her gym bag before going out the door to meet her client at the local Powerhouse Gym. "See you later."

"Bye, have a good day," Matt said before finishing off his coffee and grabbing his briefcase, coat and heading out the door himself to teach at Oakland Community College. He hoped that this semester did not give him as big of a headache as the last one did.

***

Eddie Temple had such a headache. He felt a little worse-for-wear after last night's sudden and unplanned party. In fact, he felt godawful. He drank a little too much booze and smoked a little too much weed. It was one of those spur-of-the-moment things where a few friends showed up with others in tow. While he didn't feel knock-down drag-out hung over, he didn't feel very good either. This made him irritable, which wasn't a hard thing to do.

In fact, Eddie was usually irritated about something. Most people at parties are happy and festive when they drink. Not Eddie. Liquor tended to bring out the worst in him. He was a living example of the saying: *instant asshole, just add alcohol.* When drinking, he would often become sullen and eventually outright angry about some slight, whether real or imagined. Some had come to call him "Volcano Eddie" or "Eddie the Volcano" because he could erupt up at any time over the smallest thing.

And often did.

On those occasions that he was fun-loving and happy, he still retained a mean-spirited sense of humor. He would often find a victim to humiliate, tease, and bully to the point of leaving the party in tears or wanting to fight him on the spot. That was just typical Eddie.

Eddie didn't like many people. He didn't care for minorities, especially black people. He wasn't overly-complimentary of women, either. He couldn't keep a steady girlfriend. Usually he ended up verbally or physically abusing them, or just blatantly cheating on them. To Eddie, women were useful for sex and little else.

Bosses, cops, and other people of authority weren't high on the Temple list either. This could be attributed to the many times he'd been fired and his numerous scrapes with the law.

In fact, Eddie did not like many people, *period.* Except perhaps his two buddies, Andrew "Belch" Furlong and Kevin Shannon.

Like them, he couldn't hold a steady job. He had just lost his last one for threatening a female manager and calling her the "C" word as well as other names. But that was typical of Eddie. Usually, he would supplement his income by dealing drugs, stripping cars and other illegal activities. He was intent on being his own man and not listening to some asshole telling him what to do.

Kevin typically worked at a gas station or some convenience store that he'd eventually quit after a few months. Andrew was a bit more ambitious, usually working at everything from security guard services to being a bricklayer. Yet, like his friends, he usually quit after a while to pursue some other vocation such as unemployment.

In some ways, the trio was nothing alike. Andrew and Eddie at least finished high school, while Kevin needed special education classes to do so. Andrew liked fantasy games, science fiction and shooting guns. Kevin liked sports and thought he was a better athlete than he actually was. He always felt he should have made the school's teams, but his me-first loner attitude never meshed well with the team concept. He liked to play video games and get fucked-up every weekend. Of the three, Eddie was the ring leader.

While different, all three also shared similarities. They had police records, liked to drink and get high, and seemed to continuously live on the edge. All three had also been told they would never amount to much, even by their own parents. And as all three hit twenty-eight, so far none of them had.

Eddie always figured that one day this would change. All he needed was that one big score. Right now he was waiting for his buddies, seated on the old blue sofa in his apartment. He turned on the TV and began flipping through the channels. He decided to pop some aspirins and washed them down with a lukewarm bottle of Old Milwaukee or "Old Swill" as he liked to call it. He returned to the sofa and began flipping through the channels once more, wondering when Kevin and Andrew would arrive.

Andrew said he scored some "killer weed" and that he wanted to come over and share it. He told Eddie that it was the best stuff ever. That was alright with Eddie; he didn't feel like doing much of anything today anyway.

Eddie looked at the clock impatiently and rubbed his blonde mane of hair. It was almost noon.

"Goddamn you fuckers, when are you coming over with the shit?" he muttered, still irritated by his headache. He flipped onto the Weather Channel where the weatherman was talking about a slow-moving storm system that was hammering the state of Washington with a lot of snow, ice and fog that showed no signs of dissipating and was heading eastward.

According to the weatherman it was a real monster.

***

In many ways, Cassandra Stern was a monster. Not the hideous-looking kind one found in horror movies; she was too physically attractive for that. It was her obnoxious, unpleasant and self-centered behavior towards anybody she deemed beneath her that made it so.

Which was almost everybody.

Very few did not suffer from her wrath. More often than not, she took no prisoners when it came to her vindictiveness. This general meanness was masked by her pretty face and well-developed body, which she used much to her advantage. She had cost people their jobs, or had gotten them in some serious trouble, all because they had displeased her in some way. But this was of no consequence to Cassandra.

She had also contributed to a couple of divorces, a nervous breakdown, the destructions of several individuals' friendships, and even a suicide with little care or regard.

That was classic Cassandra Stern.

For her the term "*bitch*" was more than a name, it was a great source of pride, a badge of honor she relished wearing. She enjoyed it more than anything else.

Right now, she was enjoying getting her brains fucked out by the sexual battering ram of her dreams, her rich businessman boyfriend, Drake McCormack, while her husband Max was out of town on business.

To her, Drake was the perfect man in that he was built like a Greek God, hung like a horse, and the fact that he was rich didn't hurt either.

She also figured that if Max was dumb enough to believe Drake was merely a business associate…well, that was too bad for *him*. Physically and sexually, Max, while not in bad shape, was no match for Drake. The only area where Max exceeded Drake was that Max was a warmer, more generous person.

In her own way, she did love Max. He was good to her and offered her a kind of stability and security. He never forgot a birthday or an anniversary and even sent flowers to her for no reason at all. To her, he seemed like a pushover. Then again, she knew he adored her.

Even if she didn't return the adoration.

She had desired Drake ever since their first meeting in her antiquities business. She had sold him a very old and valuable Persian rug. To complete the deal he wined, dined and bedded her. For her it had been a very nice payday topped off by one hell of a great sexual romp.

From there, the affair just continued.

Besides, after over ten years, the marriage had stagnated for her, both emotionally and sexually. She was going through the motions. With Drake there was a certain *chemistry*, a connection she did not share with Max.

All that mattered now was Drake thrusting away, helping her to achieve climax.

Almost in unison they moaned in ecstasy. A few moments later, he kissed her one last time, climbed off and fell beside her, both breathing hard.

"That was definitely a deeply moving experience," he said between deep breaths as she put her head on his shoulder.

"Mm hmm," she purred, still enjoying the moment.

"When does Max get back?" he asked.

"Tomorrow," Cassandra replied unenthused. "Tomorrow. I have to pick him up from Metro Airport."

"You still toying around about leaving him?" he asked.

"Yes," she answered. "Especially now, after each time we make love."

Drake smiled. "That's understandable." he finally said. "But don't take too long about the decision. I won't wait forever."

"It's all about timing," Cassandra said matter-of-factly. "That and picking the right moment. The time has to be right. For both of us. In spite of everything, our marriage hasn't been bad. In fact, it has been a good and steady one."

"Then why leave him?" Drake asked flippantly.

After a long silent pause Cassandra answered. "Because I want more than that. I deserve more than that. I have love. I want passion with it."

"We do have that," Drake said before leaning over and giving her a long deep kiss.

She reached down and caressed his penis, and noticed he was nearly aroused. Cassandra lowered her head towards his groin.

"What…" Drake started to asked.

"We have twelve hours before I have to pick up Max," Cassandra explained, looking up towards Drake. "And I plan on us utilizing as many of them as humanly possible."

"Oh, Drake replied, as she went down on him. "Ohhhhh!"

When it came to sex, Drake loved how Cassandra was able to make sure they got the most out of their limited time together. She definitely made sure of that. Soon they were once again having sex with an almost animalistic carnality. Desperate to fulfill as much of their own passions in a short amount of time as they could. But that was their affair in a nutshell.

Passionate.

***

Doris Madden had been very passionate in her own defense. Then again, she had to be. She was in serious jeopardy of losing her high-paying executive position. All because she'd ordered a man to his death.

Now she had to explain to the board and her superiors her version of what happened, which she did in very lawyerly fashion. The biggest problem was she felt little contrition or guilt. Deep down, she was angry and defiant about being treated like she was. Now she waited outside the boardroom, waiting to be summoned in like a little girl to the principal's office.

She seethed with what she perceived as the injustice of it all.

"You can go in now, Ms. Madden, the board is ready for you to return," the receptionist announced.

Doris stood up and silently walked in without acknowledging the receptionist whatsoever.

Once inside the boardroom, she felt like she was greeted by both a firing squad and a jury with a guilty verdict.

"Please sit down Doris," said company CEO Sam Michelson. Doris sat down at the very end of the twenty-plus-foot oak table. "We were going over the discrepancies between your account and others. Especially, the second in charge, Jim Brundage. Some of the board wondered why there was such a disparity in versions."

"I am not surprised," Doris replied.

"What do you mean?" asked the executive vice-president Ronald Bates.

"I believe there was a conspiracy against me with regards to the men and this incident," Doris said adamantly.

"Please elaborate," Michelson agreed.

"Thank you, I shall," Doris said, bordering on condescension. "I was brought in from the outside. Mr. Brundage was passed over after working here for years. I believe there was resentment from him and the men. Resentment that may have lingered and helped to magnify the event."

"Do you have proof of this?" asked Kathleen Morrison, a board member. "There were no records indicating this. There were no complaints or write-ups."

"I believe they kept it hidden," Doris replied. "I believe that is why there are differences in our stories."

"Let's say all of that is true," Bates stated. "Let's say there was a lingering resentment. How does that explain how Charlie Merrill died? You were aware he was on limited or restrictive duty right? That he had no business doing the job he was doing?"

"I will admit it was a horrible mistake," Doris said, matter-of-factly. "Even a tragedy. I wish it had not happened."

"You did not answer the question," Bates countered. "Did you know?"

Doris paused for a moment. "I may have forgotten," she admitted. "Nobody could have forseen that."

"Except Jim Brundage and four other men," Morrison said, reading over the notes on a clipboard. "We have testimony of five people saying they reminded you of his work restriction. We also have the testimony that you threatened him with a reprimand if he did not do this job."

"Is that true?" Bates asked.

Doris was silent for what seemed an eternity, but was only a few seconds. "I wouldn't say I threatened him."

"What would you call it then?" Morrison asked.

"A strong suggestion that he help out his friends," Doris answered.

"So, you told a man to do something you knew he shouldn't be doing," concluded another board member, Ken Carlson.

Doris didn't answer.

"Doris....we only ask these questions so that we may get all of the information to make a sound and just decision on this," Michelson said. "We have suspended the man who lost his temper and tried to assault you over this. We made a condition of his employment that he go to anger management classes until he is cleared by the psychologist. We cannot have that. But we don't want to lose a good employee either."

"But…?" Doris asked.

"But, we reached our decision after going over all of the stories and testimony as it were," said Michelson.

"So where do I stand with the board?" Doris asked directly.

"We were hoping that after all of this we would hear a bit more contrition and corroborating stories from you," Michelson replied. "Had we heard that, then we might have reached a different conclusion and decision."

"You mean verdict, don't you?" Doris asked.

"No, decision," Michelson said. "We did not come by this lightly. Because of circumstances and impending lawsuits, your services are no longer required. I will let Ron finish with the details."

"You will be given a severance package and a recommendation," Bates added. "Jim Brundage will take over for you. We figured it was easier to lose an executive than have a whole department mutiny and lose them all."

"I may have to weigh my legal options," Doris commented.

"You can," Bates agreed.

"I would not advise that course of action," Morrison advised. "If you go that route we will then be forced to charge you with a wrongful death suit. You will lose the severance and everything. So I advise against a wrongful termination. You will lose."

Somehow Doris refused to cry and remained defiant. "When does this take effect?" she asked.

"Immediately," Michelson answered.

"Do I have time to clean out my office?" she asked.

"It is being done now," Morrison said.

"So this was a set-up, then…" Doris commented.

"No," Morrison responded. "You set *yourself* up. It's time to take responsibility for your own actions and decisions."

"And now I'm being thrown out in the dead of winter," Doris complained. "Thanks."

"May I remind you that you are not the victim here," Michelson said with subdued anger. "A long-time and much-loved employee is the victim of your sorry-ass decision-making. Not you. I believe this concludes this meeting. Security will escort you out."

Doris sat there for a moment, seething with anger. Finally she rose. Within a half hour she was escorted out by two burly security guards with a cart holding her belongings, and seething with even more anger. It wasn't until she was alone inside her Land Rover with her offices' belongings that she broke down and cried. As she started the vehicle and drove out of the parking lot, she rolled down the window and gave her now-former employer the middle finger before driving off.

***

"Fuck you!" Richard Case exclaimed, raising his hand to give the widely-known, one-finger salute to a parent who was less-than-enthused about his language and behavior in his overzealous support of his sons' and their hockey team.

"Look, Bud, either watch the language around the women and children or I'll ask someone to have you leave," warned the other angry parent. "So….cool it with the language!"

"Tough shit," Richard barked. "You going to call a cop?"

"No, dummy," the man said. "I *am* a cop, and I'll have you removed for causing a disturbance."

"You try anything, and I'll get a lawyer," Richard said defiantly. "I have my rights."

An attractive brunette who was sitting nearby and also watching the hockey game spoke up. "Actually, Sir, you don't," she said confidently. "If the owners or the authorities ask you to refrain from the language and you do not, they are within their rights to remove you. So you have to follow their rules."

"Who the fuck are you, Gloria Allred?" Richard asked.

"No, I am deputy assistant prosecutor to the Oakland County District Attorney," the woman replied.

Richard was a bit shocked and taken aback by this small bombshell, and grumbled something inaudible.

"So, in other words, Bud, shut up!" said the man who had identified himself as a cop.

"Yeah, right, whatever," Richard grumbled before turning back around to watch the hockey game. "Goddamn cocksuckers," he grumbled in quiet frustration.

For Richard Case, that was his life. Frustration piled upon frustration. A frustrated former athlete and now a frustrated adult and parent of two young athletes. Such was the life of Richard Case. Because of the other parents, he could no longer truly enjoy the early afternoon game.

A life that always seemed filled with personal set-backs and nagging frustrations.

***

After being stuck in traffic for hours, Jim Summerlee had grown frustrated. Even moreso, now that he was stuck behind someone going slower than the speed limit. Muttering a few choice words under his breath, he damned the drivers in front of him for more than likely being on cell phones or some other technological devices distracting them from driving.

"*What was it about the white man and their electronic devices?*" he thought.

He could feel his anger rising as he made his way up one of two lanes on I-75.

Soon he began to hurl ten-and-twelve-letter names at the offending driver in front of him. He briefly wished that he had a tank to blow them off the road with a shell and then run over them. These were not words his Native American parents and grandparents had taught him as a child. It was not the Ojibway way.

After a few minutes, Jim was finally able to pass the driver in front of him. As he did, he could see that the driver was a little old man and beside him an equally-aged woman.

"Oh, God," Jim muttered to himself. "Jim, you dumbass."

He then looked over at them, nodded and smiled. They reminded him of his own aged grandparents that he was on his way to see. He felt terrible.

He thought of how his wife Fawn had gotten after him for this very same thing. Especially, when he was driving with his boys Jim and John.

Nothing this inconsequential was worth blowing your top over he decided. Especially not traffic, where it was not moving as fast as he wanted to. Yes, he wanted to get to his destination and then home, but getting that angry was just stupid.

He now felt a bit humbled and embarrassed by the experience. His heart sank a little from his own shame and guilt.

As he continued on his way, Jim wanted to see his grandparents very badly, but also dreaded it.

A Gathering Storm

Matt Torrey dreaded going into the staff building as he made his way to class. As he headed to the main office he could feel that something was wrong.

"Good morning, Sue," Matt said, greeting the office manager upon entering.

"Good morning, Matt," she replied. "Just a head's up, but Dean Serling needs to see you right away."

"Oh God, what now?" Matt asked.

"It's regarding the situation involving Professor Burns," she continued.

"Okay," Matt said with resignation. "Terrific."

He knew where a lot of the staff stood on the situation from last semester. He just didn't know what the repercussions were going to be from it.

"Just go on in," she said.

Matt entered the Dean's office.

"Good morning, Matt," Dean Serling said. "Please have a seat."

"I sure hope it's going to be," Matt replied, sitting down. "This is about Jan Burns, isn't it? How bad is it?"

"It's bad, but it could be worse," Dean Serling replied. "She wants to sue the college and you."

"That's not a surprise," Matt remarked. "I was expecting it. I'm just surprised she hasn't gone public or sought Gloria Allred's services yet."

"The problem is she can't," Dean Serling explained. "You see, she violated several of the schools' codes of conduct. We have visual proof and a lot of eyewitnesses. But, she still wants to sue you."

"She appears to have an anger management problem," Matt said. "That, or a mental disorder."

"The chancellor and the board aren't thrilled about the situation and want to investigate it further before making any decisions," said the dean.

"Look, I tried to defuse the situation," Matt admitted. "But she became verbally abusive and then physically violent, and I will defend myself as needed. It just pissed her off that I laughed at her extreme stupidity and she had no answer for it. When I avoided her flying drop kick and she fell on the floor and embarrassed herself, she became livid. She should have quit then….unfortunately for her, she didn't….decided to grab a knife and paid a heavy price."

"If she does plan on suing, will you fight it?" Serling asked.

"Hell, yes!" Matt exclaimed, starting to get slightly angry. "You cannot say you're Xena, the Warrior Princess and behave like a violent perp and then claim victimhood. Especially when the person you physically attack ends up knocking you out. I already talked to a lawyer. I'm rock solid there."

"Okay," Serling said. "That is exactly what I told the chancellor and the board. The school has decided to end her contract and pay her what she's owed for the rest. I will admit some on the board frown on violence against women. They weren't thrilled how you acted."

"They should frown about violence against *anybody*, not just women," Matt commented matter-of-factly. "She was, after all, the assailant and I acted in self-defense. They had better understand that fact before thinking of any action against me."

"I just thought you should know where the school stands," Dean Serling said. "It doesn't hurt your case that you have at least three videos of it floating around proving your story."

"Thanks," Matt said. "I appreciate the heads up. But, I am serious about any veiled warning or threat they may have as well."

"Well, it proves one thing," Serling said, with a slight smile. "You don't mess with a decorated former army ranger with martial arts skills."

"I guess," Matt agreed. "It also proves some people are terminally stupid too. I just wish it had never happened."

"So does the school," the dean agreed. "We also offered to pay her medical bills just to play nice. But please Matt, try to avoid any other altercations. The school is not thrilled with the whole situation, and it could reflect on you and your position here."

"I will," Matt responded, as he stood up. "I will heed the warning nonetheless. But I will defend myself when I am attacked, and the school had better realize that as well. It is my right to self-defense, not pleasing the politically correct."

"I understand your point." Then Dean Serling asked, "So….what is your first class?"

"Michigan History," Matt replied as he began to exit the office door.

"Have a good day," Serling called after him.

"Thanks," Matt said, and he left for his class.

While Matt knew the school would eventually support him on the incident, he was not very thrilled or excited about the veiled warnings regarding the whole thing.

Rachel Torrey was definitely not thrilled to be sitting in a doctor's office. Stuck in a small room wearing a paper gown, she sat patiently on the examining table awaiting the results of her tests. Thankfully for her, before she could get to the gym, her client had cancelled their session due to the flu. This allowed Rachel to make an appointment with one of her other clients, Dr. Samantha Ridenour.

After about fifteen minutes, Dr. Ridenour returned.

"Well?" Rachel asked.

"It's not the flu," Dr. Ridenour replied.

"Then what is it?" Rachel asked.

"You're pregnant, Rachel," Dr. Ridenour said. "Congratulations."

"You're kidding?" Rachel exclaimed, shocked by the news. "I'm 43 and have four kids already. Three of them grown."

"And you're healthy and active, with the body of someone about five to ten years younger than your actual age," Dr. Ridenour explained. "So is your husband. I ran both the urine and blood tests twice. It's accurate."

Tears welled up in Rachel's eyes. She was now even less thrilled than she had been when she first arrived.

Dr. Ridenour noticed this. "You had better take a few minutes with this, Rachel," Dr. Ridenour said, handing her a tissue.

"Thanks," Rachel said, sniffing. "Thanks for everything Sam, I appreciate it."

"That's what friends are for," she replied. "You've squeezed me in many times, it was just my turn. I wish you all of the best on this. I can recommend a gynecologist."

Rachel quietly nodded and muttered. "Thanks."

"I'll talk to you soon," Dr. Ridenour said, before leaving to tend to other patients.

Rachel sat crying for a few minutes before finally dressing and regaining her composure. She cancelled her other sessions and went home, somewhat depressed by the news.

***

Marlene Markway was depressed. She had just taken a home pregnancy test when she arrived home from school and it was negative...again.

She had taken one every couple of weeks ever since the last miscarriage, hoping for the best.

Marlene had done everything that she was told, both medically and non-medically in trying to get pregnant. She ate the right foods, followed her cycle, exercised, was definitely very sexually active with her husband and did about anything else that was supposed to help.

The only thing she had not done was relax. Try as she did to just let things happen, her desire to have children almost consumed her. No matter how hard she tried to relax, the past miscarriages were always in the back of her mind.

She hoped that their long weekend getaway during winter break would change all of this.

As she looked out the bedroom window, she thought the snow-covered ground looked barren and empty. This was how she felt about herself at that moment.

"*Winter wonderland my ass*," she thought. "*It's just snow and ice.*"

***

"Goddamn snow and ice," grumbled Milt Hudak as he struggled with his undersized, battered old snowblower, in clearing his driveway near Whitlash, Montana. "This is fucking ridiculous. Fucking storm. Come on Bessie, keep working."

Oblivious to everything except the task at hand, he had not noticed that he was being stalked as prey by an age-old horror.

Milt continued to make one pass and then another. Finally he came to a rest. He stopped, shut off his snowblower and refueled it. It was then that he noticed, as the snow continued falling, how quiet and desolate everything was. The birds and squirrels that had been around earlier were all gone.

He then noticed a very bad smell. It was a stench of rot, and decay.

"Goddamn, Milt, you had better stop eating that spicy Mexican food," he said to himself. "That is real bad."

As he started the snowblower back up, he noticed that the stench had become much worse and stronger. It was as if it had gotten closer. He knew then it was not the gaseous byproduct of his love for spicy food.

It was something else.

He stopped and looked around, seeing nothing. Just more snow and ice. He started pushing the snowblower. As he turned to make another pass, he came face-to-face with a nameless, indescribable horror.

Milt went to scream, but lost all control of his bodily functions. Before he could even move, the unknown terror grabbed him, ripping him to shreds and devoured him.

Milt's screams of agony, pain and eventual death were drowned out by the continuous roar of his snowblower as blood splattered all over the unmoved snow.

The beast had eaten and was not sated. No amount was ever enough, for it was afflicted with a never-ending hunger and greatly needed and craved more. This was its time, and the storm was its hunting ground. The dead of winter had arrived.

***

"That's why it is called the dead of winter," Jim Summerlee's grandfather Sam explained upon hearing the television news report about the suspected bear attack on a man while snowblowing in Montana. "It's not a bear, it's the Wendigo, Jim. There would be remains if it were a bear. This is the time of the Wendigo."

"Sure, Grandfather," Jim replied, not really believing it, but listening just the same.

"No," Sam Summerlee snapped from his chair. "Mind my words, Grandson. It is the time. Be wary. Be very careful out there. The Wendigo feeds on man. It is its time."

"I am sorry, Grandfather, I meant no disrespect," Jim apologized. "How are you and Grandmother doing? We've been concerned, especially being way out here and during the winter."

"We are fine, Jim," he replied. "There is no reason for worry. Please sit down and stay awhile. It has been too long."

Jim sat down across from his grandfather. "Yes," he said. "It has been."

"You have much on your mind," Sam Summerlee said. "I can tell we have much to talk about."

***

Upon leaving the doctor's office, Rachel desperately needed to talk to someone. Much of the shock from being told she was pregnant had worn off and she went through a flurry of different emotions.

Now she just needed to talk or vent.

She texted Matt that she would see him for lunch after all. She wanted to talk to him badly, but he could not talk to her now, because he was in class and of little help.

Right now, she was upset and needed a friend. She decided to call her best friend in the world other than Matt, and that was her sister Melanie. She knew that if anybody could understand what she was going through, it was her.

Melanie Becker had gone through an unexpected pregnancy at age 40 herself, with her husband David. They too already had three nearly-grown children, all boys, and they seemed to weather that storm pretty well.

Though their circumstances were different in that Melanie was pretty much a stay-at-home mom who assisted her husband with his carpentry business while Rachel had her own business, they could relate to each other's circumstances.

Now, she greatly needed her sister's shoulder to cry on, and reassure her it would be all right and comfort her.

Once she arrived back home, Rachel began dialing the number. "Please be home," Rachel said as she waited for the phone to ring.

For the first time in a while, she felt desperate and alone.

***

After only a few hours of being out of work, Doris Maddens felt a sense of desperation. Panic may not have set in, but it was damned close.

As soon as she arrived home, Doris began calling headhunters, the Ladders and other executive employment agencies to help her find another position on the level of what she had been doing.

Her severance pay may have been lucrative, but it wouldn't last forever.

Therein lied her problem, she seemed consumed by making the all-mighty dollar and a lot of them no matter what it took to get ahead.

Unfortunately for Charlie Merrill, he had the bad luck of getting in the way of Doris' determined quest for a better position with more pay. The problem was, it cost her everything.

She flipped on the television while she waited for some return phone calls and started watching the news. The weatherman explained that a major winter storm was heading eastward and it should hit the Great Lakes region by the weekend. He added that the storm already claimed three lives.

"Lovely," she grumbled. "You kill three with your goddamn predictions and get to keep on forecasting and I have one old fucker who shouldn't have been working, croak and lose a career."

The anger and resentment had not dissipated and continued to grow.

***

Eddie Temple was getting angry and growing impatient about Kevin and Andrew not being at his place already.

"Those two idiots couldn't find their own dicks with a flashlight and tweezers," he muttered as he sat flipping the television remote control. He finally settled on the weather channel, while he picked up his .45 pistol that he stored near his chair and began checking it.

After a couple of minutes, there came a knock on the door. Eddie readied his handgun and pointed it towards the door as he made his way closer to it.

"Who the fuck is it?" he asked.

"Eddie, it's me, Belch and Kevin," a voice outside the door said.

Eddie opened the door, half-pointing his pistol at his two friends. "Get in here," he said, closing the door behind them. "What the fuck took you fuckers so long?"

Andrew and Kevin looked at each other before Kevin finally spoke. "I lost my goddamn stash," he replied. "I think it was stolen."

"It *what*?" Eddie asked, pissed. "How the fuck did that happen?"

Kevin shrugged. "I think it was my sister," he explained. "I think she found my hiding spot."

"What do you plan on doing to her?" Eddie asked. "If it was *my* sister I'd shoot her in the fucking ass."

"I can't do nothing," Kevin answered. "She'd squeal to our parents, so I'm screwed."

"Jesus Christ!" Eddie snapped. "That's bullshit! She gets a free bag of shit, and we don't! Nice going dick-brain!"

"Calm down, Eddie," Andrew said. "I know a place where we can get some good stuff."

"Where at?" Eddie asked.

"Pontiac," Andrew replied. "I know a guy named Odell Gilmoe. He and his brothers deal here and there. It's not in the best neighborhood, but we'll get in and out."

"Terrific," Eddie snapped. "A bunch of niggers. This just keeps on getting better."

"It's okay, they're cool," Andrew tried to reassure Eddie.

"So when do we do this little transaction?" Eddie asked.

"Tomorrow night," Kevin said. "All we need is a hundred bucks."

"That's goddamn highway robbery!" Eddie exclaimed.

"It's worth it," Andrew said, trying to reassure Eddie. "Odell and his brothers usually treat me good."

"Okay, but I'm going with you," Eddie said. "I want to see who we're dealing with, just to make sure it goes alright. I don't want to hear any argument about it either."

Both Andrew and Kevin looked at each other, concerned. Both knew that this was not a good thing. Both had a very bad feeling about their upcoming deal.

A very bad feeling.

***

When Melanie Becker initially heard the phone ring, she had a bad feeling. Nobody ever called this time of day unless they were salesmen or the bearers of bad news. When she picked up the phone, she was surprised to hear it was her sister, Rachel.

She knew it had to be important because Rachel never called this time of day.

"Hi Rachel, it everything alright?" she asked.

Cold Front

After receiving her text, Matt wondered whether Rachel was all right and grew concerned. He attempted a call, but her phone was busy. Being preoccupied with class, he thought that he would try again later. He knew that she'd been feeling pretty sick earlier and figured that's what it regarded.

He decided to head home for lunch and check on her when he finished class.

The day had already started out eventful enough and Rachel being sick would just make it moreso. But that was life he thought, always filled with the unpredictable.

He thought about calling her again on his way home, but decided to wait because she could be resting and possibly asleep. Besides, he would see her soon enough.

Finished with his work, Matt headed for home.

***

Nathan Hurley was on his way home from a day of snowmobiling with his friend Denny Haslip in northeast Montana, about fifty miles from the North Dakota border.

Nathan had lost track of his friend on the way home in the blizzard. He figured, as the weather became worse, that Denny decided to head for home.

As Nathan made his way through a clearing, he caught sight of something sticking out of a large snow drift. As he approached, he could see that it was Denny's snowmobile.

"What the hell?" he muttered as he slowed down to check out the sight, confused by what he saw.

Nathan looked around, seeing no sign of his friend anywhere.

The he spotted Denny's white snowmobile helmet about twenty feet away. There was blood splattered all over it.

As Nathan came to a complete stop, he then saw what appeared to have been his friend's shredded boots. They looked as if they had been chewed up and spit back out by.....by *something*.

Fear ran deep through Nathan as he sensed an unnatural presence nearby. He thought he heard something out in the quiet stillness of the blizzard. He revved his snowmobile up and practically flew across the snow and out of the area as quickly as possible. There was no way that he was going to be the next victim to whatever it was that was out there.

He would not stop until he reached home. Never once did he look behind to see whatever was out there. Deep down, he knew that it was best that he didn't. Once back home and in his house, he was filled with a great sense of both loss, bewilderment, and the relief of escaping certain death

***

Doris Madden felt relieved. After being on the phone and the computer for most of the day since she arrived home, she had managed to line-up an interview. It may not have paid what she had been making, but it was close enough for now.

The only drawback to it was that particular position was way up in Traverse City and she wasn't thrilled about living or working that far north.

Doris quickly had come to wonder where all of her fair-weather friends and contacts were during this since she had not received a phone call. Then again, things were different when an acerbic personality like herself wasn't working and of no help to others. As Doris began preparing her resume and getting ready for the trip, she thought about how it could be a stepping stone to a better position.

Doris wasn't worried so much about the interview as she was about driving in the weather up there. The interviews were nothing anymore. She handled them like a professional. She knew that this time of year could be absolutely terrible.

***

The creature was still terribly hungry. Its appetite was nowhere near satisfied after devouring the careless snowmobiler that had driven right into its waiting arms. It was greatly disappointed that it could not make a meal of the other snowmobiler. It let out a growl of pain from its endless hunger.

As the storm continued eastward, the creature knew it had to find others to feed on while it could. That was the sum of its existence. It continually needed to feed. This unholy predator of man kept searching as the snow fell harder and the temperature became colder.

***

By the time Cassandra Stern had picked up her husband at the airport, the snow flurries had stopped and it had gotten colder.

"Tired?" she asked her husband Max.

He kissed her after climbing into the car. "Yeah, a little," he replied. "It's just good to be home. This traveling, especially in the winter, is getting to me."

"You'll be fine in a couple of days," Cassandra said as she drove away from the arrival area.

"I'm thinking of scaling back," Max announced. "I want to work strictly out of the Detroit area office and keep my travel down to a minimum. That way we can spend more time together."

Cassandra nodded. "That would be good," she said, while really hating the idea of Max being around more.

"I'm glad you like it," Max continued. "But it might be a little while before that could happen."

"Yes," Cassandra agreed, trying to sound encouraging while really wanting to scream about his sudden change of plans. "*Fucking great!*" she thought. "Do you want me to make any dinner?"

"Let's just pick up some Chinese," Max suggested. "We can have some wine and then go to bed."

"That would be great," Cassandra replied, not meaning a single word of it, as she drove them home.

***

When Matt arrived home, he was stunned to find Rachel, not sick, but sitting at their dining room table amd gazing into a photo album of their children as babies.

"Is everything alright?" he asked, when greeted by this peculiar sight. "I was worried you were really sick."

Rachel nodded. "No, I am fine," she said, closing the photo album.

"Well, that's good," Matt said.

Rachel stood up. "I'm pregnant," she said. "I went in for a test today. It was positive."

"What?" Matt said, trying to process what Rachel just said.

"I'm pregnant," she repeated, as she walked towards him and hugged him. "I'm between four and eight weeks."

Matt took a deep breath and exhaled. "Okay," he said, looking at her tear-filled eyes and hugging her. "Is there anything I can do? Will you be alright?"

"Yes," she said, her voice getting hoarse and froggy as she tried to keep from crying.

"You're not alright," he said, noticing a difference in Rachel. "Is there something wrong?"

Rachel looked up at Matt with tear-filled eyes. "I don't want to be pregnant," she muttered, upset.

Matt pulled away a little. "What do you mean?" he asked, unsure of the statement.

Rachel pulled away, wiped her eyes and took a deep breath. "I do truly love you," she began. "You're the best. Together we produced four happy and healthy children. Three are grown, and Dani is thirteen. But, I now have a successful personal training business and I do not want another baby. I've raised my kids and I don't want to start over at this stage. I've been pregnant five times already including the one we lost."

"Look, I know you're upset," Matt said. "But wasn't Dani a bit of a surprise after the one we lost? We'll get through this, honey."

"We?" Rachel snapped. "I'm the one going through this. You're pretty much a bystander after doing your part."

Matt just looked at Rachel stunned. "That's not what I meant," he explained.

"I'm sorry," Rachel said, realizing that she had snapped at Matt. "I didn't mean that. You didn't deserve that. I'm sorry."

"It's alright," Matt said, as he reached out and hugged Rachel. "I understand you're upset. It is a life-changing thing."

Rachel returned the hug and they kissed. He rubbed her cheek as she pulled away and began pacing.

"I don't know, Matt," she said. "I don't know if I can handle another one. Not now. Not at forty-three."

"Well this will definitely change a lot of things," Matt said. "I'm a little unsure myself at this stage. But, I think we can handle it."

"Don't I know it," Rachel said. "I know we have been pretty much pro-life and against abortion except in certain instances, but everything is just so….so…"

"Uncertain," Matt finished her sentence.

"Yes," Rachel agreed. "I don't take this lightly. I have my hands full dealing with all of Dani's drama and emotional outbursts. I don't know if I can handle another baby. Not now and not at my age."

"You managed our three boys alright," Matt countered. "And I was away a lot then. You're an excellent mom. We are better off now."

"Things were different then," Rachel argued. "I was different then. The boys were all close in age and easily occupied. I don't know if I want to do it again. I have my life and career now."

Are you saying that you want to abort?" Matt asked, shocked and starting to get angry. "Because you don't want to be? Because it's not convenient right now?"

"Yes, no, I don't know," Rachel said, crying. "No. You don't understand. I'm not explaining it right. I've worked hard to get where I'm at now. I just don't know."

"Don't you think we should think about this, before doing anything rash and that we might regret later?" Matt asked. "I do understand. I want you safe and healthy. I don't want anything to happen to you. So, yes, you're first and foremost in my life. But, shouldn't we be sure about everything first?"

"Yes, maybe," Rachel replied. "I suppose. I need to think about this. I need time."

"I'm here for you," Matt said as he moved to hold her again, only to have her push him away.

"Why do you have to always want to have sex with me every time you see me naked?" she asked, upset. "Why did we have to make love like two newlyweds between the holidays? Why didn't you get a vasectomy? Why?"

"You didn't want me to get one, remember?" Matt answered. "Because a client's husband caught an infection and had a complication afterwards. Plus, you said there was a rise in the potential for prostate cancer or something like that. As for the holidays, I don't know, we've always had a very active sex life, especially Christmas and New Year's Eve."

"I know that," she snapped. "I just want to know why me and why now?"

"I don't know, honey," Matt answered. "I guess God gives us challenges to handle. Do we tell the kids?"

"No, not now," Rachel replied. "Not yet. I'm not ready to make any announcements yet. Hell, I'm not even ready to be pregnant. I had better get cleaned up, Dani will be home from school soon and I don't want her knowing yet. At least not today. And as for God giving us challenges, I don't need or want this one at this time."

"Do you want me to join you?" he asked.

"No," she snapped, somewhat angrily.

Matt nodded upset and unsure. "So what do we do now?" he asked.

"I don't know about you, but I'm going to lie down for a while," Rachel announced. "I'll be up in time to start dinner."

Rachel headed off to bed, with Matt standing there hurt and uncertain. He headed to the kitchen, opened the cabinet and pulled out a bottle of Maker's Mark. He poured himself a drink and looked out the window at all of the snow and ice in their backyard as he took a sip.

A cold front had moved in, one that could be felt both indoors and out. He watched as the freezing north wind blew snow across the field and pond beyond their backyard.

It was already a hard winter.

***

No matter how hard the winter, or how bad the weather, you could always count on Ed Brown to be out on his favorite pond, just east of Crosby, North Dakota, ice fishing any chance he got.

It was his way of dealing with life's problems. Ed's ice shanty was his refuge from the world and people. It was big enough to almost hold all of the comforts of home. It had an army cot, a Coleman ice chest, a large battery-powered lantern and a gas heater set on several cement blocks to make it more comfortable.

As soon as Ed got out of work, he headed out to his favorite spot. As far as he could tell, he was the only one out on the pond this evening. Even old Arthur Krause who fished every day wasn't out, he could tell, because there was no light in his shanty when Ed walked by.

Ed could hear the wind howl and whistle outside his shanty as he fished. The snow had been steady when he walked out there. By now it had to be a full blizzard.

While it was warmer and much more peaceful inside the wooden shanty, he had no luck fishing. In just over an hour he had not caught a single fish. Not even a bite.

Even a minnow would have been something.

He sat and listened as the wind appeared to sound louder. But now, it seemed like the wind was howling and screaming as the weather became worse. No matter how bad it got outside, Ed felt safe inside. He had built it sturdy to withstand the strong winds and heavy snow, or almost anything else Mother Nature could throw at it.

As he continued fishing, he thought he heard something in the howling wind, but could not make it out clearly. He could swear at times that he heard something screaming out there in the snowstorm.

Whatever it was, he felt safe. If it was an animal, he had his .357 on hand for protection.

At least for now.

He could tell by the sounds of the wind that the weather was getting worse. He could hear the wooden shanty creak and moan from the high wind crashing against it.

Finally, after over an hour of fishing, he landed a small-mouth bass. It wasn't much, but it would almost make a meal for himself. As Ed stood admiring his prize, he heard the wind blow much harder. He also heard a blood-curdling shriek right outside of his shanty.

Just as Ed looked up and around, the roof to the shanty was lifted off and snow from the blizzard came tumbling in. The first thing he noticed was the horrid smell of death and decay. Before he could even react, a large gray, dead-colored hand reached in for him.

Ed screamed as he saw what the owner of the hand looked like.

He fell backwards, still grasping his fish in an attempted retreat to get away from the creature. He slid upon his back across the ice to try and get beneath the army cot to get away. But, it was to no avail.

The creature grabbed Ed by his left ankle and pulled him upwards. Ed finally dropped his fish onto the ice. He grabbed onto the side of the shanty in a vain attempt to keep from being taken. The creature then pulled the back two sides of the shanty along with Ed.

Ed's screams of horror and pain were greatly muffled by the night-time blizzard. Once finished with Ed, the creature reached inside the shanty and grabbed Ed's only catch of the day as well.

This dinner had not sated the creature. It was already in search of its next meal. It knew that it would find more as the snow continued to fall.

It always did.

Prey would be much easier for it as the storm grew worse.

***

"Richard, the weather is getting worse and the boys need to come in and do their homework!" yelled Marianne Case, Richard's wife, from their back door.

"We're working on their game," Richard called back.

"I don't care!' she yelled. "They played a game earlier. That is enough hockey for now! The boys have dinner and their homework. Enough is enough already!"

Richard knew she was right about the homework, but felt she did not understand why he was pushing their sons into something they already excelled at. He could see a lot of talent in his sons Gordon and Steve, and only wanted to give them every opportunity that he never had.

Even if at times they really did not want it.

"We need a few more minutes," he yelled back.

"Gordon, Steve get in here now!" Marianne yelled. "That's enough hockey for the day. If your dad insists on staying out there, playing with his stick and freezing to death, then *he* can."

The boys commenced to abandon their homemade rink.

"The boys need to up their game," Richard protested. "What about their training? It's important."

"So is rest, dinner and schoolwork," his wife yelled back. "You're being ridiculous. School trumps hockey, every time. You're becoming one of those ridiculous hockey dads. Boys, get in here *now*."

Once again, Richard had been undermined and angered. This time it was his wife.

He stood out in the cold, fuming for a few minutes, before finally heading inside for dinner.

***

That night had been a relatively quiet and uneventful affair in the Torrey household. With the exception of the ramblings of thirteen-year-old Danielle about the day-to-day dramas of middle school life and gossip about friends, there was little conversation. There was an uneasy quiet between Matt and Rachel.

Since he did not know what to do or say, he felt it was better to say little or nothing, except to engage in some conversation with Danielle. He knew there was little he could say that would do any good right now.

After a while, Danielle went to her room to do homework and talk on her phone to her friends.

For a moment, Matt and Rachel sat in a kind of quiet and uncomfortable silence.

"I was informed by Dean Serling that Professor Burns may file a lawsuit against me," Matt said, finally breaking the silence.

Rachel looked over at Matt sympathetically and asked, "You mean the crazy bitch that tried to stab you at that function last month? Can she do that?"

"I'm afraid so," Matt replied. "The school is looking into the matter before fully supporting me."

"Why is that?" Rachel asked. "You have the right to defend yourself."

"I told the school I would fight it," Matt continued. "It's just the PC bullshit I have to deal with. I am on solid legal ground. I also warned the Dean that if I am punished somehow for this, I will do what I have to do to defend myself there as well."

"Good," Rachel said. "I never liked her. That bitch insulted me the first time we met. She inferred that I had no brains, only looks. Maybe if she put in some effort she could find a man, and not be so damned angry and frustrated. She probably hasn't been laid since the 1990's. I'm glad you're willing to fight back on this."

"Thanks," Matt said. "I appreciate that."

"Why didn't you say anything earlier?" Rachel asked.

"Because you had more important things on your mind," Matt replied. "We both did."

Rachel nodded. "I know," she said.

"I'll get the dishes later," Matt said. "I have some work to do. If you need me, I'll be in the den."

Rachel could tell Matt was a little upset. But so was she, and the more she thought about it, the more upset she became.

She was mad about the whole situation. She was mad at Matt. She was mad at herself. She was mad at God and the world. She was even mad at life in general.

It wasn't fair.

But, to her nothing was fair right now.

Rachel went about quietly doing the dishes while Matt did school-related work. Afterwards, she watched television by herself.

"*This sucks*," Rachel thought.

***

"*This really sucks,*" Cassandra Stern thought as Max was on top, making love to her.

Or at least his version of making love to her.

Just like they always did when Max arrived home, they had a quiet dinner, relaxed a little and then went to bed.

She knew he loved and missed her. So, it was her wifely duty to make love to him when he returned. But Max was not Drake. While Max may have been almost as handsome as Drake was, that was where the similarities ended. When it came to passionate lovemaking, they were worlds apart.

Basically, she viewed Max as old reliable, safe and secure. While Drake was the sexual sports car of her dreams that really revved her up and gave her more excitement.

Sometime in the middle of making love to Max, Cassandra made the decision to leave him and be with Drake.

It was just a question of when.

***

When Brandon Markway arrived home, he found Marlene still upset. He knew almost immediately that she must have taken another pregnancy test.

"You have to quit doing this to yourself," Brandon said, concerned. "This can't be good for you. It will happen when it happens."

"I know, but when?" Marlene replied.

"When the time is right," Brandon answered. "Nothing is a given. You can do everything right and still have the wrong thing happen."

"I just want this so badly for us," Marlene said.

"I know, I know," Brandon said. "But you're almost obsessing over this. You're almost forgetting us in this."

Tears welled up in Marlene's eyes. "How can you say that?" she asked.

Brandon stood there miffed about Marlene's reaction. "Look, we can't be so focused on having a baby that we forget about ourselves here," he said. "It will still come down to us in the end, and all of this obsessing isn't any help, that's all."

"Fine!" Marlene yelled, both hurt and angry. "I'm going to bed! Goodnight!"

"Goodnight," Matt said, as he instinctively leaned over and kissed Rachel, just like he had every night he was home for almost a quarter of a century.

Until tonight.

While she did return the kiss, it was half-hearted and very distant.

"Are you alright?" Matt asked, concerned.

"As I can be under the circumstances," Rachel replied.

Matt reached out and caressed her shoulder. "It will be alright, honey," he said. "We've been pretty blessed so far and with so much."

Rachel took a deep breath, exhaled and then sighed. "Yeah," she said, before turning over onto her side.

Matt turned off the light on the nightstand. "Yeah," he muttered, both hurt and frustrated.

Snow Showers

Matt woke up early feeling even more frustrated and hurt than when he went to bed.

Rachel had rebuffed his attempts during the night to hold and comfort her. She had been angry and rude, and made it all too apparent that he was to leave her alone.

In all of her pregnancies, she had never been this way. With the exception of morning sickness and later discomfort, she had always been happy and accepting of her pregnancies. This was totally different.

While he was trying his best to be understanding and considerate, her anger, resentment and bitterness were already wearing on him and getting old quick.

Upon waking up, Matt shaved, showered and got ready for work. While getting dressed he heard Rachel in the bathroom getting sick. He wanted to help, but after last night felt it was better to just leave her alone.

After making himself something to eat, he sat down and had breakfast with Danielle.

"Would you like a ride to school?" he asked her.

"Sure," she replied. "That would be great, because I don't want to stand out there waiting for the bus. But don't you usually go in later?"

"Yes, but it's no problem," Matt said. "Besides, I need to go in early anyway."

"Well, let me go get ready then," Danielle said, finishing her breakfast.

Matt watched as Danielle left for her bedroom, still wearing her pajamas, and was amazed at how much she looked like her mother. He laughed to himself how, by the time she reached sixteen, he would have more problems with boys than he ever did with all three of their sons and girls.

As he finished breakfast he saw Rachel approach.

"Thanks for checking on me when I was puking," she said snidely. "Thanks for caring."

"Well, Rachel," Matt said. "I tried to comfort you during the night and you pushed me away and told me to leave you alone. So, that is what I did."

Rachel glared at Matt. "That isn't what I meant," she said. "I could have choked to death and needed your help in there."

"You can't have it both ways, Rachel," Matt said. "I don't play guessing games so you better be clear. Besides, I figured you could handle vomiting by yourself."

"Thanks," Rachel snapped, sarcastically.

"You're welcome," Matt said with equal sarcasm.

Rachel was a bit taken aback by Matt's response. He wasn't one to easily rile or get upset, so she knew that she must have really pissed him off.

"Will you be home for lunch?" she asked, trying to change the subject.

"No, I highly doubt it," Matt replied.

Rachel knew then she had really angered Matt. He usually made a point to come home and see her.

Soon Danielle came out dressed and ready for school. "I'm ready," she announced. "Dad, can we pick up Tracy Miller on the way to school?"

"Sure," Matt said. "No problem."

"You're taking Dani to school?" Rachel asked.

"Yeah," Matt replied. "It's too cold around here and I decided to go in early. Why?'

"Just asking," Rachel said, sadly.

"Okay, Dani, let's go," Matt said, grabbing his briefcase and coat.

Rachel watched silently as Matt and Danielle left. She thought it was telling that he did not kiss her goodbye and that he was not coming home for lunch. She knew that her anger and bitterness was pushing him away, whether she could help it or not.

Filled with great sadness and uncertainty, she started to sob.

***

Marlene Markway was still sobbing as she got ready for work. She had cried herself to sleep and now did so because Brandon never came to bed last night; he decided to spend the night out on the couch. On top of that, he left for work early without saying anything or kissing her goodbye.

Now, she was not only worried about whether or not she could ever have children, but if her obsessing over it had hurt her marriage and losing Brandon.

Marlene spent much of the morning trying to cover up the effects all the crying had done to her eyes and face. She needed to get cleaned up and regain her composure for her students at school.

She hoped this weekend getaway would be what the both of them needed.

All she knew was that today was already a long day to an even longer week.

***

For Cassandra Stern, it already felt like it had been a long day to a potentially longer week. It was bad enough that she had to spend much of the day with Max, but he decided that he had to make love to her again before breakfast, which did not thrill her.

She felt obligated, since she would be leaving him soon and did not want him to suspect anything since he was only home until Thursday. Plus, he also took her out to breakfast and a little shopping afterwards.

All the while, she found herself thinking of Drake. She found herself thinking about him non-stop since she picked up Max from the airport. Cassandra found herself half-listening to Max talk about business as he drove them home.

At one point, Max reached over and caressed her left thigh. She looked at him, and he wore a large smile. She knew he wanted more sex.

She smiled back. "*Oh, God,*" she thought, "*Not again.*"

Wishing Max was as good a lover as Drake, Cassandra looked out the window and watched the snow begin to fall harder.

***

As the morning went on, the snow began to fall harder near Fergus Falls, Minnesota. But that didn't make any difference to Edna Crouch, since she only went out when she had to, and that was usually to yell at people walking on her lawn.

Being that it was winter with a foot of snow on the ground made no difference.

She spared no insult or offensive verbage when yelling at trespassing evil-doers. She could be pretty raw and her language could get pretty blue at times, and it didn't matter if the culprit was two or ninety-two.

If anybody gave her any lip or a showed any bad attitude, then she kept her handy-dandy twelve-gauge shotgun nearby. Living just outside of Fergus Falls, she was the stereotype of a mean old battleaxe, and relished every moment of it.

Since there wasn't much else for her to do, she kept an active vigil of her property.

Today, in spite of the heavier snow flurries, Edna was able to see a little boy cross her yard. It did not matter that he only looked about six or seven, she was ready to confront him as only she could.

Edna quickly got up and went to the door, opened it and approached the boy as he was carrying a beagle puppy.

"Get the hell off my lawn, you little bastard!" she yelled.

"I'm sorry, Mrs. Crouch," the boy apologized. "But, my puppy got out of my yard and I've been looking all over for him and found him here."

"I don't give a shit!" she yelled. "Next time I'll shoot the mangy cur, now beat it!"

Just then the boy's neighbor, David Barr, showed up, alerted by the old ladies yelling. "Come on lady, give the kid a chance to at least get his dog out of your yard already," he said. "There's no reason for this. He's not going to hurt your crabgrass with a foot of snow on it."

"Aw, shut up, asshole!" Edna yelled. "Nobody asked you!"

"Let's get your dog back home," David said. "Here, I'll carry him for you."

"Thanks, mister," the boy said, with tears in his eyes. "I depreciate it."

David chuckled at the boy's comment.

"You better move!" Edna yelled again. "Or I'll get my shotgun!"

David turned and glared at Edna. "You ever threaten a little kid with a shotgun again, and I'll personally shove that twelve-gauge up your ass and pull the trigger, you old battleaxe!"

"Fuck you!" Edna yelled before slamming her front door shut.

David's sense of smell caught a horrid stench nearby, like something was rotting. He then thought he heard something screech somewhere out in the storm.

"Come on kid, let's get you and your puppy home," he said. "It's getting a lot worse out here."

Inside her house, Edna watched as they walked away. She went back to watching television when she heard something out in her yard again.

"Goddammit!" she yelled, as she got up and grabbed her shotgun. "I'll show those little bastards this time."

Edna opened up the front door, aiming her gun. "I got you fuckers now!" she said, leaning against the storm door, seeing nothing but blizzard condition snow.

As she looked around, she caught a very rancid odor drifting in the air, and contorted her face in response. Sniffing, she gazed about further until, without any warning, an unspeakable horror was suddenly standing before her, looking directly at her. Edna stumbled backwards inside of her house in sheer terror. The great fear Edna felt was so overwhelming that her heart seized and she collapsed into a heap upon the floor.

The bitchiest, scariest woman in the area had finally run into something far worse than herself.

***

With the falling temperatures and her personal issues, it was hard for Rachel to get motivated this morning. She really didn't feel like doing much of anything.

Except cry and feel depressed.

"This pregnancy is already messing me up," she thought.

She knew that she had clients to attend to, so she decided she'd better get ready and motivated pretty damned quickly. Pregnant or not, it was full speed ahead. Her clients paid her well and she had to be there. That was her job. It was time to deal with the task at hand. The rest would have to wait.

At least for now.

Rachel, after much initial delay, finally left for work. Her life hadn't been in this much turmoil since her sons were all little. With all that was going on in her life, she began to wonder what she would do next.

***

Doris Madden wondered what she was going to do next. The sudden arrival of two more job offers after breakfast had altered her plans and schedule for the week. One was in Bay City and the other was in Alpena. On top of that, she was waiting to hear back from some networking contacts who said they would be in touch with her soon.

For now, her future was looking up.

She was determined to show those assholes on the board that removed her how wrong they were. Somehow, someway, she would get even. It was all just a matter of time.

Doris began packing her clothes as she planned her trip northward. She wondered what the best route would be in the winter conditions.

"Oh well, the GPS, will tell me," she thought.

Come whatever weather, be it snow, ice or anything else, she was going to be on her way.

This was to be her redemption and she would not be denied. Nobody would stop her, she was positive of that. Even if it meant driving hundreds of miles in the frozen northern wastelands of Michigan in the winter.

***

Upon waking up, Eddie Temple surveyed the frozen snow-covered ground beyond his front window. He watched as a few cars drove by, studying how the road conditions appeared to be.

"The cars seemed to be driving well enough," he thought.

Eddie's mind was already thinking about their deal tonight. He planned on going armed, or *packing heat* as Eddie called it. He'd studied how people were driving for the sole reason that if trouble broke out, they had to get out of that place fast.

While he did not like and trust almost everybody, he felt even more so when it came to minorities.

Especially blacks.

Time had not softened his view on them. He outright hated them.

He wasn't the least surprised the drug dealers they were doing business with were black. He always expected it. In Eddie Temple's myopic world, black people were always gangsters, rappers, drug dealers, hustlers, pimps, whores or criminals of some sort.

Eddie grabbed some cold pizza and a beer out of the refrigerator for breakfast. As he sat eating, he grabbed his .45 so he could clean it for later.

There was no way he was going anywhere without being prepared. In Eddie's case, that meant being armed.

After finishing breakfast, Eddie got up and checked his coat pocket, pulling out a switch blade. He hit the button on its handle, instantly snapping it open.

Eddie smiled.

***

Lon Michelson was not prepared for what he was about to encounter while small game hunting out in the woods of northern Minnesota. While he had all of the necessities for a successful hunt of rabbit and squirrel, nothing he had would help him deal with what came next.

Unlike a lot of hunters, Lon would hunt in inclement weather. He always figured that animals had to eat regardless of the weather and they would be more vulnerable. So with the snowstorm, he had an advantage, since they would be less likely to see, hear and smell him.

This thinking had made him very successful, where he often bagged more than his limit.

Only hunting during this snowstorm was different.

Usually he could almost sneak up on deer, because of the snowfall.

As he made his way down a two-track that separated two adjacent woodlands, he saw nothing.

No deer. No squirrels. No rabbit.

Nothing.

He didn't even scare up a partridge when he deviated off of the path to check on the possibilities of animals nearby.

There was no sound whatsoever.

It was too quiet.

Almost eerie.

Lon stood motionless on the two-track, cradling his shotgun, while listening to the snowfall.

After a few moments, he caught the scent of something unpleasant. As he continued to sniff, he thought he caught the aroma of something dead and rotting.

But then he realized that being out in the cold, the likelihood of smelling something like this would be small. He wondered whether if he was near a natural gas well, but ruled that out when the smell became stronger and he had not even moved.

"What is that?" he asked, looking around.

Lon then heard the sound of something large landing in the snow. He listened intently and soon heard it again. He gazed around. Finally, he observed some movement near the tops of some trees.

"What the fu…?" he said, shocked by what he saw.

The creature let out a horrific, almost unbearable shriek.

Lon brought his shotgun up and fired, but to no avail. He was too far away for it to do any good.

He started to reload as the creature approached. He could not believe its height or its rancid smell of death. Lon backpedalled as the terrible thing approached. He fired again, unsure if he hit it, as the creature let loose with another horrible shriek.

Lon was in a full-fledged retreat. He tried in vain to reload his shotgun as he ran away. He dropped several of his shotgun shells as he blindly tried to reload.

After some distance Lon was able to stop, reload and fire at the creature that had gotten much closer to him.

This time his aim was true, hitting the monster, and causing it to shriek in pain. Lon knew that this was his chance for escape. He was only able to get a few feet when he ran into another creature like the one he'd just shot.

This other one roared thunderously. Lon fumbled in vain for shells to reload his shotgun. The creature grabbed it, bending it like a pretzel, before throwing it some distance away. Before Lon could blink twice, this creature reached out for him, just as the one he shot arrived and they both overcame him together.

Fortunately for Lon, his heart stopped from sheer terror of seeing these creatures up close and before they ripped him apart in their horrific feeding frenzy. So thorough was the creatures' feeding that only a few drops of Lon Mitchelson's blood hit the snow.

Only the baying of some hounds in the distance sensing danger gave any notice to Lon Mitchelson's death, as the snow beat down harder and the temperature plunged. As the storm and what came with it moved eastward, it continued to cause havoc to anything in its path.

***

Rachel Torrey could not believe how much havoc this pregnancy was causing her in such a short time.

During two of her sessions with clients, she began to cramp up and had to take a breather. One caused her to double over briefly. It was bad enough to have her client ask if she was all right.

On top of that, she was still angry with Matt. She thought the only reason he went into work early and not come home for lunch was because he didn't want to deal with her and this pregnancy. Normally he would have come home for lunch and, time permitting, they would have indulged in a little afternoon delight, before heading back to work.

She thought it was cowardly of him to both go in early and not come home today.

She did not want to be pregnant and was pissed at Matt.

As Rachel drove home, she began to consider something she once thought unthinkable.

An abortion.

She already had her kids. She was in her early forties and now a professional. She did not have time for another baby.

In a sudden and irrational decision, she decided to head to the nearest women's health clinic.

It was her choice and her body after all. Matt may have gotten her pregnant, but she would be the one carrying it, not him. So, it was her decision.

As she pulled into the parking lot, she looked for a space. Finally finding one, she parked her car and shut off the engine. She watched as a couple of teenage girls walked in.

Yes, Matt had gotten her pregnant, but he wasn't a stranger. He was her husband. Her best friend, lover, and soul mate. He was her world and she was his. She knew he loved her and she loved him.

They had been through too much together. He had been there through all of the children's births and even the miscarriage. He had been her rock and there for her.

Rachel broke down and cried.

She could not go through with it.

At least not now.

Traveler's Advisory

Cassandra Stern began to wonder if she really could do it, and leave Max. Yes, he had been good to her and loved her. There was never any question of that. He had been a good and faithful husband. Max had always been giving, attentive and loving to her. With no children, she had been on the receiving end of this kindness.

Then Drake came into her life.

Unfortunately, Max's being a good husband wasn't enough for her. She needed and wanted more.

A lot more.

And Drake was the one she thought could give her that. He could fulfill all of her needs.

So, while Max was working on something in the home office related to work. She decided to sit down and compose her "Dear John" letter to Max.

It was the only way she could muster enough courage to do so, otherwise she would never be able to do it. While brave and fearless everywhere else in her life, with Max she was almost cowardly and submissive.

She thought long and hard whether this was what she really wanted and decided that it was. As good as she had it with Max, she knew in her heart it would be a lot better with Drake.

She was absolutely certain of that.

***

Filled with uncertainty about everything, Rachel Torrey drove home. It had already been a long and emotionally demanding day and she was tired from it.

She desperately needed to talk to Matt some more and hoped he was willing, especially after the way she had treated him during the night.

Now she felt guilty for being so angry with him.

Rachel felt more guilt about even considering an abortion as a possible solution. She had always been against that kind of thing. It was just not like her.

Once home, Rachel showered, through on some sweats, and laid down for a nap. Sleep came easily to her.

***

Jim Summerlee could not sleep. No matter how hard he tried, it was not happening. He had too much on his mind.

He was concerned about his grandparents' advancing ages and how to care for them, as well as his own family.

He had also heeded his grandfather's concerns about the Wendigo. While not as superstitious as his grandfather was and his tales and beliefs in the old ways, Jim knew he had been right about a lot. He also knew his grandfather had a kind of sixth sense. He knew that his grandfather was right about his warning. He explained to him what the Wendigo was and how bad it was. Jim also sensed something dreadful was coming in the future as well. He just didn't know where or when.

As he continued to toss and turn endlessly, his wife Fawn noticed this and joined him. She closed their bedroom door, took off her clothes and climbed in bed with him.

Jim felt Fawn's warm body next to his. He opened his eyes, gazed at her and smiled. She kissed him. Soon they were in each other's arms making love. Lying afterwards in each other's arms relaxed and comfortable, Jim was finally able to fall asleep.

Fawn gently kissed his forehead as he slept, silently climbed out of bed, dressed and departed to get some much-needed rest.

"*Works everytime,*" she thought, smiling warmly at her husband, closing the bedroom door behind her.

***

"Every damned time I get a couple of days off, it seems like I have to leave before my time is up!" Max Stern exclaimed loudly disappointed. "Every goddamn time!"

"What's wrong?" Cassandra asked, upon hearing Max's shouting.

"Oh, I have to fly to Houston tomorrow for a week to help them out with some problems they're having," Max explained.

"Really?" Cassandra asked, trying very hard to mask her excitement at the news. "That really sucks. You've only been home a couple of days."

"I know, I know," Max said, as he reached out and hugged Cassandra. "That means we'll just have to make up for lost time before I go, baby."

"Oh, joy," Cassandra thought, with an utter lack of enthusiasm and Max kissed her and groped her left breast.

Max held her and led her to the bedroom. "Let the bedroom games begin," he laughed.

"Terrific," Cassandra said blankly.

Cassandra was divided emotionally and mentally. While she wasn't thrilled at the idea of spending a lot of the day in bed with Max today, she was ecstatic that he was leaving early and she could finally be with Drake.

Having sex with Max was a minor sacrifice that she would gladly make if that meant ending up with Drake.

"Funny how things have a way of working out," she thought with a wicked smile as they entered their bedroom.

***

"It will work out," Kevin Shannon said, trying to sell Eddie Temple on his drug dealer friend and his brothers. "Odell Gilmoe is cool. You'll see. He's alright…"

"For a nigger," Eddie chimed in, sarcastically. "He better be."

"I don't think Kevin would tell us differently," Andrew Furlong said.

"Yeah," Kevin said, defensively. "Odell's alright. His brother Jearvis Gilmoe is an expert. He's the, the, the…"

"Pharmacist?" Andrew suggested.

"Yeah, that," Kevin said. "He's cool too. The only one we have to watch out for is their brother Marvell. He's kind of a hothead."

"Ain't they all?" Eddie asked. "Seems like they're always rioting or pissed off about something."

"Just be cool, Eddie, and we'll be alright," Kevin pleaded.

"I'm cool," Eddie said. "Those niggers just better be civil and cool, otherwise there'll be problems."

"Just be cool and we'll get our stuff and get home alright," Kevin said.

"I heard you," Eddie said. "Shut the fuck up already!"

"Okay, Eddie, okay," Kevin said, trying to not piss Eddie off.

"Are we almost ready?" Andrew asked.

"Let's have a few beers first," Eddie announced, going to his refrigerator and grabbing three beers. "No way, I'm going there in the daylight. Too easy to be seen and I don't want to be seen there."

"You think there'll be any trouble?" Andrew asked, opening his beer.

"No," Kevin replied, opening his beer and taking a drink.

"Well, if there is, there's going to be some dead niggers in there," Eddie commented.

"Let's just be cool, buy our stuff and get back home," Kevin said.

***

When Matt Torrey arrived home, he did not know what to expect from Rachel. He definitely did not want a repeat of earlier. He knew she was upset, but did not expect her anger and resentment. He hoped she was in at least a better mood and emotional state.

He knew her well enough to know that she would probably want to talk some about this. He just had to get over the anger and frustration of how she acted towards him during the night. He had to do this, because he knew that she really needed him right now.

Once home, he made his way to their bedroom where he found her stretched out and asleep. Instinctively, he leaned over and kissed her.

She opened her eyes. "Hey," she said, softly. "How was your day?"

"It was okay," Matt replied. "Are you alright?"

"I'm fine," Rachel replied. "Just a little tired, that's all."

"I'll make dinner," Matt offered.

Rachel sat up. "No that's alright," she said. "I can do it."

"You sure?" Matt asked. "It's no problem."

"Yes," she answered. "Thanks for offering. It's alright. I want to."

Matt sat down next to Rachel, holding her hand. "Are we okay with this?" he asked.

Rachel knew what he meant and hesitated for a moment. "I don't know," she finally answered. "I really don't. I hate to admit this, but I pondered the idea of an abortion."

Matt looked at her stunned and surprised. "Really?" he asked.

Rachel nodded 'yes' with tears in her eyes. "I even drove the clinic nearby and parked there."

"You really considered that?" he asked, hurt by her admission. "Because you were upset and thought about doing this to us?"

"Yes," Rachel admitted, now crying, and her voice scratchy. "But, I couldn't do that. I just ended up sitting there crying in my car."

"I'm trying to understand and be there," Matt said. "But, I just don't know. I knew you were upset, but I didn't realize how much or how mad you were at me. But to consider that without telling me. I don't know."

Rachel could tell Matt was both hurt and angry. "I'm sorry," she said. "I still can't believe I did that myself. I wasn't thinking."

Matt sat silently as Rachel leaned on him crying. He held her, but Rachel noticed something different in his touch. He was not really holding her, as much as she was leaning on him. She noticed an uncomfortable tension in him, that she had not felt other times when she was upset or sad.

"You're mad at me, I can tell," Rachel observed, through her tears.

Matt took a deep breath and exhaled. "I don't know what I am any more, Rachel," he finally said. "I try to comfort you and get pushed away. I try to tell you it will be alright and you consider aborting our child. Tell me what I should do because……I just don't know anymore."

Rachel continued sobbing. "I'm sorry," she said. "I know I really hurt you and I never meant to do that. I am truly sorry."

"I never thought our careers would replace our family in priorities," Matt said. "That's why I stayed where I was, so I had a flexible schedule to be with our family, see you and be at our kids' important events. I guess I was some kind of fool."

"I just wanted to talk about this," Rachel explained.

"What's there to talk about?" Matt asked. "We talked already. You let me know how unhappy about this you were. We're married. We're healthy and we're having a baby. What else is there? I don't know what else to say and do. Help me out here."

"I know," Rachel said. "I haven't been fair. I just don't know."

"Then how in the hell am I supposed to?" Matt asked, frustrated.

"Please Matt, don't be upset," Rachel pleaded.

"Why?" Matt asked, standing up to leave. "You were mad at me earlier. What's the difference? Hell, you even blamed me. I'm not a good person to talk to right now. Because, I no longer know what to do or say here. I'm all out of answers right now."

"I said I was sorry," Rachel said, her eyes red from sobbing.

"I know," Matt replied, as he stood near their bedroom door. "But, that was after treating me like shit and because you probably felt guilty about considering an abortion. Maybe you need to talk to someone else, because I don't know what to say. Do what you have to do, I guess, because I give up. I'm not very happy right now myself……"

"Matt," Rachel said, crying again. "Please don't be like that."

"I'm trying damned hard not to," Matt snapped. "But, I don't have an answer. At least one you would like."

Matt shook his head and left the room, frustrated, hurt and angry.

Rachel sat crying for a few minutes. She knew he was deeply hurt and angry, not easy things to do to him, yet somehow she did just that.

She decided to start dinner and then wondered what she would do next. She knew that while Matt was upset with her, he deeply loved her. He had always been there for her and now wondered if he always would. It did not help that she gave him mixed messages. Rachel knew that it was unfair of her to do that.

Rachel also knew that Matt was right about one thing: she needed to talk to someone, and that was her sister, Melanie.

***

Marlene Markway was unsure of what to say or do when she arrived home. She had not heard from Brandon all day and knew that he was irritated with her last night.

"Maybe, he was right," she thought. *"Maybe she was obsessing over having a baby."*

When she arrived home, she found Brandon sitting in his easy chair with his left leg up and his wrist and ankle bandaged. Her mouth hung open for a moment.

Are you alright?" she asked, surprised.

"Yeah," Brandon muttered. "Sorry I didn't call, but I was a bit indisposed. We had a run and when I was helping some people down a stairway, it gave way and I fell through."

"Oh, my God!" she exclaimed as she ran over to him and kneeled down beside him.

"I'm alright," he said. "Fortunately, I only sprained my ankle and wrist. So, I couldn't really call. The guys didn't want me to make you worry unnecessarily."

"Oh, dear," Marlene said. "I am so sorry."

"It's alright," Brandon said. "The good news is, I am home for two weeks. The bad news is, I won't be skiing on our weekend up north."

"We don't have to go," Marlene said. "We can stay home."

"Honey, I only hurt my wrist and ankle," Brandon said. "Everything else still works fine. So after you play snow bunny on the hills and I get some drinks in you, there'll be plenty of time for a lot of sex."

Marlene smiled. "Is that all you think about?" she asked.

Brandon looked at her seriously and replied, "Yeah."

"So….what do we do for dinner?" she asked.

"Let's order a pizza and eat it in the whirlpool tub," he suggested. "I could use it for medical reasons, since I'm a little sore. Plus we could have dinner, sex and relax."

"You have a one-track mind," she said, standing up.

"I know," he said, struggling to get up also. "And that's a good thing."

"Are you sure you can make it?" Marlene asked, trying to assist him.

"Hell, yes," Brandon said. "How do you think I got in here?"

At that moment the doorbell rang.

"Who the hell is that?" Marlene asked.

"The pizza delivery guy," Brandon answered, smiling at Marlene. "I already made our dinner reservations."

Marlene smiled at him as he hobbled off to the bathroom, whistling. As she went to pay the delivery man, she knew their argument was over and forgotten.

She also knew that for the moment, everything was all right and felt much better.

***

Eddie Temple felt much better knowing that Andrew Furlong was also packing heat as they approached Odell Gilmoe's house. Not that he would have felt a lot better had Kevin Shannon remembered to bring one as well. The problem was that Kevin was almost too damn dumb to use one anyway. Eddie wouldn't admit it, but the neighborhood kind of creeped him out.

All three men approached the house that neighbored three other deserted and ransacked houses.

Kevin knocked on the Gilmoe residence door. It soon opened.

"Odell told me to come here to get some good shit," Kevin said. "I'm Kevin Shannon and I have my two buddies who want to buy some as well."

"Hurry up and get the fuck in here then," said the man.

Kevin, Eddie and Andrew all entered the dimly-lit house's front porch.

"I'm Jearvis Gilmoe, Odell's brother," the man said. "Odell said you'd be here."

"Cool," Kevin said as Jearvis led them into the rest of the house.

Upon entering, the men saw a couple of battered lime-green and gold couches, an old recliner, and a large-screen television against the wall.

Once they got closer, Kevin could see Odell Gilmoe unconscious on one of the couches, strung out from some narcotics.

"He okay?" Kevin asked.

"Yeah," Jearvis Gilmoe replied. "Fucking Odell's had to sample some new shit."

Soon Jearvis led them into an adjoining dining room.

There, at a table with a sawed-off double barrel shotgun and several large bags of marijuana on it, was an angry-looking black man wearing a white wife-beater and baggy jeans, while cleaning a hand gun.

Instinctively, Eddie did not like the man. He could tell the man did not like him either. Both men quietly glared at each other, sizing up their potential adversaries. In reality, they were carbon copies of each other. The only difference was color.

"That's my brother Marvell," Jearvis announced.

"How much is it?" Kevin asked.

"One fiddy," Jearvis answered. "It's our good stock."

"One fifty!" Eddie exclaimed. "That's a little high, isn't it?"

"You doan like it, get the fuck out!' Marvell said. "Them's the prices, mutherfucker. Take it or leave it."

"What's your goddamn problem?" Eddie asked. "You not get your welfare check?"

"You mutherfucker!" Marvell replied. "Buy the shit and get out. We doan need no white trash 'round these parts. We got standards."

"Cool it, Marvell!" Jearvis ordered. "We don't need you scaring away customers."

"Come on, man, be cool," Kevin said to Eddie. "Let's make the deal and get outta here."

"Could we at least see what we're getting for our money?" Andrew asked.

"No!" Marvell snapped. "Take it or leave it, mutherfucker. Sight unseen."

"Lighten up, Leroy," Eddie said. "He was just asking."

"The names Marvell," Marvell exclaimed. "Not all of us are named Leroy 'cause we're black."

"Whatever," Eddie said, callously as the others watched the tense exchange.

"Don't be disrespecting me in my house, boy, or you'll get a shotgun up your ass," Marvell warned, opening and closing his shotgun.

"Cool it Marvell," barked Jearvis. "Kevin here is a friend of Odell's an' we can show him. Follow me."

Kevin followed Jearvis into the kitchen, while Marvell fumed, staring daggers at Eddie. Eddie just returned the look with equal disdain and hatred.

"You eyeballing me?" Marvell asked.

"Yeah, so what?" Eddie asked. "You're eyeballing me. Can't take it or what?"

"I doan like white boys eyeballing me," Marvell said.

"Damn Leroy, you really need to lighten up, brother," Eddie said sarcastically, as he slowly eased his hand behind his back to grab his hand gun.

"I ain't your goddamn mutherfuckin' brother," Marvell said. "And if you call me Leroy one more time, I'll shoot you in the ass."

"Listen nigger, don't go making no threats with that mouth your ass can't cash," Eddie warned, eyeing Marvell as he had pulled his 45 out from his pants.

"You mutherfucker!" Marvell yelled as he grabbed for his shotgun.

Before Marvell could really bring his shotgun to bear, Eddie pulled his .45 upward and fired, hitting him in the chest twice.

As Marvell was hit, he spun to one side and accidently fired his sawed-off shotgun, which hit Jearvis in the upper torso and head as he approached from the kitchen. Jearvis let out a shriek from being hit by the errant shotgun blast.

"Mutherfucker!" Kevin yelled with surprise and pain as he caught some of the pellets that passed by Jearvis.

Seeing Odell stirring on the couch, still out of it, Andrew plugged him twice in the head. "What do we fucking do now?" he asked.

"Grab any money and as many drugs as we can and get the fuck out of here," Eddie commanded. "Come on Kevin, start grabbing some shit!"

"What the fuck, man!" Kevin shouted. "What the fuck happened?"

"That damned nigger Marvell started trouble," Eddie explained, as he moved over to Marvell's still-quivering body. Marvell raised his hand in futility as if to try and ward off what was going to happen next. "Not so tough now are you, Leroy?"

Eddie then proceeded to empty the rest of his .45 into Marvell Gilmoe. He then began to set fire to the place as he took his cigarette lighter to the curtains, loose paper and other flammable items.

Eddie, Kevin and Andrew grabbed all that they could before running out into the night. They jumped in Andrew's car and quickly took off. They could hear the distant sound of police and fire alarms.

"Are you alright?" Andrew asked Kevin as he checked over his minor wounds.

"Yeah, yeah, I'm fine," Kevin replied. "Those fucking pellets hurt like hell."

"How about you, Eddie?" Andrew asked.

"Marvell-less," Eddie snapped, with a wicked smile on his face. "Simply Marvell-less."

Andrew broke out in hysterical laughter as he drove them away. "Man, that is fucking funny!" he laughed.

Eddie and Kevin roared with laughter, while Kevin grimaced in pain and picked shotgun pellets off his clothing and arms. They made their way home.

***

Janet Elkins was on her way home from her job in Ironwood and was just west of Bessemer, Michigan when she noticed two cross-country skiers hurrying across an open field. Due to the conditions, she was only traveling a little over ten miles per hour herself.

As she drove, she would occasionally look over at the skiers. Even with the poor visibility, she thought it looked as though they were being chased by something by how fast they were moving.

"*Probably a bobcat or a coyote,*" she thought. "*Maybe even a horny buck.*"

As she continued driving along, she looked over again and only saw one skier. Figuring she drove a little further out of visual range and due to the bad weather, Janet didn't think anything about it.

Janet looked over again and noticed the other skier kept looking over his shoulder while continuing his frantic pace. She figured he was just trying to beat the storm in.

As she refocused on her driving, she looked over again, and saw no signs of the other skier.

Suddenly a couple of red drops fell on her windshield.

"Shit!" she yelled, thinking a bird had either crapped on her car or at the very worst, crashed into a power line and spilt a little blood.

As Janet turned her vehicle onto her road, the blizzard worsened. At one point, she thought she glimpsed something large in the distance, but could not be sure. As she continued onward, she caught sight of a broken ski sticking out of snow drift. As she warily eyed the broken ski, she heard a blood-curdling shriek somewhere out in the snowstorm.

She had no idea what it was, but it sounded very large and she did not want to be around to find out. Whatever it was, she knew it had to be horrible.

"That is horrible!" exclaimed Danielle Torrey when her parents informed her about the pregnancy at dinner. "When did you find out you were having a baby?"

"The other day," Rachel admitted.

"So that's the reason you've been crying off and on," Danielle surmised.

"Yes," Rachel said.

"Well, I think it's a horrible idea," Danielle continued. "Especially at your age. Aren't the two of you too old to be doing it?"

"Well, we're not dead yet, Dani," Matt interjected. "So we're supposed to stop after we reach a certain age? That is ridiculous."

"I'm not very thrilled about it either," Rachel said. "And no, I'm not too old."

"Mom, you're too old to be having a baby," Danielle argued. "You're almost 50. That is too old. You old people shouldn't be having sex. Don't you have to worry about heart attacks or dying? This is so embarrassing."

"I'm forty-three, thank you very much," Rachel retorted. "That is a few years away from 50."

"No Dani, you can have sex into old age," Matt replied. "And if you're healthy, you don't have to worry about that."

"Ewwww!" Danielle screeched in disgust at the idea of her parents having sex. "That is so gross. This is so embarrassing. What will my friends say?"

"Since when does it matter what they think?" Matt asked.

"It's still embarrassing," Danielle protested. "Mom's too old to be having a baby."

"Tough shit!" Matt exclaimed. "Deal with it. We didn't ask your opinion and we don't need your permission. For that matter we don't need your friends either."

"This sucks!" Danielle said, before stomping off to her room.

Rachel looked sad and nodded. "See she agrees, that I'm too old," she said.

"She's a thirteen-year-old brat," Matt said. "She worries too much about what her friends think. What does she know?"

Rachel lowered her head and nodded. "I'm forty-three," she muttered. "Until today, I didn't feel old. I never thought about my age or even felt it. We were always active and had fun. Now she has me in a wheelchair and ready to collect social security."

"Forget it," Matt said. "She's a kid. They think thirty is over-the-hill."

"Matt, I'd like to go see my sister," Rachel said. "She had a baby at forty and I need to talk to her. Maybe I could get a little perspective."

Matt nodded in agreement. "I think that is a great idea," he said. "When do you want to go?"

"Tomorrow," Rachel answered. "If that's alright with you."

Matt nodded, knowing it was best she did. "Do whatever you think you have to do," he said. "If you think it will help you, then yes."

"Matt, is Dani right?" Rachel asked. "Am I really that old?"

Matt looked at her and smiled. "No," he finally said. "As far as I'm concerned, you have gotten more beautiful and sexier with age. You're like a rose in full bloom, as beautiful as ever, if not moreso. I love seeing you naked. I always look forward to making love to the most beautiful woman I have ever known."

Tears welled up in Rachel's eyes. "Thank you," was all she could spit out, choked up by Matt's compliments.

"You had better call your sister and let her know," Matt said, reminding her as he moved over and kissed her forehead. "I've got lesson plans to make. If you need help packing, let me know."

***

"Thanks for letting me know," Melanie Becker said. "It's no problem. I'll see you sometime tomorrow. Love you. Goodbye."

"Rachel?" asked David Becker, Melanie's husband.

"Yes," Melanie replied. "She's coming up for a couple of days with Dani."

"Oh, okay," David said.

"She's pregnant," Melanie announced. "She's having a tough time with it and needs our advice."

David looked at Melanie somewhat resigned. "That's good," he finally said. "Then maybe you can tell her what we're going through. Because her being pregnant isn't as important as our news."

"I'll tell her about our news when she gets here," Melanie said.

"I will distract Dani with snowmobile rides," David offered. "But you had better tell her and no chickening out this time."

"I promise to tell her," Melanie said. "I know I have to."

***

"I have to take a piss," Eddie announced. "We're out of Nigger Town, so stop here."

"Kennedy's Irish Pub?" Andrew asked.

"Yeah," Eddie said. "It's a good place and there are a lot of hot waitresses."

"Sounds like a plan," Andrew said, wheeling his car into the parking lot.

"We'll just chill out for a bit and see if we made tonight's news," Eddie said.

"Sure," Andrew agreed. "What do you say, Kevin?"

"Yeah, sure," Kevin said, rubbing his wounds. "I don't care."

The three men walked into Kennedy's Irish Pub and saw only about ten customers in it. After using the bathroom, the three men bellied up to the bar and ordered three Budweiser's.

As they nursed their beers, the three men paid close attention to Fox2News' Ten O'clock News. The news announced the developing story of a possible drug deal gone bad in Pontiac that led to the deaths of Marvell, Jearvis, and Odell Gilmoe. The newscast told of how they were murdered and their house was set ablaze. The anchor reported how the police believed it was a drug deal gone bad, and not done by rival dealers.

The news anchor also reported the police said witnesses saw a mid-1990's green Grand Am in the area occupied by two or more white males driving nearby.

Eddie, Andrew and Kevin all looked at each other stunned.

"Holy shit!" Andrew said to Eddie softly. "Somebody saw us."

"Calm the fuck down," Eddie said in a hushed tone. "They saw a car like ours, not us."

"How can you be so sure?" Kevin asked.

"I'm not," Eddie admitted. "But if we fucking panic, we're dead. So let's have another beer or two or three or six and watch the eleven o'clock news and see if there is more."

"I'm for that," Andrew said.

"Yep," Eddie said.

They continued to drink in quiet silence as they watched the eleven o'clock news. Once the news was over, they left Kennedy's Irish Pub. Outside the bar could hear the distant din of sirens in the night.

As Kevin climbed into the backseat of Andrew's car, he suddenly had a terrible feeling about everything.

Snow Flurries

Even while Max was making love to her, Cassandra Stern did not feel bad in the least about her plans to leave him. While it initially nagged at her in the beginning, it quickly dissipated each time they had sex. Max was not Drake when it came to lovemaking and while she played the role of the willing wife with as much enthusiasm as possible, her mind to leave him was made up already.

Once Max rolled off her, he quickly fell asleep. Meanwhile, Cassandra rested in bed next to him thinking about her plans. She knew Max would want some more sex before finally getting ready for his trip. She just had to put up with him a little longer before ending up with the real man of her dreams.

All she had to do was drop Max off at the airport tomorrow and she would be on her way.

***

Doris Madden was on her way. She had one interview down and was on her way to the next one in Alpena. The Bay City chemical company had been merely a warm-up for the other interviews.

She knew that she excelled and easily impressed the interviewer with her answers and resume. But, she also knew that she did not want the position. In all likelihood, she would turn it down. That was, unless she didn't get any other offers, and that was highly unlikely.

She thought the position was beneath her; it didn't pay enough and had little prestige. This was merely a feeling-out process. She knew the real opportunity would be either in Alpena or Traverse City.

But for now, she was on her way up US23 to Alpena, where she would spend the night, so she could be fresh and ready for tomorrow.

Even at this late hour, she enjoyed the scenic drive with the snow and Lake Huron to her right. She enjoyed this route, even if it did take longer.

Doris knew tomorrow would be a new opportunity and the start of a new career.

It may not be a second chance, since she was long past that. But it would be *another* chance, and after burning some of her bridges, she needed all of the extra chances she could get.

As she continued northward on US23, she checked her cell phone for messages.

Nothing.

She turned on the radio and found little other than country music channels, which she did not really like. Even with the scenic drive, and Willie Nelson crooning *You're Always on My Mind*, it was going to be long night.

***

"It's going to be a long night," Kevin Shannon announced from the back of Andrew Furlong's car after checking his text message on his cell phone.

"Why?" Andrew asked "What is it?"

"My sister just texted me," Kevin replied. "She said the cops visited my parents. They were asking questions about Odell."

"Why the fuck would they do that?" Eddie asked, pissed off.

"I'll call and ask her," Kevin answered.

"No!" Eddie snapped. "Don't do that!"

"Why not?"

"Because the fuckers are probably listening in," Eddie replied.

"Huh?"

"What do you think happened?" Andrew asked as he wheeled his car towards Eddie's home.

"The only thing I can figure is those niggers had your name on something," Eddie said, talking to Kevin. "They must have had your name and number somewhere."

"Fuck!" Kevin exclaimed. "That's right, Odell had my number. I forgot."

"Nice going shithead!" Eddie said, more irritated. "What kind of a retard gives his number to a drug dealer for Chrissake? Belch, drop us off at my place. We'll get some of my shit, then hit your place, get some of yours and then head up north."

"Are we going to hit my place so I can get my stuff?"

"Are you nuts?" Eddie asked. "Hell no! The cops were already there! Are you that stupid?"

"Sorry," Kevin apologized. "I wasn't thinking."

"No, shit!" Eddie said. "You doing too much of that shit has affected your brain."

"Eddie, my cousin has a place up north," Andrew said. "We could stay there for a while. He's like us."

"What's his name?" Eddie asked.

"Jeff Sanderson," Andrew replied. "He'll help us. We were pretty close. His dad and him moved up there to get away from the criminal element and the minorities."

"So he don't like niggers either?" Eddie asked.

"Yeah," Andrew admitted. "We can stay there until things die down a bit."

"Cool," Eddie said. "That sounds like a plan."

"Shit man, can we stop somewhere and get some bandages?" Kevin asked. "These shotgun pellets are kind of hurting."

"Hell, no!" Eddie said. "It's because of you, we have to do this. So you have to wait."

"It hurts, man" Kevin whined.

"Tough shit," Eddie said. "We'll get you some whiskey and band-aids at my place."

Andrew dropped Eddie and Kevin off and waited in his car. While Eddie gathered his belongings, Kevin cleaned his multiple pellet wounds as best as he could and bandaged where he could. They loaded Andrew's car as quickly as possible. They then headed to Andrew's, loaded his belongings and headed up north.

***

Rachel and Danielle Torrey were all packed and ready for their trip up north in the morning. Danielle in particular was excited about the trip and the prospects of snowmobiling, skiing and enjoying the winter wonderland of the North. It was decided that they would leave after breakfast and after Matt went to work.

Matt loaded Rachel's Chevy Trax with their bags, then went to bed without saying a word.

Rachel knew this was unlike him and that Matt was still angry and hurt.

When Rachel finally decided to go to retire for the night, she took off her clothes and climbed into bed next to Matt. They had always made love the night before one of them was going away and she knew that she had to, especially now.

As she slid closer to Matt, she leaned over and kissed him. Matt felt Rachel's naked body next to his, turned and kissed her. Soon they were in the midst of passionate lovemaking. Sometime later, they were asleep in each other's arms, exhausted.

Before breakfast, Matt and Rachel made love again, though not as long or with the intensity as a few hours earlier, due to the constraints of time. Both had schedules to keep.

Soon, both were up, showered, dressed and eating breakfast.

"Well, I have to go," Matt said, before kissing Rachel goodbye. "Call me when you get to your sister's. Tell everybody I said hi."

"Bye," Rachel said, a bit sadly as Matt left for work.

Once Rachel finished doing the dishes, she and Danielle were on I-75 and heading northward. While it was nice to going away with Danielle for a few days and to see her sister, Rachel was filled with some misgivings and a bit of melancholy.

***

During the night, Kevin Shannon's misgivings gave way to pain and anger. As they headed northward, he continued to pick an occasional shotgun pellet out of his body and clothing that he had earlier missed.

He knew that it could have been much worse. If Jearvis Gilmoe hadn't been where he was to take the brunt of the shotgun blast, he would have been lying on the floor severely injured or even dead himself. Kevin still had continuous visions and flashbacks of Jearvis getting hit with the shotgun blast. That alone was bad enough.

Still, his body ached and he was in pain from his wounds. He was even a little angry.

His anger and resentment had grown when Andrew and Eddie wouldn't stop anywhere so he could buy something to treat his wounds. He bet if it were either of them, that they would have.

Kevin finally had a chance to buy some gauze and antiseptic ointment when they stopped at a Forward's service station at exit 202 just off of I-75. The only reason they stopped was because Eddie had to take a shit.

Kevin staggered into Forwards and chose what he needed for his wounds, while Andrew topped off his gas tank and after Eddie ran into the bathroom.

While Kevin waited in line, Eddie finished using the bathroom, walked by and muttered, "Hurry the fuck up or we'll leave your ass behind."

The cashier gave a look of surprise. "Some friend," she commented.

"Yeah," Kevin muttered, before paying for the items.

As Kevin headed back to Andrew's car, he began to question his friendship with Andrew and Eddie.

Soon they were heading back onto I-75.

***

Richard Case made great time in his Ford Escape as he drove the boys up I-75 to their tournament in Traverse City. It was a very peaceful drive with both of them being asleep. He enjoyed the quiet time and listening to sports talk radio. It was his quiet time.

And after this week, he thought he needed it. His wife, Marianne, had put her foot down about his making the boys practicing outside with him after their regular practices. She made them do their homework, rest and eat dinner before any more hockey. On top of that, he needed to get his battery or alternator checked and he forgot. He hoped it held out until he got back home.

They had some major running arguments about that the last couple of days.

On top of that, she expressed even more disapproval of how he was acting and carrying on at their hockey games. She told him that it was embarrassing and causing problems. She really did not want them going to this tournament. But his mind was made up that they would do it. Even if that meant sneaking out in the wee hours like they did, without her permission. Richard felt she just didn't understand and appreciate what he was doing for his sons. He would deal with her displeasure later after the fact. It would all be easier then, because

Marianne could only stay angry for so long. He was positive that what he was doing was all for the best.

***

"All for the best, my ass," muttered a drunken Harry Langdon, as he staggered home several hours after leaving the bar in Bessemer. "I ain't that goddamn drunk. They didn't need to take my keys."

Harry slowly staggered and stumbled down the snow-covered road towards his home. He deeply resented the fact that the bar took his car keys from him after he fell in the men's bathroom and pissed all over the place.

Even more miraculous was that he didn't piss on himself, much to his and the barstaff's surprise. Every now and then in his drunken state, Harry would laugh about the humor of it and then grumble some more how they took his keys and he had to walk home.

"Fuckers," Harry grumbled after going another mile down. "They just did it so I have to come back and get my car and buy more drinks. It's a goddamn consptra… a goddamn conspirt…..a goddamn conspirticy…..it's a goddamn trick."

Harry knew that he would have made better time if he did not have to stop and piss every so often. At one point, he even staggered back to a convenience store in town to take a shit. He even laughed about whether he remembered to flush or not.

It was full daylight, and about breakfast time when Harry hit the dirt road that led to the two-track road he lived on. Even so, the overcast sky and steady snowfall kept the daylight to a minimum.

As he started down the two-track, Harry had a sense of being followed. He turned around and looked, but saw and heard nothing. Even drunk, he could not help but notice how quiet and still everything was.

Even drunk, he could not shake the sense of being followed and would turn around and look every so often.

Nothing.

Still sensing that he was being followed, Harry turned around and shouted. "Alright you, fuckers! I carry a gun, so if you don't want me to shoot you in the ass, you'll stop following me! I'm serious. I'll shoot you fuckers!"

After a few moments of seeing nobody or nothing, he turned around and continued on his way.

Finally after hours of staggering and tripping his way home, he was within eyesight of his house. Even if it was a glorified shack, it was still home. As he picked up the pace, and he had a momentary sense of mental clarity, he noticed a horrid, godawful smell fill the air. It was perhaps the worst thing he had ever smelled.

The horrific, overpowering odor caused Harry to gag and then vomit on the ground. When he finally recovered, he felt a presence nearby. Instinctively, Harry ran for his house. But in his still semi-drunken state, along with the weather and road conditions, he could not go very far or fast without stumbling.

After about fifty feet, he fell and rolled over, coming face to face with the horror he moments earlier sensed nearby. It was horrid and looked like something from his worst nightmare. On top of that, it smelled ungodly. He let out a loud scream and scrambled across the ground, finally getting to his feet. Within just a few feet of his front door, the creature grabbed and pulled him upwards, with Harry trying to scream, but only managing to puke some more, and shit his pants in abject fear. His fright so complete, he died from the shock before the creature devoured him.

The horrific creature screamed in agony and pain from its insatiable and endless appetite as Harry Langdon's death was drowned out by the eerie quiet and stillness of the snow falling on the northwestern woods of Michigan's Upper Peninsula.

Winter Storm Watch

"Welcome to the deep woods of Michigan's northwest lower peninsula," Andrew announced as he pulled into a driveway that was little more than a two-track. "Here we are."

The three men looked out and saw an old wood-sided cottage, basically in the middle of nowhere with an old blue Ford Bronco parked nearby.

"You weren't shitting about them living out in the woods, were you?" Eddie asked, but was more of a comment.

"Yep," Andrew replied. "I'm just surprised we didn't bottom out. He must have had it plowed and graded recently."

"That's not very reassuring," Kevin said. "I'd hate to be stuck out here."

The three men quietly climbed out of Andrew's car and slowly made their way to the front door. Eddie laughed upon seeing a sign that read *Trespassers will be shot. Survivors will be shot again*. Once near the front door, Andrew knocked.

There was no answer.

"Try again," Eddie ordered.

Andrew knocked again.

"Okay you fuckers, hands up!" ordered a voice from behind them.

"You've got to be shitting me," Kevin asked aloud. "What next?"

"Turn around real slow, fuckers," the voice ordered. "And don't start no bullshit."

Slowly the men turned around, and came face-to-face with a scruffily-bearded man with a face like a clenched fist, that was holding a twelve-gauge shotgun on them.

"Drew?" the man said, surprised

"Jeff?" Andrew replied.

"What the fuck are you doing up here?" the man, identified as Jeff, asked. "What the fuck has it been, a year? So what's going on?"

"It's a long story," Andrew said. "We had a deal go bad on us in Pontiac. Oh, these are my friends Eddie and Kevin."

Jeff lowered his shotgun. "Nice to finally meet you two," he said. "I've heard about you. Sorry about the shotgun, but you never know."

"I hear that," Eddie agreed.

"So, why are you up here in the winter?" Jeff asked, as he opened his front door. "Come on let's go inside."

The three men followed Jeff. Once inside they looked around, seeing an old brown couch and loveseat, a couple of large recliners, a television with aluminum foil on rabbit ears and a rectangular in the dining area with four chairs.

"So what happened exactly?" Jeff asked.

"Well, we were buying some drugs from a friend of Kevin's," Andrew explained. "Anyways, the guy had two brothers. One had an attitude and shit hit the fan. Eddie shot him, before he could get us with his shotgun, and he accidently shot his brother with it when he got hit."

Jeff shook his head. "Mmm, mmm, mmm," he muttered. "Man you should know better than to go into Nigger Town and buy from them. Nothing but trouble. That's why we moved up here. You find more ways to get in trouble down there."

"Speaking of which, where is your dad?" Andrew asked.

"In jail," Jeff replied. "He had a dispute with the DNR and lost. He'll be out in a year or so, with good behavior."

"Oh," Andrew said. "Anyway, can we hide out here for a while?"

"Yeah, sure," Jeff said. "It will be great to have company again. Why don't you go grab your shit out of the car?"

"We'll get it," Eddie offered. "Fill your cousin in on the details of everything, Andrew."

Eddie and Kevin went back out to get all of their belongings. By the time they returned, Andrew pretty much filled Jeff in on the details of what happened.

"Well guys, I'm impressed," Jeff admitted. "You took care of business. It figures it was niggers though. It seems like committing crimes is all they ever do."

"Yeah," Eddie agreed. "We appreciate you putting us up. We'll pay our share when it comes to groceries and all."

"No problem," Jeff said. "If Dad were here, he'd have bought you drinks for what you did. Anyway, we have a spare room where there's a cot, when one of Dad's buddies comes by and gets drunk and then there's Dad's bedroom. Someone can take the couch. You arrived at the right time, if you arrived two weeks ago you would have bottomed out. I just had the drive and the road leading plowed."

"I have to crash guys," Kevin announced as he plopped down on the couch, grimacing as he removed his coat, revealing specks of blood.

Jeff noticed the blood. "You look like a man who got hit by some buckshot," he said. "You still hurting?"

"Oh, yeah," Kevin answered. "I'm more tired from it than anything."

"It's partly from the shock of being hit," Jeff surmised. "If you need some bandages, or ointment or whatever they're in the bathroom. I can take a look at you later to make sure they're all out."

"Thanks," Kevin replied as he lied down on the couch. "I'm beat, we've been up for twenty-four hours."

Kevin was asleep in a matter of moments, snoring.

"He's a regular sleeping beauty," Andrew commented. "But he's right. I'm beat. I'm going to crash in your dad's bed, Jeff. Wake us up if anything changes."

"Will do," Jeff said. "Otherwise, I'll get you up at dinner time."

Eddie looked out the front window surveying the area and the scenery. "I could get used to this," he said. "It's beautiful, and peaceful."

"It ain't much," Jeff commented. "But it will do. I like it. But don't let it fool you. We get some really bad storms and winds off of the lake up here. Not to mention the animals."

"I have to get some sleep too," Eddie said. "Where to?

"Just go towards where Andrew went and it's across the hall on the right."

"Thanks," Eddie said. "We appreciate all this, man."

"No problem," Jeff said, as Eddie headed to the room. "I'll keep watch. So rest easy."

"I could get used to this," Eddie thought as he climbed onto the cot and started to doze. *"What a place. Beautiful, peaceful and quiet. It's almost heaven."*

***

"Wow, it's almost like heaven up here," Danielle exclaimed as Rachel pulled into her into her sister and brother-in-law's driveway that led to their large cabin with a wrap-around covered porch. "It's so beautiful."

"Yes, it is," Rachel admitted, taking a deep breath and exhaling. "It's like a live version of a Currier and Ives Christmas card."

As they got out of the car, Rachel's brother-in-law David Becker came out to greet them. "How was the trip, ladies?" he asked.

"It wasn't too bad," Rachel replied, thinking David looked a little tired.

David and Rachel hugged each other. "It's good to see you, Sis," he said, as he looked over at Danielle. "My God, Dani, you're looking more and more like your mother every time I see you. Your dad's going to have to get a big stick to beat the boys off with soon."

"Oh, Uncle David," Danielle said, a little embarrassed by the compliment.

"So, where's Melanie?" Rachel asked.

"Oh, Mel's in the bathroom," David explained why his wife didn't come out to greet her own sister. "Pop the trunk and I'll carry the bags."

Rachel hit the trunk button on her keypad, and David grabbed their bags.

"How are you doing?" David asked, as he carried their bag towards the cabin.

"Pretty good, considering," Rachel said, knowing that he was asking about her pregnancy, as she closed the trunk and began to walk with him up to the cabin. "How's Mel?"

"She's doing okay," David replied.

Rachel noticed something in David's response that did not sound right, but decided against saying anything. "How's the kids?" she finally asked.

"All are doing well," David said as they hit the door to the breezeway near the kitchen. "Jonathon has his artwork all over the refrigerator."

Rachel smiled. She remembered those days fondly. "So, he's a regular little Rembrandt," she said.

"More like a Picasso of the finger painting world," David chuckled. "Dani, we'll be snowmobiling a little later after Jonathon gets out of school. Just making a few test runs to see if they're working for tomorrow. I hope you bought clothes for it."

"I sure did!" Danielle exclaimed, proudly. "I'd never forget them!"

"Good," David said as they arrived at the breezeway door. "How's Matt?"

"He's doing well," Rachel said. "He sends his regrets. He said he'd come up next time."

"That's good because we're overdue to go out and have a few drinks," David joked.

"Oh, God," Rachel moaned. "The last time you two did that you had a hell of a lot more than a few. I'm surprised you didn't get arrested. You both were so drunk and singing *When the Saints Go Marching In* at that Super Bowl party at the bar. I still can't believe you two from that night."

David laughed. "Yeah, we were pretty ripped that night," he admitted. "Oh well, you know how us old army guys roll. We're good for one now and then."

"I think you two did enough for a couple of years then," Rachel laughed, as she and Danielle removed their boots before heading in.

Once inside the cabin, they were greeted by Melanie, who moved to hug Rachel immediately. "Oh, God, it's so good to see you," she said. "I missed you."

"Me too," Rachel said, tears welling up in her eyes.

Melanie pulled away and hugged Danielle. "My God, Rachel, she's your clone," she exclaimed. "You're beautiful!"

"Thanks, Aunt Mel," Danielle said, blushing.

"I'll take the bags to their rooms," David announced, as he walked by carrying the bags.

"You've lost some weight," Rachel said, noticing that her sister looked much thinner.

"Oh, a little," Melanie said. "Let's go sit down and visit a little."

Melanie led the way as they passed through the kitchen. Rachel noticed the finger paintings on the refrigerator like David mentioned. She noticed one in particular that looked like it had an I.V. bag and a red cross hooked up to a character that had an arrow pointing to it that said "Mommy" on it.

Rachel had questions, but figured Melanie would tell her about it later. For now, she was just glad to be there.

***

In spite of being tired from the long drive, little sleep, the cold weather and bad conditions as well as the job not being what she really wanted, Doris Madden was still glad to be where she was.

The position was an excellent opportunity and a step up, but wasn't as prestigious as she hoped. The pay was very good, but when it was all said and done, it was a factory. Albeit a smaller and more modern one, but a factory or shop, just the same.

Doris figured if the opportunity in Traverse City didn't pan out and she received no other offers, then this would be an acceptable choice. Otherwise, she knew she didn't want it.

She knew all this as she aced the interview with flying colors. When she walked out afterwards, she received a text message about an interview for a potential opportunity in Troy next week.

Doris responded immediately. She then received an answer almost as quickly. Doris acknowledged the response, finalizing the interview for next week.

Doris decided to follow through with the interview in Traverse City anyway. She never believed in putting all of her eggs in one basket, at least not when it came to opportunities. Besides, she figured, she could use them as leverage against each other.

Doris drove away with a new-found sense of enthusiasm. Her future now seemed brighter. All she had to do was drive a number of snow-covered roads to get to Traverse City. At this point she would have driven through Hell, because she was that excited.

***

When Richard Case and his sons arrived at Howe Arena in Traverse City, he was almost as excited as his sons were to have finally arrived there.

With much enthusiasm and energy, the boys piled out of the truck, opened up the rear end and grabbed their equipment and gear.

"You two ready for the tournament?" Richard asked, already knowing the answer.

"Oh yeah," Gordon exclaimed. "I don't care who we'll play because we'll pulverize them."

"Yeah, we'll kill them, whoever it is!" Steve agreed, with as much energy and gusto as his brother.

"Well let's go in and find your teammates," Richard said, as they headed for the main doors. "I'll go find our hotel when you're between games. That way we don't lose any time."

"Okay, Dad," Steve said.

As they walked through the doors and entered Howe Arena, Richard saw some familiar faces, and his heart sank. It was the cop and the deputy district attorney that had gotten after him the other day. He hoped that they didn't see, him, but before he could help it, the cop had locked eyes with him. Even worse, he tapped the shoulder of the deputy district attorney and pointed him out. She then said something to the cop. Richard didn't know what was said, but he knew that it was about him.

"Shit," Richard muttered under his breath, unhappy about being in the same arena with them.

"There's the team," Gordon said, pointing over to a corner where their team was at.

"Come on, Dad," Steve said. "They're over there."

"You boys up for this?" Richard asked as he walked over to the team with his sons.

"I'm ready to go," Gordon replied.

"I'm good and ready to go," Steve said.

***

"Cassandra," Max called out softly to his wife. "Cassandra, I have to go."

"What?" Cassandra asked groggily as she began to wake up.

"I have to go," Max repeated. "It's time."

"Oh, okay," Cassandra said, as she sat up and started to get out of bed.

"No, no, it's alright," Max said. "You're tired. I can take my car and drive myself to the airport and leave it there for a few days."

"Are you sure?" Cassandra said, trying to fight off a yawn.

"Yeah, I'm sure," Max replied. "It's the least I can do after all of the sex lately. It's the least I can do."

"Okay," Cassandra said with a tired smile, as she leaned over to kiss him goodbye. "Have a safe trip."

"Hopefully it's only a couple of days. Go back to bed and get some sleep."

"I will," Cassandra said through a yawn as she lied back down. "Bye."

Max grabbed his travel bag, computer laptop case and briefcase, and exited the room.

Cassandra stayed awake long enough to hear Max leave, close the front door and start up his car and pull out of the driveway. She then nodded off, sleeping the sleep of a very content woman.

After a few more hours of sleep, she would feel rested up enough for her trip north.

***

Jim Summerlee felt rested and ready for his next run north after almost a couple of days home with Fawn and his sons. Even rested, he was filled with an overwhelming sense of foreboding and the need to see his grandfather.

He knew that his grandfather was one of a very few who could explain why he felt this way and what he possibly could do about it.

"You feel better?" Fawn asked, as she was doing dishes. "You slept for almost a whole day."

"Yeah," Jim replied, smiling. "Thanks, and I do mean for everything."

Fawn smiled. "Well, I am a nurse after all and it's the only thing I know that seems to work when you're over-tired and worried," she replied. "Besides, I know how overly tired I get working a shift at Mercy. It's hard to get to sleep when you're stressed sometimes."

Jim leaned against the counter next her. "You do have that power over me," he said. "And I'm glad you do. It seems to always work."

"I haven't seen you sleep that hard and like that since you had the flu a few years ago, she said. "No, not even then. This was different. You were sick then, this was very different. Something must be really troubling you."

"There is, but I don't know what," Jim admitted. "I am troubled, but uncertain why."

"You need to see Grandfather," Fawn said. "I sense he needs to see you too."

"I know," Jim said. "I will stop by after my run. He's the only one who can help."

Fawn reached out and gently touched Jim's arm. "Be careful," she warned. "I fear something bad is coming and very nearby."

"I know," Jim admitted, as he reached over and hugged Fawn. "I do too. That's why I need to see him. Will you and the boys be okay?"

"Yes," Fawn replied. "They're staying at the Arthur's for the weekend and I have to work at the hospital the next couple of days."

"Good," Jim said, relieved. "I worry about you when I'm away. This way I know you're all safe. You are everything to me."

Fawn leaned up and kissed him. You had better go," she said. "I love you and be very careful. There is more than just a storm coming."

Jim pulled away and grabbed his coat from the wall coat hanger nearby. "I know," he said. "I love you too. I will be careful."

"Call me when you can," Fawn said. "Remember I'll be at Mercy Hospital in Grayling."

Jim put on his coat and headed for the door. "I'll see you in a couple of days," he said. "You and the boys be very careful too."

Fawn quietly nodded as Jim closed the door. A tear ran down her cheek. Her sense of foreboding was overwhelming.

Blizzard Warning

Upon awakening, Cassandra Stern was filled with an almost overwhelming sense of joy and relief. Max was finally out of town and she soon would be, joining the man of her dreams. After making breakfast, she showered and packed her bags with all her most cherished and valued possessions.

Cassandra made sure that she placed her "Dear John" letter prominently where Max would see it, in the center of his office desk.

She felt no remorse. Especially since she thanked him for their time together and how much she appreciated it, and how in her own way she would always love him. It sounded phony, but it was the best she could do under the circumstances. She explained how she needed more passion and adventure in her life than what her current stable marriage could give her.

She just hoped he understood.

In her mind, she had moved on emotionally. Cassandra hoped Max would in due time.

As she finished packing her last bag and then carried them to the front door, she tried to make a mental note not to forget anything. Each trip carrying her bags to the front entranceway, she took in memories she had of the place. She then threw on her coat and carried two of her suitcases out to her car. After starting up her car, she made two more trips for the other suitcases, all the while going through her mental checklist.

She debated about taking their wedding album with her, but decided against it. She thought Max might be more sentimental about it and want to keep it. Plus, there was also the fact that she did not need to add anymore baggage than she already had to a new relationship.

Cassandra took one last, long look around the house, before finally leaving for good.

After leaving the emotional debris of her marriage behind, Cassandra Stern was undertaking a much-desired and new adventure.

***

Marlene Markway felt certain her long weekend with Brandon promised to be exciting and full of adventure as they drove north. She was thrilled to finally be getting away for a few days.

Best of all, Brandon's leg was not hurting as bad, so driving and moving around would not be too difficult for him. While he would not be skiing, he could still enjoy the trip and the company just the same. Besides, not all of their friends skied a lot anyway.

They both woke up early, made love, ate breakfast, loaded up their SUV and were soon their way.

"How's the leg holding up?" Marlene asked as Brandon passed the I-475 exit to Flint on I-75.

"Not bad," Brandon said. "I still can't dance, but it's holding up alright. I might need to get out and walk on it in another hour or so."

"Stop when you need to," said Marlene. "We're not on any schedule."

"Sounds good," Brandon replied. "I just hope the weather doesn't get too bad. The weatherman said there's a storm rolling in soon."

"Well, if we get snowed in, we can just stay up there and stay in bed," Marlene said, smiling.

"Works for me," Brandon said as he continued northward. "Either way, we're going to have fun."

***

"Go have fun, while Aunt Mel and I visit," Rachel said to Danielle about going with her uncle David and cousin Jonathon snowmobiling.

"Alright!" Danielle exclaimed, half jumping and running to get her winter clothes on and head out.

"She's just like you at that age," Melanie said, sitting on the couch next to Rachel after Danielle left.

Rachel smiled. "I guess," she said. "Though most of the time she's a bratty thirteen-year-old."

"I have news for you, Rach," Melanie commented. "They're all that way anymore. She's just typical."

"I guess," Rachel said.

Just then Melanie's son Jonathon ran in excited. "Mom, Dad said to tell you we'll be back by dinner."

"Okay, be careful," Melanie said.

"I will," Jonathon said, as he ran back outside.

"Wow, he's a bundle of energy," Rachel said. "You must have your hands full."

"At times," Melanie admitted. "But, not as much as when he was a baby. So, how far along are you?"

"Four to six weeks," Rachel replied.

"So, what is the problem?" Melanie asked. "You're in great shape. So is Matt. You're both comfortable financially. What is the problem then?"

"I just do not want another baby," Rachel admitted, with tears welling up in her eyes. "Not at this point in my life."

"I don't think you have a choice now," Melanie said. "How did Matt take it?"

"He said we can handle this," Rachel said. "He's okay with it and says we'll get through it."

"And?" Melanie asked, knowing there was more.

"Initially, I blamed him," Rachel admitted. "I was mad at him and pushed him away. It wasn't just him for getting me pregnant, but I was mad at the world. Mad at God. Just plain mad at everything."

"How did he take it?" Melanie asked, after taking a deep breath.

"He was okay," Rachel answered. "He was understanding. That is until…"

"Until, what?" Melanie asked. "What did you do? What did you say?"

"I admitted to thinking about an abortion," Rachel said. "I admitted to thinking about it enough to stop by the women's clinic."

"You what?" Melanie snapped, recoiling in anger and finally standing up. "How could you?"

"I was so angry," Rachel continued, as she stood up and began to pace back and forth. "I felt so guilty about it. I had to tell him. I couldn't stand it. I know he's angry with me. I can sense it. I leaned on him crying and needing him to hold me and he didn't. He was that mad at me."

Melanie just shook her head in disdain. "How could you ever consider that?" she asked. "Have you really become that selfish and self-centered? No wonder Matt is pissed. I can't say as I blame him. That baby is half his."

"I know," Rachel said, tears flowing down her cheeks. "I wish I had never done it. But I was just so upset. I had worked so hard on my personal training business. I just don't want another baby at this point in my life."

"We're not always given the choices we want at times in our life," Melanie said, still shaking her head. "I just can't believe you. That is just damned ridiculous on your part. I would never have thought that you would do something like that."

"I thought maybe you would understand," Rachel said, upset. "You know how tough it is having a baby at forty."

"Yes, it was tough," Melanie admitted. "It was much tougher than the ones in my twenties, that's for sure. But he was a blessing. I wouldn't have traded him for anything."

"I'm not you Mel," Rachel commented. "I'm not a stay-at-home mom like you. I have a career now."

Melanie took a deep breath and exhaled. "You're lucky you're still married at this point," she said. "So far it's been all about you. Me, me, me. My God, what is wrong with you Rachel? What the hell happened to you? Yeah, I am now a stay-at-home mom. But, I gave up my career because I wanted to, not because I had to. I did it for my family. I made the choice."

"That's not what…" Rachel started to say.

"It's not like you're a single mom, or you were raped," Melanie continued. "You and Matt made love and made a life. Why don't you appreciate what you have?"

Rachel was getting angry at Melanie. "You honestly mean to tell me that if you had it to do over again, you would have decided to have Jonathon?" she asked. "Now, be honest."

Melanie looked at Rachel seriously. "Yes," she replied. "More than ever. Especially now."

"What do you mean by that?" Rachel asked.

"It means that I would have been able to leave my husband with another part of me," Melanie explained, as Rachel listened intently.

"What?' Rachel, asked, confused and uncertain.

Melanie turned and looked out the front window, taking another deep breath. "I have cancer Rachel," she finally said. There was a long silent pause. "It's rare and I have a fifty-fifty chance."

"What?" Rachel asked, shocked and crying. "Oh, my God! I am so sorry."

"That was what my weight loss was from," Melanie explained.

"That was why Jonathon's picture had an IV in it on your refrigerator," Rachel said, remembering the picture on the refrigerator. She walked over and hugged her sister. "My God, I am so sorry."

Melanie returned the embrace. "Now you know why I gave you hell," she said. "David will have someone to care for and love if I am not around. He will have a reason to go on and not retreat into some kind of shell, mourning. Jonathon has kept me going through this."

"You don't know that you won't be here," Rachel said, trying to reassure her sister. "You will beat it."

"I have to prepare for the worst," Melanie countered. "Rachel, we give love and we give life. That is our most important job. I know it sounds very old-fashioned, but it is true. That is why I have no regrets about having a baby at forty. Jonathon was made out of our love for each other. How can I regret that? He's been one of the best things in my life. Look at what we made together."

Rachel looked down at the floor. She knew Melanie was right.

As the roar of the snowmobiles engines broke the silence of the snow-covered ground outside, the two sisters cried and held each other tightly. Both watched as a couple of snowmobiles sped by with three passengers as it began to snow.

They never felt closer than they did at that moment. Both appreciating this time together more than either one could ever say.

Both knowing what was really important and neither one wanting it to ever end.

***

"Man, will it ever end?" Kevin asked after waking up and looking out the window. "All it does is snow."

"It's winter, what do you expect?" Eddie answered from his cot.

"It won't end until spring," Jeff replied. "Just be glad you ain't in the upper or closer to the lake."

"So, how are you feeling?" Eddie asked, climbing off of his cot.

"I'm not tired anymore," Kevin replied. "I'm still a little sore though."

"Should I wake up my sleeping beauty cousin?" Jeff asked.

"No," Eddie responded. "Let the fucker sleep. He drove through most of the night, so he's beat."

"Well, I got some good news and bad news for you," Jeff announced. "The good news is we got plenty of food. Enough to last us until spring. The bad news is we're almost out of beer. We've only got six left."

"Man, that's terrible," Eddie laughed. "We might have to make a beer run."

"I'll do it," Jeff said. "I have to pick up a few things anyways and I have a truck."

"We'll kick in some money for some beer too," Eddie said. "Enough for at least two cases."

"I'll go just after dark," Jeff said, as he got up and looked out the window. "I'll take whatisnuts, er, Kevin there with me. It might even be sooner as opposed to later."

"Maybe you should go now, before it gets any worse," Eddie suggested.

"You might be right," Jeff nodded in agreement. "Come on Kevin, saddle up. We're going for a ride."

"Okay," Kevin said, putting on his coat. "Let's go."

***

"Go, go, go!" yelled Richard Case, as his sons had a breakaway and were flying down the ice behind almost all of their opponents.

His son Gordon had one defenseman to beat before the goaltender. As the defenseman moved towards him, Gordon passed the puck to Steve. The defenseman shifted towards Steve, who passed the puck to another teammate who shot it and missed.

"Yeah, aw shit!" Richard said, at first excited thinking the shot went in, but realized almost immediately it had missed. He pounded the plexiglass in frustration. "Jesus Christ!"

"The one bright spot the team had and they muffed it," he thought.

Richard already knew he was going to light into his sons for not taking the shot themselves. They were two of the best players on the team and it was time they started acting like it.

"The team was already getting killed out there, even though the score was only 3-0, what different would it have made had they taken the shot?" he thought.

Richard continued to watch in disgust as his son's team was being outplayed in every way. They were being outhustled, out-muscled and just plain outclassed in every facet of the game.

For Richard, it was unbelievable.

He was surprised he stayed as restrained as he had been. He hadn't even said "fuck" once.

When the horn finally sounded at the end of the game, he stood there and muttered. "Un-friggin-believable. I drove up all this way for this shit! Unbelievable."

***

For Doris Madden, the drive had been unbelievably long and tedious because of the slippery and snow-covered roads as she made her way from Alpena to Traverse City. Because of the patches of ice and snow and the lack of visibility, the drive had taken twice as long as it normally would have.

After she passed through Gaylord, the road and weather conditions worsened. She began to doubt whether she really wanted to work in Traverse City because of her driving through this.

She decided she would stop at the next service station, to not only fill up her gas tank but to stretch her legs. The long tedious drive and sitting for this long length of time was killing her and she needed to walk around and move some. She was getting tired and sore from all of this driving and was beginning to really hate it. In spite of this, Doris felt very fortunate that she didn't slide off the road, crash or have an accident.

Up here, and not near a town or population center, an accident could be serious and even deadly….

Snow Squalls

Fortunately for Matt Torrey, the accident wasn't too serious. His vehicle, a Jeep Patriot, had been totaled on his way home from work, all from some stupid young girl who thought she could text and drive a Hummer at the same time.

He was pretty shaken up, but at least he was alive. And he was coherent enough to check and make sure he was alright. He knew his arm was broken. He could feel that. He had broken his leg some years ago and his arm felt that way now.

Matt saw that his legs were intact, could feel them both, but as he went to move his left leg, it was very sore. He could move it and he knew it wasn't broken, but it hurt. As he felt it to see what was wrong with it, he knew the pain grew more intense around his thigh.

He gazed over at the other vehicle and saw that it was just as damaged as his, if not moreso.

He could hear sirens approaching and saw people running over to his and the other vehicle.

"You alright buddy?" a man asked, who had run up to the vehicle.

Matt nodded. "Yeah, I'm just a little shaken up."

"That's good," the guy said. "Because it looks like that other person is a lot worse."

"Can you help me out of here?" Matt asked.

"I don't know about that, the door is smashed in pretty good," the man said. "Wait, the police are here."

Matt nodded.

The police, the fire department and all of the emergency services arrived. After some minutes of prying, the medical and emergency personal were able to help Matt out of his vehicle. With only a little assistance, he was able to hobble his way over to the ambulance.

"Is the other driver alright?" Matt asked a police officer and medical personal.

The men looked at each other and did not say anything. Matt knew then that the other driver was in pretty bad shape.

"Officer, my wife and daughter are out of town, could you call my sons?" Matt asked.

"Yes," the officer replied. "I just need their numbers."

Matt gave the officer the phone numbers before he was transported to the hospital. While lying on the gurney as he was being transported to the hospital with his injuries, his body ached all over, every muscle throbbing with pain. In spite of this, Matt knew how lucky he really was.

***

After the revelation of Melanie's cancer, Rachel felt very lucky and started to count her blessings. She knew that both Melanie and Matt had been right, and that she had behaved badly about everything. As she began to assist Melanie with dinner, she heard her phone ring in her purse. Rachel walked over and looked at her cell phone.

It was her son Mathew's phone number.

"Hi Mathew, what's going on?" she asked.

"Hello Mathew," Melanie said in the background.

"Mom, Dad's been in a car accident," Mathew explained

"Oh, my God!" Rachel, exclaimed, as tears flowed down her cheek. "Is he alright?"

"He's not hurt bad, but he's got a broken arm, a badly-bruised leg, bruised ribs and a concussion." Mathew continued. "He's fine, Mom. Don't panic. The police and EMS said he's pretty tough. That he limped over to the ambulance with only a little help from a police officer."

"So, he's not hurt too bad," Rachel, asked, her voice quivering.

"He said his body hurts pretty bad," Mathew explained some more. "He said that his body felt like it was jarred around and whiplashed pretty good."

"What is it?" Melanie asked in the background, as Rachel listened. "Is it Matt?"

"It's Matt, he was in a car accident," Rachel said to her sister "Where is he at? Can I talk to him?"

"Dear God," Melanie said, shocked.

"No," Mathew replied. "They're taking Dad for some tests. Mark and John are with him. They're keeping him overnight for observation. He's at Beaumont Hospital in Troy."

"So a broken arm, a concussion and a badly bruised leg," Rachel repeated. "What exactly happened?"

"Apparently some idiot thought she could text and drive, and ran a stop sign," Mathew explained. "She was killed. I guess she was DOA. He'll be fine Mom, so don't worry."

"Thank you," Rachel said. "I love you. Call and let me know how he's doing."

"Love you too, Mom," Mathew said. "I have to go, bye."

"Bye," Rachel replied, before ending the phone call.

"So what happened?" Melanie asked.

"Mathew said some girl ran a stop sign while texting and hit Matt," Rachel explained.

"Those idiots and their devices," Melanie spat. "They're dangerous to the point of stupidity."

Rachel nodded in agreement. "Apparently, the girl was killed," she said.

"Well at least she only got herself killed being stupid," Melanie said, with a bit of anger.

"This sure puts things in perspective," Rachel admitted. "This and what you're going through."

Rachel broke down and began to cry uncontrollably. The fear of losing Matt and her own guilt over the way she had behaved were overwhelming. Melanie wrapped her arms around Rachel to console and comfort her. Rachel embraced her sister as tightly as she had earlier for what seemed like minutes. After a while, Rachel regained her composure.

"Are you alright?" Melanie finally asked.

"I feel so bad, Mel," Rachel confessed. "I have been such a terrible wife and person lately. I could have lost Matt without him knowing….with him being angry at me….oh, Mel, I've been so wrong."

"It's alright," Melanie said, trying to comfort her. "What do you want to do?"

Rachel took a deep breath and exhaled. "I need to go home and be with him," she finally said. "I need to be there. I'll leave sometime in the morning. Maybe after breakfast."

Melanie nodded. "You should," she said. "Under the circumstances, I would leave if it were David. You have to be there too."

"As soon as he's alright, I'll come back and help out any way possible," Rachel said.

"Thanks," Melanie said. "I appreciate that. Are you okay now?"

Rachel quietly nodded. "I love you, Sis," she said.

"Love you too, Rach," Melanie said.

Both women embraced each other tightly, drawing strength and comfort from each other as they dealt with the physical, mental, and emotional turmoil that was going on in their lives right now.

It was all they could do at the moment.

***

All Doris Madden could do when she arrived at the motel was take off her clothes and collapse on the bed. She was sore and exhausted.

Because of the weather, the drive from Alpena had been overly long and tedious. That didn't even account for the fact that she had to be sharp and alert for the interviews, thus compounding the mental fatigue.

Though very tired, Doris was mentally prepared for the next day's interview. She had not driven over a hundred miles through a frozen, snow-covered hell to screw it up now. Doris knew she was as ready as she possibly could be.

Her head ached and throbbed terribly as she lay in bed trying to sleep. She knew it was from exhaustion and stress. Driving through the snow didn't make things any easier.

After tomorrow it would be alright. She knew it and believed it.

She had to.

As the headache finally began to dissipate, she noticed a horrid smell outside. It was like the smell of death. At this point she was too tired to care. After a while, Doris finally fell asleep and began to dream about tomorrow and the prospects that it offered.

Outside, a distant wind howled, masking the shrieks of something ominous as the snow began to fall harder.

***

The horrific winter tempest was crossing Lake Michigan and began to assault Beaver Island. The storm that had started out west had showed no signs of letting up and even intensified. It had gone from a bad snow storm to a blizzard from Hell as it made its way eastward.

Old Jess Murphy sat in his old, somewhat rickety cottage just south of Bonner's Landing on Beaver Island, just riding the storm out. As he drank down another Pabst Blue Ribbon, he wished that he had winterized his place instead of waiting for the next summer.

Even with satellite television, the reception didn't come in very well, all because of the ferocity of the storm.

"Goddamn blizzard," he grumbled after draining the last of the contents from the can.

As Jess sat in his recliner, he heard the wind howl and scream outside as it came off of the lake. He thought it almost sounded like a living creature shrieking somewhere out in the snowstorm.

As Jess continued watching the news, a powerful wind gust came off the lake and blew his satellite dish down, knocking the television off the air.

"Shit!" Jess exclaimed loudly. "Can it get any goddamn worse, I ask you?"

Just then, another gust came screaming off of the lake and knocked his power out.

"Goddammit!" he muttered in disgust. "Thanks a lot, God!"

Jess finally got up and walked over to his front window to check out how bad the storm was. As he stood in front of his window, scanning the early evening outdoors, he could barely see. The snow and the fog obscured almost everything more than a few feet away.

As he continued to scan the outdoors for anything at all, he noticed a horrific smell that was almost overpowering.

"Goddamn, what died?" Jess sniffed at the putrid smell. "That's godawful."

Suddenly, he heard a bloodcurdling shriek nearby. As Jess gazed into the direction of where he'd heard the noise, he caught a glimpse of some movement out of the corner of his eye. As he turned to look, he was greeted by the terrifying face behind made the shriek.

Jess recoiled in horror and abject fear. His own fright and disgust was so strong that he shit his pants as he stepped backwards. Jess clutched his chest as a sudden sharp, stabbing pain radiated throughout his upper torso from the shock of what he'd just witnessed.

The overwhelming pain caused him to fall to the floor as the monstrous creature peered through the window at him and shrieked again. It was more than Jess could bear and his heart finally stopped, an expression of sheer terror frozen upon his face.

The horror outside had caused another death during the terrible blizzard. Unfortunately, this victim could not be claimed and taken. The creature continued to shriek in pain from its unending hunger.

America's Emerald Island was now a snow-covered mound surrounded by a frozen Lake Michigan. The blizzard continued eastward, bringing death with it while making the roads and visibility worse.

***

As Cassandra Stern drove north on I-75, the roads and the snow gradually became worse. North of Flint, she'd made little headway. She felt like it took hours for her to even get past Saginaw.

As Cassandra pulled into a rest area to pee, she received a phone call from Max. Once parked, she listened to the message: Max said he'd be home early, perhaps tomorrow night.

Cassandra smirked at the news as she headed into the bathroom. She knew Max would be in for a big surprise when he arrived home. That was a phone call that she would not be returning.

***

Kevin desperately needed to call home. He had to know what was going on and what the police were asking about. He decided that when Jeff was grabbing some items down one aisle, he would make his phone call.

When he was out of sight and far enough away, he made the call to his sister Karen.

"Hello, Karen?" he asked, when she answered the phone.

"Kevin, where the hell are you?" she asked. "What the hell did you do? The police are looking for you and your friends. Where are you guys?"

"Oh, we're up near Traverse City, chillin'," Kevin replied. "Why?"

"Well, the police seem to think you were involved in the shooting in Pontiac," Karen explained. "They said one of the men that was killed had your information on him. Mom and Dad told them you hung out with Andrew and Eddie."

"We don't know nothing about that," Kevin said, flatly as if programmed. "We just went there and bought some drugs, that's all."

"You're lying, Kevin," Karen said. "You always sound the same way when you lie. Besides, why would you go up to Traverse City this time of year? The police say they have the evidence."

Jeff came around the corner of the aisle. "Who are you talking to?" he asked.

"My sister," Kevin answered. "Bye Sis, I have to go."

Kevin hung up.

"Man, don't be calling nobody," Jeff warned.

"I was just trying to find out a few things, that's all," Kevin explained.

"You tell her anything?" Jeff asked.

"No," Kevin said, shaking his head.

"Good," Jeff said. "Let's grab our shit and get out of here."

As they went through the checkout line, Kevin began to wonder about what he said.

"Did I tell her where we were at?" he asked himself. He could not remember whether he did or not.

As they climbed back into Jeff's truck, Kevin was once again filled with a sense of dread.

Blizzard Conditions

The drive north had been dreadful for Jim Summerlee. Somehow in spite of the snow, wind, poor visibility and shitty drivers, he was almost to his grandfather's. The only trepidations he had was when he was driving over the five-mile span of the Mackinaw Bridge.

The way the wind had been blowing, he wouldn't be surprised if the authorities decided to close it until the worst of the storm passed.

But driving over that paled in comparison to the fear and dread than ran through every fiber of his being. While he couldn't put a finger on it, he sensed that it was something terrible.

Very terrible.

Jim knew that his grandfather could help him. He was sure of that. Jim just could not figure out how to deal with whatever it was he feared and dreaded.

He knew his grandfather would know what to do. While he might not to put his mind at ease, Jim knew that his grandfather's wisdom would both guide and help him. That alone was comfort enough.

Finally, after hours of driving in miserable conditions, Jim arrived at his grandfather's home. Jim took a deep breath and exhaled. While the drive had been mentally tough on him, he felt much better reaching his destination.

Just being there filled him with a great sense of relief.

***

Cassandra Stern was both relieved and excited to have finally arrived at Drake McCormack's place. It felt like it had taken her all day to get there and she was filled with a great deal of anticipation.

As far as she was concerned, their reunion would involve little talking and a lot of sex. She could hardly wait.

She made her way to the front door.

While she didn't have a front door key, she remembered where Drake told her he kept a spare one. She reached behind the back of the outdoor light next to the front door and pulled it out, unlocked the door and let herself in. Upon entering, she could tell he was home as some of the interior lights were on.

As Cassandra made her way into the living room, she first noticed roaring flames in the fireplace. She saw no signs of Drake, but heard moaning, groaning and near-animalistic grunting noises coming from somewhere nearby.

Cassandra moved forward to see what the noises exactly were and where they were coming from. Moving closer to the couch that faced the fire, she saw two naked people on the floor going at it.

The woman called out in ecstasy as the man grunted and continued thrusting away inside her.

"Drake?" Cassandra called, dropping her purse and overnight bag.

"Drake," the woman called out, as he continued his thrusting away. "Drake. There's someone here. We've got company."

Cassandra gazed on in shock as the man who was having sex with the woman *was* Drake.

"Shit!" Drake said, right after doing one last thrust. He slowly got up and faced Cassandra, stark naked. "Cassandra."

The woman who Drake was having sex with soon stood up as well. Cassandra noticed she was a very attractive and well-endowed blonde.

"What in the fuck is going on?" Cassandra yelled. "And who in the hell is this lady?"

"Well, this is Marla," Drake said.

"Are you married?" the blonde asked.

"No, I'm not," Drake replied.

"An old girlfriend?" Marla asked.

Drake shook his head no.

"Who in the hell is she, then?" Marla asked.

"Melanie, this is Cassandra Stern," Drake finally answered. "She's a good friend."

"Good friend!" Cassandra shouted. "Good friend! I'd say I'm a hell of a lot more than a good friend. We've made love enough times to be more than good friends! I catch you cheating with this blonde bimbo airhead and all you can call me is a good friend! If that's what you want you can have her."

"Who are you calling airhead, lady?" Marla protested loudly. "I am a newscaster and we aren't together. We only hook up when my husband is out of town. It's nothing serious."

Cassandra was livid. She noticed an expensive vase nearby that she had sold to Drake. She grabbed the vase and threw it at him. Melanie and Drake both ducked as the vase smashed against the fireplace behind them.

"Holy shit!" Marla said, almost too scared to move

Cassandra quietly walked over to Drake.

"You should have called first," Drake said, coldly.

"You bastard!" Cassandra shouted as she pounded her fists on Drake's well-defined chest. "Goddamn you! I left my husband for you! I finally left Max to be with you! I left and I find you fucking another woman. Not just a woman, but another married woman! My God, you really are a bastard!"

"Yes, I am," Drake finally said, grabbing her hands to stop her pounding his chest. "You knew that and didn't seem to care. What does that say about the married women who let me fuck them, huh?"

"I left Max for you," Cassandra said with tears in her eyes and seething with anger. "I loved you! I gave up everything for you! Let go of me, goddammit!"

"Okay," Drake said as he let go of Cassandra who then walked away.

Cassandra stood in near the doorway just shaking her head. "I was so stupid," she admitted. "How could I have been so foolish? We were so good together. I thought you were my soulmate."

"I guess you thought wrong," Drake commented. "It's unfortunate, but you missed your chance."

"Yeah, thanks for that information now," Cassandra said sarcastically. "I could have used a better head's-up."

"Point taken," Drake replied.

"I used to enjoy fucking you, Drake," Cassandra admitted. "Unfortunately, being fucked by you this time wasn't anywhere near as enjoyable. Which is a shame, that very well could have been us making love on the floor."

"I guess neither one of us are ready for love," Drake admitted. "Only passionate and great sex."

"I guess not," Cassandra sadly agreed, looking at Drake's naked body one last time. "What a waste of two people's lives. Goodbye Drake. He's all yours, Marla."

Cassandra picked up her purse and overnight bag and headed to her car. Once outside, she quietly climbed in and slowly drove off. The vindictive, self-centered woman had finally been generous with someone other than herself, had karma bite her in the worst and most painful way.

About a mile down the road, Cassandra stopped her car, putting it in park, and began crying uncontrollably. She was devastated. The only man she'd ever truly loved had broken her heart and the pain was almost unbearable.

***

Staying almost exclusively in the ski lodge bar had been unbearable for Brandon Markway. At first it was torture just sitting there with his leg propped up on a table while the others were out skiing. He felt like a kid stuck inside with the chickenpox or some other malady while his friends were outside playing.

So, Brandon stayed inside with his gimpy leg, nursing a cold beer trying to make the best of the situation.

At least he could take comfort in not being alone. There were a number of other people inside whose only skiing experience was stepping outside of the ski lodge bar. The closest these people came to skiing was that they were at the lodge.

Brandon figured it wouldn't be too much longer before Marlene and their friends returned. In the meantime, he would socialize and observe the drunken wannabe ski bums and bunnies inside.

He finished off his beer and sat on a large couch relaxing.

Another beer was placed on the table in front of him. "Everybody drinks, goddammit!" said a familiar voice. "Nobody has an empty glass. So you need another round, brother."

Brandon looked up and saw Marlene's older brother. "Mark!" he exclaimed. "Glad you made it. Good to see you!"

"I know," Mark replied, as he sat down next to Brandon. "Now the party can really start. Don't get up, you damned gimp. I thought you would need the company. Besides, I needed a wing man to lie for me."

"I take it you aren't going to ski," Brandon surmised.

"Hell, no," Mark said. "Until I find a lake on the side of a hill, there is no skiing for me."

Brandon laughed. "So, what do you need me to lie about?" he asked.

"Just tell the bodacious ski bunnies around here that I'm a fireman and I helped bring you out of the house after you were injured," Mark continued. "They like the heroic type. You know that."

"Okay, but on one condition," Brandon said.

"Yeah, what's that?" Mark asked, before drinking some of his beer.

"You don't use the lines 'I have a big hose and I'll put out the fire with it,'" Brandon replied.

"Well, shit!" Mark exclaimed. "I am the king of bad pick-up lines. You have to let me use that one. I'll buy you some beer."

"Oh, alright," Brandon mildly protested. "Okay, I'll give you that one. But if you do, use the 'I'm used to standing next to hot things'. I'll let you expound on the rest of it as needed."

"Good," Mark said. "So where is everybody? Still outside?"

"Yep," Brandon said as he picked up his glass and drank. "They've been out a while and are due in."

"So, I came along just in time to rescue you from the boredom and drudgery of sitting in here, huh?" Mark asked, before taking a drink.

"You could say that," Brandon said. "So, no date for the weekend? What happened to whatshername? You know, the actress?"

"She's out of town doing an independent film," Mark answered. "I thought I'd play the field. So how's the leg?"

"Better than it was," Brandon replied. "It's still attached, thank God. But I won't be dancing, skiing or working for a while."

"You were lucky," Mark said.

"Yeah," Brandon agreed.

"Well, here's to good luck," Mark said, raising his glass of beer to toast.

Brandon did the same and touched it to his brother-in-law's glass. "Amen to that," he said.

Both men took large drinks of their beers afterward. Mark let out a large belch. "Jesus, that one had chunks," he commented.

Brandon laughed. "You're all class, Mark," he said. "You'll really wow the ladies doing that."

Mark belched a "Thank you."

"Well at least you didn't fart," Brandon remarked.

"Just keep me away from the Mexican food and nobody gets hurt," Mark joked. "So, how are you two doing? Is my sister still bugging you about having kids?"

"She's been better lately," Brandon admitted, before taking another drink. "For a while she seemed obsessed about it, especially after the miscarriages. Those were pretty tough on her."

"Yeah, I know," Mark agreed. "That was tough. She gets that way sometimes, especially when she wants something badly. We might not agree on much, but she'd make a good mom."

"I think so too," Brandon agreed.

"Well it looks like we're getting company," Mark said, as they saw the Marlene and their friends coming in from skiing. "So much for our intimate conversation, brother."

Marlene came over and wrapped her arms around Brandon from behind and kissed his cheek. "Did you miss me?' she asked.

"With every shot," Mark joked before Brandon could speak.

"Shut up!" Marlene laughed. "You're not funny, only funny-looking."

"I love you too, Sis," Mark said.

"Anyway, we're going to get cleaned up and will come back down for dinner," Marlene said. "Why don't you stay here while we're getting ready and reserve us a table?"

"Sounds like a plan," Brandon said. "So how is it out there?"

Marlene responded. "The visibility's getting bad. It's really terrible out there."

***

"You guys were terrible out there!" Richard Case exclaimed. "You call yourselves hockey players? That was about as bad as I've ever seen."

"We did our best," Gordon protested. "The other team was just better than we were."

"That's a piss poor attitude!" Richard said, loudly. "I don't know how you can think of even wanting to go out with your team for pizza after playing like that!"

"To have fun, Dad," Steve said. "We need a break. We played three games today."

"And lost them all!" Richard said. "You don't get rewarded for losing! You two should be working on your game, especially your puck handling."

"Dad, I'm tired," Gordon protested.

"I don't want to hear excuses," Richard argued. "I want results!"

"Okay, we'll do better tomorrow," Gordon suggested.

"We should work on your game tonight," Richard said. "Get your stuff and let's go."

"The coach told us to rest up for tomorrow," Steve said. "He wanted us fresh."

"Tough," Richard said, getting more belligerent. "He's not your father. I am and I say you need work."

"No, Dad, no!" Gordon snapped. "We played three games today! We're tired. We need to rest!"

"Shut up!" Richard snapped. "You'll work on your game or no more hockey."

Gordon and Steve looked at each other silently.

"Then I guess I'm done with hockey!" Gordon said. "I quit!"

Richard lost his temper and slapped Gordon across the face. "None of my sons are quitters!" he exclaimed. "Only pussies quit."

Gordon's eyes welled up with tears, but he refused to cry. He gave Richard a look of both hatred and hurt. Steve also looked at his father with fear and hurt.

"Go to bed!" Richard ordered.

There was a knock on their room's door. Steve walked over to it. He looked at his dad.

Richard nodded. "Answer it," he said.

Steve opened the door, it was their coach. "You guy's coming for pizza?" he asked. "The rest of the team is waiting."

The boys looked at their dad. "Yeah, we're coming," Gordon said, before Richard could answer to spite him.

"I was thinking the boys should be working on their game tonight," Richard said. "They looked pretty bad today."

"I think they've had enough hockey today," the coach replied. "We don't want to burn them out on it."

"Go ahead," he said to his sons. "I have a headache and am going to stay in tonight."

"Okay, are you sure?" the coach asked.

Richard nodded. "Yeah, I'm sure," he said. "They don't want me to join them. Go on."

"Come on boys, let's go," their coach ordered. "Let's go."

"Alright!" Steve yelled as he grabbed his coat.

Gordon just quietly glared at his father as he walked by and grabbed his coat and closed the door behind them. Richard quietly seethed with anger, feeling undermined by the coach and betrayed by his own sons.

Because of this perceived personal betrayal, he now felt justified in his own mind about hitting Gordon.

***

Eddie and Andrew were both filled with a sense of betrayal when Jeff told them of Kevin's phone call to his sister. Eddie in particular was upset over Kevin's stupidity and carelessness. He initially wanted to shoot Kevin, but hesitated since they were at Jeff's place and he was helping them and Eddie did not want to jeopardize that.

"You are one dumb mutherfucker!" Eddie yelled. "What in the goddamn hell is wrong with you? I swear smoking all of that shit has made you dumber!"

"Don't worry man," Kevin pleaded. "I just wanted to find out what was going on. I didn't tell her nothing."

"And what did you find out?" Eddie asked, skeptical of what Kevin just told him.

"I found out the cops know about us being there," Kevin explained. "Odell had my name and phone number. Karen said we're suspects too."

"Great!" Andrew said sarcastically. "Just fucking great! Do they know *we* did it?"

"I don't think so," Kevin replied.

"They must know something or they wouldn't have showed up to this asshole's parent's house," Eddie observed.

Andrew and Eddie look at each other with concern and uncertainty.

"I don't know," Kevin explained. "Karen didn't tell me that. I have no idea how they found out anything other than that."

"Probably finger prints," Jeff stated. "That or they found out from your family who his friends were.

"Fuck!" Eddie exclaimed, frustrated and pissed. "If I could get away with it without making a mess, I'd shoot your dumbass!"

"Eddie, it will be cool," Kevin pleaded. "Maybe we can go out of state somewhere."

'Terrific," Eddie muttered.

"So what do we do now?" Andrew asked. "What's the plan?"

"I don't know," Eddie said, still seething with anger. "We have to think. At least us two do…dumbass here can't."

"Well, you're safe for now," Jeff said. "You can stay here, if he didn't tell his sister where you're at. You're okay for now. So far nobody knows you're here. You should be alright for a day or two."

"Okay," Eddie agreed. "Thanks. You really think we're alright for now?"

"Yeah," Jeff replied. "I don't think anybody's coming out here in this weather. It's gotten a lot worse out."

Lake Effect Snow Advisory

In spite of her personal devastation, Cassandra could see the weather was getting much worse. She realized that she had been there long enough and needed to leave. With tears still flowing heavily down her cheeks, she finally drove off.

Emotionally and mentally drained, Cassandra continued driving for as long as possible. After driving for some distance, she couldn't go on any further. She stopped at a Motel 6 off of M72.

While it wasn't a place she normally would have stayed at, because places like this were beneath her, she knew she had to. Drake had taken everything out of her, and she badly needed to rest, even if for a short time.

The drive north had been tiring enough. She just needed to sleep even for a few hours.

She hoped she got home before Max did, especially with the weather getting progressively worse. Emotionally drained as she was, Cassandra hoped with a few hours of sleep she would feel a little better afterwards.

***

Melanie Becker was tired. It had already been a long day for her. The cancer had pretty much sapped her of the strength for doing everyday things. She was grateful that at least tonight Danielle was keeping Jonathon occupied with playing games in the family room.

"I'm going to turn in early," Melanie announced. "I want to be able to see you off in the morning."

Rachel nodded and hugged Melanie. "I understand," she said. "Get some rest. If you need me to help or do breakfast, I will."

Melanie nodded. "I love you," she said. "Goodnight."

"Love you too," Rachel said, as she watched David help her off to bed. A few minutes later he returned.

"How is she doing, really?" Rachel asked.

"The fatigue and weakness have been pretty constant," he replied. "She hasn't been physically sick. So we've been lucky that way. But weakness and fatigue have been the worse. She's a fighter."

"Yes, she is," she agreed.

"She even insists that we continue having our personal time together," he admitted. "She insists on it. I feel guilty, but she wants things as normal as possible. She says we will not be denied by her cancer."

"It's for her peace of mind," Rachel explained. "I understand it. Because if the worst did happen, she's loved you as mightily as she could. I know I would with Matt."

"So…what about you and Matt?" David asked. "Are you two okay?"

"We will be when I get home," Rachel replied. "This sure puts things in perspective. I was so stupid. I was such a bitch to him."

David walked over to the window. "Look at it come down," he said. "Are you sure you need to leave tomorrow? It's pretty bad."

"I have to," Rachel said. "He's hurt and I need to see him. I don't want to be away from him now. Not after arguing like this. It was so stupid of me. Arguing and being mad over such stupid things."

***

"Come on Marlene, this is just stupid," Brandon pleaded with his wife outside upon the deck as snowfall blanketed over them. "You're making a mountain out of a mole hill. It wasn't a big deal."

"It was to me," Marlene said, still upset.

"Look, Mark and the guys were just joking," Brandon explained. "We all were. Now you're upset by it. Can't we just get over this and put it past us? Let's have fun."

"Is that all you think about?" Marlene asked. "Fun?"

"It is when I drove a couple of hundred miles to partake in it," Brandon answered. "So when we're on a fun outing, it's *supposed* to be fun, not work. Besides, people get drinking and say and do things. They get loud and try to be funnier than they actually are."

"Yeah, but Mark joking about how us women get obsessed about wanting babies wasn't funny," Marlene continued. "And you guys laughing and joking about it. You saying we should just have sex for fun or recreational purposes and whatever happens, happens….*plus*, you guys called it '*mommyitis*' like it was some damned disease."

"So, what?" Brandon asked. "We were joking. Now you're mad at me and the guys over this nonsense?"

"It's not nonsense to me," Marlene argued, with tears welling up in her eyes. "My two miscarriages weren't nonsense. Also, you said I obsessed about this before."

"Don't you think I know that?" Brandon asked. "But if we can't laugh at ourselves and life in general, then where is the enjoyment and humor? It's how we get by sometimes. It's our way of dealing with life's stresses. You're letting little things upset you when you don't need to."

"So, now I'm being overly emotional and too sensitive?" Marlene asked.

"In a nut shell, yes," Brandon surmised.

Marlene glared at Brandon. "I want to go home," she snapped. "Now!"

"No," Brandon said. "We've both been drinking. It will have to wait until tomorrow."

"I can't believe I married such an ass," she snapped. "Someone who laughs at people's miseries."

"Okay," Brandon said, in a frighteningly calm voice. "We leave in the morning. I've had enough of this goddamn fun. You can shove this kind of fun up your ass. I've had enough of all of this bullshit in general. I've had enough of all your bullshit too. I'm goddamn tired of walking on eggshells. I'm going to bed. Goodnight."

"What?" Marlene asked, stunned.

"I said I was done," Brandon responded. "I've had enough of little things setting you off. It's never-ending and pretty goddamn exhausting. I am tired of it. If you aren't insulted, you are always hurt when the subject of children is brought up or joked about. You can't control everything in life, no matter how hard you try. Life isn't a kindergarten classroom. I've had a little too much to drink and I'm tired. I am tired of this shit. It's consuming you. So, if that makes me an ass, so be it. I am done with this. I'm going to bed. Goodnight."

Brandon left for their room, while Marlene stood outside on the deck, crying and shocked. She knew all too well what he meant when he said he was done. Even the two miscarriages did not hurt as bad as what she perceived as the possible dissolution of her marriage. After a few minutes of crying, she dusted the snow off her and retreated inside.

Filled with overwhelming hurt and sadness, it felt like it was the longest night of her life.

***

It had been a long night of drinking, making plans and general storytelling for Eddie, Andrew, Kevin and Jeff. They talked about what they should do next and what their options were, which were somewhat limited.

The plans they talked about most entailed either fleeing to Canada or Mexico. They were the early favorite plans. The only drawback was they all did not have a visa or an enhanced license. So that proved problematic.

The next and most logical idea was for them to head down south or out west and lie low, while trying to get lost in the population. Jeff said that was probably their best chance. The only problem there was, they weren't sure they had enough money to make it for very long. Even with a pretty good amount of stolen drug money, they still had to eat, sleep somewhere and get gas for their vehicle. That didn't even allow for the possibility of buying another car, clothes, and other intangibles.

As Andrew and Kevin were laughing and telling funny stories, Eddie began to contemplate the possibility of eliminating one or both of them. It was survival of the fittest for him. It was a very real possibility.

He knew that Kevin was the obvious weak link. But Andrew was more of a direct threat. Andrew didn't hesitate to shoot Odell Gilmoe, so he in turn might not think twice about killing him. The problem with that was, Andrew was a good second and a trusted friend. He never had to worry with Andrew at his side.

Eddie thought Kevin was just plain stupid. That became more apparent when Kevin suggested they go to Hawaii. While they all laughed at the idea, Eddie thought this guy has just done too many drugs to really be worth a damn.

While still extremely pissed at Kevin, Eddie knew that he had to play it smart. He would let Kevin think everything was alright and just fine, for him to let his guard down and then get rid of him. He was dead weight and an untrustworthy witness.

Either way, Eddie knew it had to be done. The questions now were just when, where and how.

One by one, the others crashed or went to bed. The alcohol had taken its toll on them. Eddie strayed up for a while longer thinking. He knew they had to leave soon. Staying here would be problematic. Sooner or later, someone would discover their whereabouts. Whether it was tomorrow or the next day, they had to find a new hideout. If they stayed any longer, they would be pressing their luck.

Eddie finished off his beer and then climbed into his cot. Before nodding off, he knew this was something they had to decide on first thing in the morning.

***

Morning arrived and the snow had not let up.

After sleeping almost twelve hours, Doris Madden finally woke up. Even after all that sleep, she still felt tired and her body ached.

"Oh, God," she moaned, before rubbing her eyes and face.

Slowly she sat up, resting on the side of the bed. As she collected herself and her thoughts, Doris thought she had better look outside. After a couple of minutes, she walked gingerly over to the motel room window and pulled back the curtains.

Doris was shocked to be greeted by the blizzard from hell, still falling on the frozen tundra of Northern Michigan. She could not believe how covered with snow everything was outside.

"Shit!" Doris snapped, disgusted by continued snowfall that had covered her car, making it look like a small hill.

She wondered how she would be able to live and work up here during the colder months. Finally, she walked back over and sat on the bed. There was no way in hell she was going to clean all of that snow off her car.

Doris picked up the room phone and dialed the office number. "Hello," she said. "I am in room three and I was wondering if I could get someone to clean off my car for me. I only ask because I have a job interview this morning. I will gladly pay five dollars if someone would do so."

"I'll send someone," the Motel Manager said.

"Okay, thanks," Doris said. "Could I have them warm up my car for me if I give them my keys too?"

"Sure, they'll be right there," the manager said.

"Thank you," Doris said before hanging up. Then, "No way, I'm fucking *doing* it."

About five minutes later there was a knock on the door. It was a maintenance worker. To Doris, he was like a cross between a character on Bob Newhart's old show with the two brothers named Darryl and a real dufus.

"Are you the lady who wanted her car cleaned off and warmed up?' he asked.

"Yes, I am," Doris replied. "Here they are, and here is your money."

"Which one?" he asked.

"It's the one right there," Doris said, pointing towards a large pile of snow that was covering an unseen automobile.

"Okay," he said. "I'll get it."

Doris then proceeded to close the door and get ready for her interview. She decided to wash up at the basin instead of showering because of the cold weather and snow outside.

Several minutes after getting dressed and checking over her appearance, Doris headed outside. Her car was running and mostly cleaned off. She saw no signs of the employee when returning her room key to the office.

When Doris returned to her vehicle she noticed the shovel lying nearby, broken, and the scoop part of it looked….looked *shredded.* She did not look close enough to notice the bloodstained snow a few feet beyond that.

As Doris opened her car door, she noticed a horrificly putrid smell.

"My God, that's *rotten*!" Doris exclaimed, grimacing in discomfort from the smell.

Doris finally climbed into her car, and slowly maneuvered the vehicle out of the parking lot and down the narrow strip of road.

***

Jeff Sanderson watched as the sheriff's department vehicle slowly pulled into his driveway. It was lucky for them that he woke up to take a piss when he did, or they would have been taken by surprise. Thinking quickly, Jeff woke the others and had them get dressed and ready for anything.

Jeff watched as the officer climbed out of his vehicle and headed to the front door. He recognized him as Deputy Justin Ryan. Jeff, while not a friend of his, was acquainted enough to know him. He decided to greet him outside.

"Morning, Deputy, to what do I owe this visit?" Jeff asked.

"I stopped by to see if you might know the whereabouts of your cousin, Andrew Furlong," Deputy Ryan replied.

"Andy?" Jeff asked. "What's he done?"

"Well, it seems he and some friends of his are suspected of being involved in a shooting in Pontiac," Deputy Ryan continued. "Their names are Edward Temple and Kevin Sullivan. I know that car over there belongs to Furlong."

"Yeah, it's his," Jeff admitted.

"We know he's your cousin," Deputy Ryan said. "Is he here?"

"That is true," Jeff admitted again. "He's my cousin. He's not here. He stopped by yesterday and asked if he could leave his car here for a while. His friends stopped by later and picked him up."

"Do you have any idea where they might be headed?" Deputy Ryan asked.

"Nope,"

"Would you tell me if you did?" Deputy Ryan asked.

"I don't know, is there a reward?" Jeff asked.

"No," Deputy Ryan replied.

"Probably not then," Jeff said. "But, I really don't know where they're headed."

"You know we're going to have to impound your cousin's car," Deputy Ryan said. "So I will be back."

"Okay," Jeff said. "But I might not be here, so do what you have to do. Is there anything else, Deputy?"

"No," replied Deputy Ryan, warily. "Good day, Mr. Sanderson."

Jeff could tell the Deputy did not believe him. He watched as the Deputy climbed back in his vehicle, started it, turned around and slowly drove back down the driveway before finally hitting the main road.

"It's clear guys!" Jeff announced, after going back inside.

Eddie, Andrew and Kevin all piled out of the bedroom.

"Are they gone?" Andrew asked.

"For now," Jeff replied. "But those fuckers will be back."

"How do you know?" Kevin asked. "He might have bought your story."

"No," Eddie said. "He was checking on us."

"We don't know for sure," Kevin argued.

Jeff shook his head. "No," he said. "He knew I was lying. I could tell. He knew it too."

"Okay, let's get the fuck out of here," Eddie barked. "You want to join us?"

"Yeah, I might as well," Jeff said. "I'm an accomplice now. We'll take my truck. It holds more. I can bring some of my guns with us, just in case."

"Good," Andrew said.

"Can we at least eat breakfast first?" Kevin asked.

"No!" the others yelled in unison.

"We don't have no goddamn time for no fucking breakfast!" Eddie exclaimed. "Pack up and let's go. We'll eat breakfast on the road."

***

Rachel and Danielle were on the road almost immediately after breakfast. She was thankful David had cleaned off her car and plowed the driveway before she left. While she hated leaving Melanie so soon, she needed to be with Matt.

Rachel knew that Melanie understood this. Before she left, both women had embraced each other tightly and longer than either could ever recall. It was the hardest time she ever had leaving, but finally managed to do so.

As Rachel listened to the radio while driving, she learned that the worst part of the storm was due to hit soon and that it was the worst storm since 1978.

"*The worst part?*" she thought. "*What the hell? Driving through this is bad enough.*"

While Danielle occupied herself by texting her friends, Rachel gripped the steering wheel tightly as she drove down the road. She was more concerned about Matt than the weather conditions.

As she continued down the road, she thought the weather was as bad as any she could remember.

Blowing Snow

Cassandra Stern momentarily forgot where she was when she woke up. At first, her surroundings were unfamiliar and alien to her. But with the dim morning light, it all came back to her. Last night's encounter with Drake had sapped her emotionally and mentally. While still licking her emotional wounds, it now seemed a distant memory, even though it was less than twelve hours ago.

Cassandra knew that she overslept. When she checked her cell phone she discovered it was well after nine a.m. As she was checking the time, she noticed a text message from Max. the message informed her he would be home early this evening.

Cassandra's heart sank.

"Oh, God," she moaned.

Cassandra knew that her only saving grace was to beat him home, destroy the letter and act as if nothing had ever happened. It was better to have someone who was stable and that truly loved her than no one at all.

She then heard the wind howling as it came off from the lake. As she looked outside, fear filled the pit of her stomach. Last night's blizzard had become worse.

Cassandra knew it would be a race not only against time, but the elements, on whether she got home first.

As Cassandra gathered her belongings and went out the door of her motel room, she cursed herself for being so stupid.

She knew it would be the longest trip of her life.

***

For Marlene Markway, it was already a long trip home and they had not even left yet. She knew Brandon was still pissed at her. Plus, it didn't help that her own brother gave her holy-hell for being over-sensitive and stupid. What made matters worse was that on top of her brother, her friends thought she was not only wrong, but well on her way to wrecking their marriage.

Even her girlfriends, whom she thought would side with her, had told her that she was being a fool.

Brandon, while polite and courteous, had hardly said ten words to her all morning. He was distant.

Very distant.

Marlene was at a loss. She did not know what to say or do to try and repair the damage she'd inflicted. That was what was most depressing to her. The realization she had been the one to screw up was emotionally devastating to her. She was overwhelmed by it.

As Brandon loaded their vehicle, she quietly climbed in after hugging her girlfriends goodbye. Once inside, Marlene let out a sad, painful sigh, as she felt her whole world falling apart.

A trip that had begun with so much promise had turned out to be an epic disaster.

As they drove home, Marlene could not believe what had happened.

It all seemed so unbelievable.

***

"Un-fucking-believable!" Richard Case exclaimed as his sons' team was in the process of being routed in the first game of the day. "Jesus Christ! That's what happens when you spend the night eating pizza."

He watched as his son Steve received a pass and had a breakaway. As he skated down the ice, he was hit by two of the other team's defensemen at once, sandwiching Steve in between them.

Steve went down in a heap on the ice from the physical hit. The other team then took the puck down the ice and scored.

"Shit!" Richard yelled, not noticing Steve's injury at first. "Come on ref, what are you, blind? Call those, goddammit!"

Richard noticed Steve still lying on the ice motionless. His heart sank. Finally, the referees and his coach made their ways out onto the ice. After a few moments, Steve was finally assisted off the ice by the coach and some medical personnel. Richard's heart continued to sink further.

***

Doris Madden's heart sank when she discovered that her interviewer was a cousin to Charlie Merrill, the man she'd inadvertently ordered to his death in her last job. She found this out when the interviewer, a man named Roger Merrill, mentioned how he lost his cousin and how they were proud of their safe work record, even with a couple of limited ability employees there.

When asked about her time at her former position and why she left, Doris explained that it was a mutual parting of the ways and that she needed a new challenge.

She could not tell whether the interviewer believed her or even liked her answer, which bothered her for some reason.

Doris knew one thing almost immediately after the interview had begun, that was this was not going to be the right position for her. While not as lucrative as she'd expected, the pay was better than the other two positions she had interviewed for.

But it was more than that.

She sensed that her interviewer, or in this case her interrogator, knew more about her than than he let on.

Doris sensed that the only reason she received an interview was for him to watch her squirm.

She knew there was no way for her to ever work there. By the time the interview ended, Doris felt she'd driven all this way for nothing.

She really had nothing to show for all her efforts, and now faced a long road back home in absolutely terrible weather conditions.

***

In spite of the terrible weather, Jim Summerlee knew he had to press on. His grandfather had told him so. He was on a mission. One, his grandfather had told him he must undertake this, because it was his *calling* and *destiny*. No sooner had he arrived at his grandparent's, and they were sending him on his way again.

Jim was no fool. He knew when to listen and when to act on things. And while hesitant, he knew that his grandfather was right. He knew that he would be needed somehow to keep people out of harm's way.

He could feel it with every fiber of his being.

Jim knew that he would have to confront evil, so when his grandfather gave him his old deerskin pouch, he knew what he had to do. Inside the pouch there were jars of red clay, consecrated earth and a very sharp silver knife.

"The Wendigo is *real*," his grandfather said before sending Jim back. "It is the very worst and most terrifying being of the Anishinaubae peoples. It is the worst kind of being for *all* peoples, including the White Man. This is the time of the Wendigo. After many winters, it has returned. It is ravenous, and its hunger grows. The evil smell of the Wendigo is in the air. It is faint now, but you will know its presence is close by this. Go and protect those most innocent and who do not know of its existence. You will know when, Grandson. May the Great Spirit be with you."

The words hung with Jim as he made his way back towards the Lower Peninsula. He just hoped that he would know when and where he was needed and if he could actually be of any good against a supernatural entity.

Like his grandfather, Jim knew it was nearby. He could feel its presence, even if he could not see or smell it. He knew what was expected of him. While he was not really afraid of what he had to face, he was very concerned. He did not want to fail.

As Jim continued onward in his Jeep Wagoneer, he stayed focused on what he needed to do. While the weather conditions deteriorated, he knew what lie ahead was going to be even worse.

***

When it came to neighborhood bullies, Buddy Hinson was the absolute worst. At least in this part of the small Michigan town of East Jordan. At twelve year's old, he was much larger than other kids around his age and feared by almost everybody who was at or below his height. He was just plain mean, mainly because he *could* be. He took full advantage of it.

His reign of terror as a bully began when several of the older kids either moved away or graduated and were no longer there anymore to keep this budding tyrant in check. This was a golden opportunity for him to run amok.

Buddy was proud of the fact that he had beaten up every kid around that was his age or younger. He made sure that they did not defy, question or challenge his authority in his self-proclaimed petty tyranny.

At least until about a week ago.

The defiance had come from an eleven-year-old boy named Tim Lawrence who had become weary of Buddy's destructive ways. Tim made several snowmen that stood side-by-side in an empty lot near his house, knowing that Buddy would be around to smash them. Tim decided to build a snowman over a fire hydrant as his way to get Buddy.

The plan worked. Just like clockwork, Buddy came around and knocked down the snowmen one-by-one, first pushing the larger ones and kicking the smaller ones. When he reached the camouflaged fire hydrant. Buddy gave it a mighty kick. Once his foot made contact with the hydrant, he collapsed in a heap writhing in pain and crying. Tim and some of the other kids that witnessed it laughed out loud at their tormentor's misfortune.

Buddy cursed at the kids, especially Tim, as tears flowed down his face. He vowed revenge the first chance he got.

Today, during the snowstorm, would see Buddy Hinson's revenge. He watched as the other kids built a huge snow fort, with Tim Lawrence as the main architect. One by one, they drifted home as the snowstorm grew worse.

As Buddy made his way over to an unaware Tim, he thought about what he was going to do to him. His reputation was at stake and he had to retaliate.

While Tim was working on the top part of a snow wall, he had his back turned to an approaching Buddy. He was totally unaware that he was being stalked.

"Okay asshole," Buddy exclaimed, announcing his presence, grabbing Tim by the shoulders, turning him around. "Get ready to face my vengeance."

Tim was surprised and didn't say anything at first. Then, "What..?"

"Did you just shit your pants?" Buddy mocked, sarcastically, as he grabbed Tim's collar. "Because it sure stinks. Not so brave now, are you shithead? After I kick your ass, I'm telling everybody that I made you shit your pants. You won't be building no more goddamn snowmen again."

Tim looked up and gasped in sheer terror and managed to pull himself free of Buddy's grasp and screamed. Tim then ran for home as fast as he could.

"Where do you think *you're* going, pussy?" Buddy yelled. "You can run but you can't hi…"

Buddy then became aware of the guttural groaning sound of something behind him and noticed that the rancid smell had grown stronger, even after Tim had taken off. He turned to look at what he heard and smelled and was greeted by the most horrific sight he'd ever witnessed. Instead of Tim losing control of his bodily functions, it was Buddy who both urinated and defecated in his pants at the terrible sight.

Buddy Hinson's heart mercifully stopped out of the sheer terror, paralyzing and killing him, sparing him the agonizingly painful death of being ripped apart and eaten alive by the Wendigo. The bully of the neighborhood had finally gotten his comeuppance, joining the ranks of missing children who disappeared without a trace, never to be found.

The bully and terror of the neighborhood had nearly become little more than an appetizer to an evil being with an insatiable hunger, yet his heart and fright had killed him first, and the Wendigo once more had to search for yet another live victim to feed its endless hunger as the snowstorm grew worse.

***

"The weather is getting a lot worse," Kevin announced, as they loaded Jeff's blue Ford Bronco for a trip.

"Very observant, numbnuts," Eddie snapped. "Tell us something we don't know."

Jeff loaded a duffle bag of his belongings into the back of his truck. "It's alright," he said. "It will make us that much harder to find. The cops will be having their hand's full with accidents."

"Let's hope so," Andrew said, as he tossed his bag in the back.

"Do we have everything?" Jeff asked.

"Almost," Kevin replied, loading another bag in the back.

"Well, hurry up stupid," Eddie muttered. "You move as slow as a woman getting ready for an evening out. Let's go, already."

"I am, I am," Kevin feebly protested as he put the last bag in. "Okay, done."

"Okay, let's go," Jeff announced.

All four men quietly climbed into the Bronco.

"Where to?" Andrew asked.

"Who gives a fuck?" Eddie commented. "As long as it ain't here and it's warm."

"I hear that," Jeff said as he started down the driveway to the main road.

As he stopped at the main road to make sure no traffic was coming, they saw the sheriff's department vehicle that had visited earlier on the other side of the road. All four men knew that he was onto them without saying a word.

"I hope you can lose him," Andrew said, concerned.

"So do I," Jeff responded, as he pulled out onto the road and looked back one last time at the sheriff's department vehicle before taking off. "So do I."

"Let's get out of here," Eddie suggested. "I think he knows too much."

As they drove down the road, they were engulfed by the snowstorm and a deep sense of foreboding.

Winter Weather Advisory

Jim Summerlee was filled with a fearful apprehension he had never felt before. As he crossed the Mackinaw Bridge in the middle of the snowstorm from hell, he kept thinking about what his grandfather had told him. Right now he had two missions. The first one was just getting over the bridge in this weather, and the second was facing the Wendigo.

Driving over the bridge was bad enough. As Jim glanced to his left and right, he saw nothing but snowflakes engulfed in a white foggy haze. It was more like evening than morning.

He could also sense its presence nearby.

The question was where and when.

Jim's grandfather said he would know the time and the place.

After finally crossing the Mackinaw Bridge, Jim felt a little more at ease. The drive over the bridge had been tough enough in this weather. Now, he had to mentally prepare himself for the next few hours. He knew it was just a matter of time until he would have to face off with an almost unbelievable evil. As Jim drove through Mackinaw City, the words of his grandfather echoed repeatedly through his head.

In this quest, they offered him great comfort.

***

Reaching I-75 was of little comfort to Rachel Torrey. The weather had been consistently bad since leaving her sister's. While the interstate was in a little better shape than the side roads, the visibility was getting worse and the snow was already accumulating on the previously-paved highway.

"Slow and steady," Rachel said softly to herself.

"You say something, Mom?" Danielle asked, not really paying attention.

"No," Rachel replied. "Just talking to myself."

"Oh, okay," Danielle said, before going back to texting her friends.

"Shit," Rachel muttered.

"What? Danielle asked.

"I forgot to charge my cell phone," Rachel replied. "Maybe I won't need it."

"Yeah, me too," Danielle said. "Mine's getting low on battery too."

"Here's hoping we don't need them," Rachel continued.

Rachel took a deep breath, continued driving and wondered if she had made a mistake leaving when she did. Fortunately, there wasn't much traffic on the road.

"*Slow and steady,*" she thought to herself. "*Slow and steady and you'll be back home safe and sound and everything will be alright.*"

At least she hoped that would be true. Right now, she felt like a desperate, middle-aged woman whose regrets were almost as deep as the snow outside. Plus, the guilt she now carried regarding how she treated Matt was almost as thick as the fog that was beginning to obscure the visibility.

Yes, the conditions were bad, but she needed to repair the damage she'd done to her marriage. She loved Matt that much.

As Rachel continued south on I-75, she didn't dare drive more than forty-five as the visibility and the road conditions were progressively getting worse.

***

"Jesus Christ, can this shit get any worse," Doris Madden muttered more as a statement than a question, as she approached the I-75 exit, only to end up behind someone going barely over 20 miles-per-hour. "Come on dumbass! Speed it up a little, huh?"

Nothing irritated Doris more than when she ended up behind someone on the road that was going much slower than necessary. While she could understand going a little slower because of the conditions, she thought this was ridiculous.

Doris' irritability was greatly exacerbated by the fact she was indeed sore and tired from all of the driving, and that she had to pee badly.

She reached the I-75 exit with the vehicle in front of her going even slower.

"For Chrissake asshole, come on!" she yelled, before finally getting fed up and passing the slow-moving obstacle as soon as she hit the expressway. "So long, suckers. See you next year, because you'll still be here the way you drive."

As Doris headed down I-75, she was racing time and her bladder.

"The first rest stop I find, I'm stopping," she thought.

She hoped that she could make it.

***

Racing against time and weather conditions, Cassandra Stern hoped and even prayed a little that she would make it home before Max. Driving home in terrible weather conditions, she felt both vulnerable and desperate.

Two things she had never felt in her entire life.

Both feelings were unfamiliar and yet very upsetting to her. She did not really know how to deal with them. Cassandra just knew she had to.

Now desperate to try and repair the biggest mistake in her life, she drove dangerously close to being way too fast for the conditions.

If Max arrived home before she did and found the letter, Cassandra knew her life as she currently knew it would be over. He had loved her enough to help her get her business started with some major financial backing. If he found out, he would take everything. She knew him well enough to realize that. Deep down, she wouldn't blame him.

Desperate and scared, she continued to race home. In this race, there were no prizes for coming in second.

And the consolation prize was jack *shit.*

If Cassandra didn't win this, she knew that she was totally screwed, and her comfortably-pampered life would be over.

***

"He's done, Mr. Case," the coach said matter-of-factly. "I'm afraid the tournament is over for him."

"Are you kidding?" Richard asked. "Why? He just got his bell run, that's all. He can still play, for Chrissake."

"League rules," the coach explained. "Any player that suffers an injury, particularly a head injury, they cannot play until they are medically cleared."

"You're shitting?" Richard protested. "That's stupid."

The coach looked at Richard handily. "Mr. Case, it's an attempt to lower brain injuries and concussions. We don't want to see anybody's career shortened or any permanent damage," he finally said. "We have to think of their futures too."

Richard looked over to his son. "Tell him you can play, Steve," Richard ordered. "Tell him you can go."

"My head kind of hurts, Dad," Steve sighed. "I don't feel real good."

"You sound like a pussy," Richard remarked. "Tough it out."

"Mr. Case," the coach said, a bit irritated. "Even if he could go and tough it out, I would not allow him to play. That is the league rules and I will enforce them out of concern for my player."

"Well they're stupid rules," Richard argued.

"That may be," the coach replied. "But he is not playing until he is cleared. So, I suggest you take your son home to see a doctor."

Richard just shook his head in disgust as the coach turned and walked away.

"Dad?" Steve muttered. "Dad? Dad?"

"What?" Richard replied, very annoyed.

Steve then threw up all over Richard's new boots.

"Shit," Richard said with disappointment and disgust.

***

"Shit!" Jeff exclaimed, looking in his rearview mirror.

"What is it?" Andrew asked.

"The sheriff is following us," Jeff announced. "I think he either suspects or he knows."

"That's just fucking great!" Eddie muttered, while glaring at Kevin. "Thanks mutherfucker! Why didn't you just call them and let them know where we were at?"

Kevin just looked sheepishly at his feet. He knew it was better to not say anything. It was always best to just shut-up and take Eddie's verbal wrath.

"Settle down Eddie," Andrew said. "He's still a fair distance behind us."

"Yeah, hopefully I can lose him," Jeff said. "I know the area pretty well. We might be able to disappear into this blizzard somewhere."

"If you say so," Eddie grumbled. "I just hope you can shake this guy."

"I do too," Jeff admitted. "We might just be able to drive right out of his jurisdiction being a sheriff and all."

"Works for me," Eddie said. "You better hope it works for us too."

"What?" Kevin asked, confused.

"I mean if we get into trouble, you're in deep shit," Eddie explained.

"He's right," Jeff agreed. "You're calling home pretty much gave us away."

"Yeah," Andrew agreed. "You had to have told your family where we were."

"I didn't mean…" Kevin started to say.

"It doesn't matter," Eddie said interrupting him. "You did. Now we're in trouble."

"He's getting a little closer," Jeff announced. "We had better think of plan to deal with him just in case."

"How far are we from I-75?" Eddie asked.

"A couple of miles," Jeff replied. "We should be there soon."

"I have one," Andrew said.

"What?" Jeff asked.

"Drive faster for now," Andrew replied.

Jeff nodded and pressed his foot down on the accelerator. After a few minutes, they had lost their pursuer as they drove further into the snowstorm. Jeff soon slowed down due to the poor visibility.

"What is it?" Andrew asked.

Jeff shook his head and said, "We've driven into the snowstorm from hell."

"Damn," Brandon Markway muttered.

***

"Well, don't blame me," Marlene responded, still hurt from last night's argument and trying to make some kind of conversation with Brandon.

"I'm not," Brandon said, disdainfully. "Why would I? You don't control the weather. This rests solely with me. I should have paid better attention to the weather forecast."

"What do you think we should do?" Marlene asked.

Brandon took a deep breath and exhaled. "Keep driving, I guess," he finally said. "Hopefully we can drive out of this shit."

Marlene wondered if he meant the storm itself or the current state of their marriage. She tried to take it as his meaning the snowstorm, but like she tended to do, she wondered if he was implying something else.

"*Stop it!*" she thought to herself. "*Quit reading more into this, than was actually meant. That's what started all of this.*"

She knew that Brandon was not this way. He usually said what he meant and meant what he said. There was no reading more into his statements. He had always been pretty direct their whole marriage. That was the way he was. She knew that.

He had been kind, considerate and there with her through it all.

Marlene knew it had taken some doing on her part to piss him off like she had done. She knew he had been right about continuing to live their lives in spite of their losses or regrets.

She had also been overly sensitive about almost everything since the miscarriages. She knew that. Marlene had basically made it so everybody, especially Brandon, had to walk on egg shells around her and that had been horribly unfair.

That unfairness and over-sensitivity was what had finally pushed him too far. He'd tried and even bent over backwards in helping her deal with everything. But, it still had not been enough for her.

She knew that she had to quit doing all of this, especially if she wanted to save their marriage. Right now she knew it was in jeopardy by her own doing and self-centeredness about wanting to have children. Marlene wondered how and if she really could make things right. Hopefully she could figure out how. She hoped it was not too late.

Only time would tell.

And that was running out.

Right now, the future and her marriage were about as clear as this blizzard.

White-out Conditions

The blizzard was the perfect hunting ground for it. The falling snow camouflaged its sight and sound. The harder the snowfall, the better hidden it remained. With the exception of its strong putrid smell, it moved stealthily throughout the storm, stalking its prey.

While its prey was not as plentiful as the storm grew worse, what was out there had no idea of its presence or even existence.

Even after it had feasted on its victims, the hunger that tormented it continued to grow. Its need to gorge itself continued to grow with each and every victim. The more it ate, the more it had to eat.

A vicious cycle.

Fortunately for it, there were more victims for it to feast on.

The sweet aroma of Man had filled its nostrils, making its mouth water. It grew even more hungry knowing man was nearby. It stalked mankind as it had always done under the perfect cover of snowfall.

The warmer air temperatures mixing with the frozen ground helped to create a low-lying fog that was perfect for it to hunt in….

***

For Doris, this had been the worst blizzard she'd ever experienced, let alone drive in. It was taking her an eternity to get a measly ten miles to the nearest rest area.

What should have only taken a few minutes seemed to be taking more than an hour.

To keep her mind occupied, she counted down the mile markers as she eventually passed them. 10…9…8…7…6…5.

"My God, it's taking forever," she thought. "4…3…2…1..." And then, "Hallelujah, thank you Jesus!" she exclaimed. "I'm going to make it."

The pain of having to go was almost excruciating. Doris hit the exit ramp without even slowing down, feeling like her bladder was ready to explode. As Doris pulled up to the rest stop, she parked her vehicle and ran for the bathroom.

It wasn't until Doris finished going that she realized that the rest stop was deserted.

She knew *somebody* had to have been around because the walkway was recently cleared and salted. What Doris didn't notice was the blood-smeared snow of custodian Elmo Krielack on the opposite side of where she'd parked.

Doris decided she needed to stretch her legs a bit and bought a cup of coffee from the vending machine. After taking a sip, she let out a sigh of relief. It felt great not being cooped-up in the car for a while.

As she continued to sip her coffee, she checked the map to see exactly where she was. The 'You are here' indicated she was just south of Grayling.

"Good," she thought.

After a few minutes, she finished her coffee. She really didn't have to be anywhere, so she decided to relax a bit.

Even though it wasn't the best, she purchased another cup of coffee from the vending machine. Right now, it would do just fine. She decided to take her time and finish it before venturing back out into the snowstorm.

***

Let's get out of this snowstorm for a while," Jeff suggested upon seeing the rest area sign outside of Grayling.

"Yeah, I need to take a shit," Eddie commented.

"Only ten miles to go," Jeff said. "What do you say Andy?"

"Sounds good," Andrew said. "I need to use the can too."

"How about you?" Jeff asked Kevin.

"Yeah, man, whatever," Kevin responded.

Eddie just shook his head in disgust and irritation, still extremely pissed at Kevin. He really wanted to shoot him, but knew it was best not to. Unfortunately for now, they were stuck with him.

***

"Stuck!" Doris yelled. "How in the fuck does one get stuck in a goddamn rest area? Jesus Christ! What next?"

Doris tried to gun the engine and rock herself out of the deep snow. She then heard a loud pop, and then the engine just running hard and doing nothing.

"Goddammit!" she spat, angrily.

Doris knew she was stuck there for the time being. She also realized with the heat not working, she would have to go back inside the building. She slowly opened the car door and climbed out. She trudged through the tire tracks her car had made in the snow, cursing with every step.

As she neared the sidewalk that led to the building, she was caught in two beams of light quickly bearing down on her.

"Oh, shit!" she muttered.

***

"Oh, shit!" Jeff yelled, as he suddenly caught sight of a woman in the parking lot of the rest area. Jeff managed to swerve at the last minute, but nevertheless clipped the woman, sending her sprawling. He parked the vehicle and all four men climbed out.

"Is she dead?" Kevin asked.

"How the fuck do I know?" Jeff responded.

Doris got up on her knees and finally stood up. "You stupid bastard!" she shouted. "Don't you know how to drive in a parking lot? You could have fucking *killed* me!"

"Sorry lady, but we didn't see you until the last minute," Jeff tried to explain.

"Well, I'm calling the cops after a call for a tow truck," Doris announced. "I'm calling the cops to report an accident. You need to be locked up the way you dri…"

Eddie connected with an overhand right to Doris' face. "Fuck that idea, bitch!" he said, as Doris collapsed in a heap on the ground.

The others just stared, shocked by Eddie's reaction.

"What do we do now?" Andrew asked.

"Fuck it," Eddie snapped. "We don't need her calling the cops on us. Besides, I still need to take a shit."

The others shrugged, laughed and then followed him into the building as Doris lied semi-conscious in the snow. When they had finished using the facilities, all four men checked the map that told them where they were.

"Boy, we have a bit of a hike," Andrew commented, as Eddie and Jeff nodded in agreement.

"Let's get out of here, before that pain-in-the-ass in the snow wakes up," Eddie said.

"Sounds like a plan," Jeff agreed. "I have to warn you, we need to hit a gas station soon."

Just as the men were agreeing to leave, Doris was recovering. Still groggy and semi-conscious, she moaned and grimaced in pain. Her head hurt like hell. At first, she didn't remember what happened. After a few moments, it gradually came back to her.

Still groggy, she clumsily got up from the snow-covered ground and headed towards her car. Facing away from the building, she didn't see the men get back into their truck and start to leave. She was still too dazed to notice that as she stumbled around like a zombie in *Night of the Living Dead.*

"Hey. Eddie your girlfriend is back," Andrew joked.

"Fuck her," Eddie spat. "I wouldn't even fuck that with Kevin's undersized dick."

The men all roared with laughter.

As Jeff reversed the truck and then began to creep forward, Doris turned around.

"Fuck you!" she hissed as she stood in their path, giving them the finger.

"Why that rotten…" Jeff started to say, as he drove towards her with increasing speed. "Better move, bitch!"

Doris didn't believe that they would deliberate hit her. And then…

"Oh, shit!" she exclaimed, just before the truck collided into her.

Doris then found herself sprawled out upon the ground. She watched as the truck sped off, disappearing into the blizzard. As Doris lay in a clump upon the ground, she knew instinctively that her leg was broken. As she tried to move, the pain was intense.

She knew that she had to get inside or risk hypothermia. Slowly and painfully, she began to drag her injured body back inside the rest area. After a few feet of crawling across the snow on her belly, she had to stop and rest.

She was sore, tired and in great pain. Finally, after a few excruciating minutes, she resumed crawling, grunting and groaning all the way.

She then heard something nearby. She naturally assumed that it was the men who'd hit her, returning to torment her as she crawled along the ground.

"How about a hand here?" she asked. "You pricks owe me that."

There was silence.

"Did you retards hear me?" she asked. "You fuckers can at least help me up."

Once again silence, this time followed by a low guttural growl.

"You pricks really are pathetic," she continued. "Getting your kicks watching me crawl around here, damn near helpless. I got one more thing to say to you assholes. Fuck you!"

Doris turned and raised her hand, giving them the finger. But as she turned, she was greeted by the most horrific sight she'd ever seen.

All she could manage to do was gasp. There were no words. Even if she could speak, there was no describing the monstrous creature that towered over her. Quickly, Doris turned and began to crawl away. At one point, she tried to get to her feet and limp away, but only managed to fall back down.

The horrific creature let out a shrill wail and moved towards Doris, who had wet her herself in fear. Just as she reached the curb, the creature grabbed her by her good leg and lifted her upwards.

"Oh, Sh…" she screamed.

The creature bit her head off in mid-scream. Finally, the creature finished off the rest of her, as the falling snow covered Doris's blood that had dripped onto the ground.

The self-proclaimed bitch of the business world and heartless head honcho had finally run into something worse than herself. She was devoured with about as little effort as one would eat a chicken nugget.

Once again the Wendigo feasted, and once again its hunger was still not sated. But it knew there was more prey nearby, so it would not be long before its next meal.

It could smell it.

The hunger drove it forward.

Drifting Snow

Richard Case could not believe how quiet it was in the blizzard. In an ironic way, the silence was almost deafening as he checked over his vehicle's engine. The quiet was eerie and disturbing to him as he looked around to see if there was something amiss. This was the first time recently that Richard thought of something other than hockey.

Once again he was frustrated. This time, it was by his sons' lack of great play and eventual injuries. He grumbled almost incessantly that they were forced to leave because of Steve's concussion. When Gordon came up limping a short time later, the coach insisted they be taken home to get the proper attention.

So they had to leave the tournament. Richard knew that if the boys were to play hockey again, he would have to take them to their doctor and get them cleared.

Now a few hours later, his vehicle died somewhere in the middle of Bumfuckville Nowhere on I-75, adding to his already-compounded frustrations.

"Why the fuck couldn't you have died in the middle of downtown Grayling or closer to town, you piece-of-shit?" he thought.

"Turn the key!" he barked to Gordon inside the car.

Gordon turned the key in the ignition.

Click.

"Turn it again!" he ordered

Click.

"Again!"

Nothing.

"It ain't working!" Gordon protested.

"Again, goddammit!" Richard ordered, only hearing a click. "Fuck!"

Gordon just shrugged his shoulders, dumfounded, as Steve sat in the back with his eyes closed, just listening.

Richard walked back to the driver's side of the vehicle. "Well, come on then," he said. "Let's hike it back to town."

Gordon looked at his father like he had two heads and was completely crazy. "Dad, I can't make it," he said. "My ankle hurts too bad."

"And my head still hurts," Steve muttered, grimacing in pain.

Richard just stared coldly at his sons. "My ankle hurts,' he said, mockingly. "My butt hurts, my finger nail hurts. Jesus Christ, are you guys wussies. Makes me wonder if I had sons or daughters."

Gordon was taken aback. "I quit hockey," he said. "I really hate it lately. It isn't fun anymore."

"Same here," Steve agreed.

"You will quit when I say you can," Richard snapped. "It isn't about fun, goddammit. It's about winning. I will be back and we will finish this conversation. So you had better be ready for it. You will do as I say."

Gordon just glared. "I don't care," he finally said. "I don't like hockey anymore."

"Same here," Steve said, as he rubbed his aching head.

"Yeah, well we'll see," Richard threatened as he grabbed his gloves and hat. "I will see you two later."

Richard slammed the car door, huffing and puffing in anger and frustration as he did so.

"Lock the door, Gordie," Steve said. "Just in case there's something out there."

Without hesitation, Gordon quietly did what his brother asked.

Once again, Richard was frustrated. This time it was his son's mutiny from hockey. It really upset him that they couldn't see he only wanted them to be as good as they could be and to have opportunities that he never dreamed of.

He thought they were just too young and stupid to see it.

As Richard continued northward on the shoulder of the expressway, he could hear his boots making a muffled semi-crunch sound.

He turned around and could hardly see his vehicle in the thick snowfall. As Richard started walking again, he thought he heard something large nearby step into the snow. He looked around and did not see a thing. He continued onward.

After a few steps, he was confronted by a horrid, godawful smell of rot and decay.

"What the fuck?" he muttered, wondering what could smell that bad. He wondered if it was the carcass of a dead animal.

***

"My God, did you fart?" Gordon asked Steve. "It smells like something died."

"I thought it was you," Steve said. "It's awful. It's making me sick. Oh man, I think I have to hurl. Unlock the doors."

"Oh no," Gordon said. "Don't puke in here. Dad will be pissed."

Steve quickly threw open the back door, leaned over and vomited on the snow-covered ground. "Oh, God," he muttered after getting sick. He stayed, leaning over to make sure he didn't get sick again.

After a few moments, he felt a little better. It was then he realized how overpoweringly horrid the smell was. Steve also heard the low guttural growl of something large nearby. Steve then looked up, only to see what nightmares were made of.

Steve screamed in terror, and in one swift motion closed the car door just in time as the creature reached down, attempting to seize him.

"Lock the door!" he ordered. "Lock the door!" Lock the door!"

"What is it?" Gordon asked.

The creature let out a wail in frustration.

"I don't know," Steve answered with tears streaming down his cheeks. "But that's where the smell comes from."

While neither boy could see it clearly, they knew something was outside, probing for a way to get in. They heard it try the door handle, then press and pull in other areas but to no avail. After a few minutes, it gave up, the smell dissipating with it.

***

Richard heard the wail, but couldn't figure out what and where it was. It sounded like it was all around. For once he was unsure of what to do. He hoped the boys would be alright. As he continued onward in the blizzard, he wondered if he was on a fool's errand since the conditions had drastically worsened.

Even the horrid smell he'd noticed earlier had gotten worse.

Then there was dead silence.

It was disturbing.

Richard wished he had his handgun. He decided to return to the vehicle. He knew the boys were alone and they might need him after all.

As he turned to take a step, he heard something large press into the snow with a "poof" sound.

"*There is something out there,*" he thought. "*What in the hell is it?*"

"Hello?" he called out, but only received silence in return. "Hello? Hello?"

Once again silence.

Richard became wary and suspicious. Slowly, he made his way back to his vehicle. Then he heard the "poof" sound of something very large stepping into the snow. It was then the repugnant smell became almost overpowering. He then heard the low, guttural growl from something in the blizzard.

As he stood listening, some king of liquid dripped upon his shoulder. As he wiped it off his coat with his glove, he inspected it……it was syrupy and see-through and reminded Richard of dog drool.

He immediately looked up as more of the substance hit him in the face. When he finished wiping it away, he was greeted by the most horrible sight he could ever imagine. For a long second or two he was physically stunned by the terrifying sight of this creature.

Richard went to scream, but could only manage a noiseless gulp followed by a gasp. The loudest, most obnoxious parent in the hockey arena was frightened into complete silence. Even the threat of lawful eviction from an arena had never silenced him like this horror had done.

Richard took off on the best dead run he could muster in the snow and ice, with fear driving him every step of the way. After about a hundred yards, he could see the outline of the Escape. He could feel the creature in close pursuit.

"*Dear God,*" he thought. "*I'm going to make it…*"

He then slipped and fell into a small drainage ditch, just as the creature attempted to reach out and grab him. He rolled over and struggled to his feet, where he fell down again. His hands and knees ached badly and throbbed. Finally, he crawled upon his hands and knees out of the ditch and towards his car. It felt like it was taking forever. He sensed the creature had momentarily lost track of him and hoped he had time to get into his vehicle.

Richard finally reached the Escape, still on his hands and knees. He tried the handle frantically, but it was locked. In desperation, he pounded upon the lower part of the driver's side door.

Finally able to regain his voice, he began to yell. "Let me in, boys. Let me in. Let me in!!!"

"It sounds like, Dad," Gordon said. "What do I do?"

"Do you see Dad?" Steve asked.

"No."

"Then it probably ain't Dad," Steve said. "It's probably that thing trying to trick us, somehow."

"Okay," Gordon said. "That bad smell is back too."

Richard cried out as the Wendigo dragged him away by his leg into the snowstorm.

Without much fight and screaming like a little girl, the tough-talking Richard Case was ripped apart and devoured by a legendary evil creature few knew of or believed in. Once again, it wailed loudly in pain and anguish from its never-ending hunger.

Dense Fog Advisory

"Oh, my God, I can't see a damned thing," Rachel said, slowing down the car as the peak of the storm hit. "I bet I can't see more than a mile in front of me."

"What's the matter, Mom?" Danielle asked as she finally stopped texting her friends.

"We've driven into a white-out," Rachel replied with some apprehension. "It's when there is both fog and snow."

"Oh, are we stopping?" Danielle asked.

"No," Rachel answered with some concern. "I'm just going to creep along at a real low speed. Hopefully, we can get through this alright."

"Boy, I ain't ever seen it like this before, have you?" Danielle asked, amazed.

"I have," Rachel said calmly, while scanning the fog-covered road for any sudden surprises. "When I was pretty young. It was 1978, I think. It made the news. A lot of cars were piled up after crashing into each other. I can't remember all of the details, but it was bad."

"I wish we could have stayed at Uncle David and Aunt Mel's," Danielle opined. "This is kind of scary."

Rachel took a deep breath and then exhaled. She thought the same thing, but finally said. "As long as we keep going slow and steady, I think we'll be alright."

***

"It's alright, boy," David Becker said to his beagle Brody as it looked outside and wimpered.

David knew that he sensed something out in the storm. It wasn't like his dog to whimper at nothing. Brody whimpered again when the wind howled. This time he went over to pet his dog and listen carefully.

"It's okay," he said, trying to comfort and soothe his dog's fears. "The storm is at its zenith."

David got up and went over to the side door of his garage. He stood in the doorway, where he watched and listened intently. He sensed something was in the area. He could feel it, only not as keenly as his dog. David also caught the stench of something pretty bad. The aroma of death and decay hung in the air, a short distance away.

He knew the smell was not normal either. Very seldom did one smell a decaying animal anywhere in the dead of winter. That was usually in warmer temperatures. Usually predators and other scavengers finished off any dead carcass.

For some strange reason, David thought of the stories and legends about certain Manitous that smelled bad and fed on Man that he'd heard from some of his Native American friends. He had never given them much credence, until now.

As the wind howled across the nearby field, he thought he caught the sound of something shrieking in the distance.

"Come on, Brody," he said. "It's time we closed up shop and headed in."

Brody looked at his owner affectionately as David turned off the garage's lights, and closed the door behind them as they headed inside the house. The dog ran ahead and looked back at David to hurry into the safety of the house.

"In for the duration?" Melanie asked upon seeing him and the dog. "You want a treat, Brody?"

Brody barked, knowing what that meant.

"Yeah," David answered. "Have you heard from your sister?"

"No," Melanie replied. "Why?"

"Well, as bad as the storm is, maybe you should check on her and see how she's doing," he replied. "Just to make sure they're alright."

Melanie looked at David handily. "You're really concerned, aren't you?"

David nodded. "Yeah," he said. "This storm is terrible. It's a real monster."

***

With a terrible headache, in a monster storm, Cassandra Stern had finally reached I-75. The stress and tension of driving and the situation had been the cause of her headache. She told herself that if she was fortunate enough to beat Max home, headache or not, she would gladly have sex with him if he demanded it. That was the bargain she was making with herself and her conscience.

But all that was moot right now.

She had to get home first. And as fast as she had to get home, she still had to stop for gas, use the bathroom and get something to eat and drink to sustain herself. This would cost her valuable time.

Valuable time that was already very limited as it was now.

Cassandra was determined to go as long as possible without stopping.

The biggest problem was the severity of the snowstorm and how it was hampering her progress. She felt better when she passed road signs that read; Exit 251 5 Miles and Road 127 Exit 10 Miles. This would be a perfect opportunity for her to gas up, go to the bathroom and get some food in one stop. Right now she was making pretty good time in spite of the weather. That was the good news.

The bad news was, the blizzard was not letting up and she still had a hell of a long way to go.

***

"How much longer do we have to go?" Kevin asked, almost whining from the backseat.

"Well, that depends," Eddie replied.

"On what?" Kevin asked.

"On where we decide to go," Eddie continued. "The cops are looking for us for killing those niggers. So, it depends. We have to be somewhat careful and strategic on where we go."

"Yeah, but I didn't kill anybody," Kevin said. "Shit, you and Andy did that."

"You were there too," Andrew said. "So, that makes you an accessory."

"He's right," Jeff said as he continued driving. "Your ass is grass, just the same as if you pulled the trigger. So, is mine for harboring you. Though I may get a little less for that. Either way we're in deep shit."

"Yeah, so don't delude yourself into thinking you're not part of this," Eddie snapped. "You're in this whether you like it or not."

"Well, I don't like it," Kevin admitted. "It really sucks getting blamed for shit I didn't actually do."

"Tough shit!" Eddie cursed. "We'd have been free and clear if you hadn't told your sister where we were."

"Not to mention giving the Gilmoes your contact information," Andrew chimed in. "That was pretty stupid."

"In other words, we don't care if your dumbass doesn't like it," Eddie said.

Kevin sat in the back seat quietly fuming. He knew the guys were still very pissed at him, but he no longer cared. Deep down, he knew that the first chance he had, he would take off and leave them. He didn't care if the police got them or not at this point. He didn't care if he got in trouble as well. They were assholes, and he was beginning to not like them at all.

"*No, hate them was more accurate,*" he thought.

Kevin might not have been the smartest person in the group, but he could still make some plans for himself if he had to. He just had to know when to do it. He sat quietly in the backseat listening and watching the others while he waited for his opportunity.

Kevin might have been dumb, but he wasn't stupid.

"Why don't you pull off on the next exit?" Andrew suggested. "We can get our bearings and figure out what to do next."

"Right now, my concern is if that bitch we hit tells the cops about us," Jeff said. "I wonder what she might say. Did we leave any clues or anything for them to go on?"

"That's if she's even alive," Eddie commented. "Hopefully she's not. Maybe she's a bitchsicle."

"Still, we have to assume she is," Jeff continued. "We have to assume the worst and that she is alive."

Eddie nodded in agreement, knowing that Jeff was dead right.

"Jesus Christ," Eddie muttered. "I can't see a goddamn thing. How are you still able to see anything?"

Jeff stared straight ahead intently. "I am following older tire tracks as best as I can," he responded. "I don't know how much longer I can do it. This damned storm is not letting up."

"Belch might be right," Eddie "admitted. "Maybe we need to stop and take a breather and figure out what we're doing."

"Wow, look at the fog," Kevin gasped, astounded.

"Boy the visibility is getting worse," Andrew agreed.

***

"I really can't see now," Rachel admitted. "The storm is at its worse. I'm moving into the slow lane. That's if I can find it."

Danielle looked around both fascinated and horrified at the general lack of visibility from the blizzard and fog. "Holy shit," she finally said.

Rachel, who usually scolded Danielle for her language, ignored the remark. She was too focused upon driving in the terrible conditions to really bother with one little swear word. It really wasn't important at the moment. She knew that Danielle was right. In fact, she had thought it herself, as their vehicle was crawling along at about 20 miles per hour as the top speed.

"We may have to find an exit and pull in somewhere," Rachel concluded. "That, or a rest area to ride this out."

"This weather really sucks," Danielle snapped.

***

"Man, this sucks," Brandon Markway said, driving past other vehicles that were having a more difficult time than he was navigating through the storm. "The visibility is getting worse. It's getting dangerous."

"We could have stayed at the lodge," Marlene replied, pointedly.

Brandon nodded in agreement. "Yeah," he finally said. "We could have. I would have gotten drunk with your brother and you would have been pissed off and miserable. We can be that at home."

Marlene knew what he meant and understood his reasoning. She knew better than to push his buttons any more than she already had. Besides, he was right. He would have gotten drunk with her brother and she would have been miserable and angry.

Marlene was in 'repair' mode for her marriage and did not want to do any more damage than she already had. She wanted to fix her strained marriage.

She had to.

So, for now, she would not say much. At least not anything that could be construed as argumentative. She had done enough of that.

"What do you want to do?" Brandon asked after a few minutes.

"I don't know," Marlene replied. "But I trust your judgment."

Brandon looked over and smiled at her. "Thanks," he said

Marlene smiled back. "*Maybe there was a chance,*" she thought.

Wind Chill Factor

"What are the chances of that happening?" Eddie exclaimed as Jeff pulled from the exit and into an Amaco Convenience Station parking lot. "Two fucking cop cars. And State boys no less. Go fucking figure. We get all of the goddamn luck."

"Shit," Andrew muttered. "So, what do we do?"

"Just be cool," Jeff said, parking next to the gas pumps. "Act like there's nothing wrong and we'll be fine. We're just four guys needing to make a pit stop. They're probably out helping people in this weather, so they might not pay much attention to us."

"Yeah," Eddie snapped as he turned and looked directly at Kevin. "Don't do anything stupid."

"Who, me?" Kevin asked.

The others all turned, looking at him and almost in unison said. "Yeah, you."

After a few moments, the men climbed out of the truck. Jeff went to the bathroom, then paid for a Pepsi and gas while the others went looking for their own food and drink. He quickly headed outside and began pumping his gas.

Eddie and Andrew kept a wary eye on Kevin.

Kevin felt like he was being watched. He would look up now and then only to find that Eddie or Andrew was looking at him. Eddie and Andrew found what they wanted and headed up to the counter.

Standing near the counter talking to the store manager were two state police troopers. Both had large cups of coffee and were built like pro football linebackers. Both Eddie and Andrew glanced over and nodded respectfully. They thought if they didn't, that the troopers might have gotten suspicious.

Meanwhile, Kevin was taking his sweet time looking around. He was tired of riding in the back seat and wanted to enjoy this time outside the truck.

"Come on, dummy," Eddie muttered after getting through the check-out lane. "We need to go."

"I'm coming, Eddie," Kevin replied, loudly. "Hold on already."

Eddie cringed upon hearing Kevin say his name out loud in the middle of the store. He tried not to show how upset he was about it in his body language, but on the inside he was livid. If he could have, he would've killed Kevin right then and there.

But Eddie knew better and was smart enough to not say or do anything. It also wasn't lost on him that the state troopers noticed Kevin as well.

"Hey Andrew, do you have a buck?" Kevin asked, as he approached the counter.

Andrew winced when Kevin called his name, but quietly handed him a dollar. One trooper quietly excused himself and went out to his vehicle. Eddie and Andrew sensed that the troopers were checking on them and quickly headed out to the truck.

"Everything alright?" Jeff asked.

"Get us out of here, fast," Eddie said. "Numbnuts in there practically told the cops who we were."

"What?" Jeff asked. "How?"

"Just get in and we'll tell you," Eddie barked.

"Okay guys let's get out of here!" Kevin said as he headed to the truck and climbed in.

Once everybody was in, Jeff took off. "So what happened?" he asked.

"Stupid here said our names out loud with the cops around," Andrew explained.

"Oh, shit," Jeff said. "That's why the cop looked over here before he got in his car. Should we leave him."

"Fuck no," Eddie replied. "I want to beat the shit out of him before I shoot him in the ass."

"What?" Kevin asked.

"Jesus Christ, do you have any goddamn sense?" Eddie asked. "Are you that goddamn stupid?"

"What?" Kevin asked, ignorant to what was wrong.

"You said our names inside with the police around, you moron," Andrew explained. "Are you really that fucking stupid? I mean really?"

"Oh," Kevin grunted.

"Oh?" Eddie shouted. "Oh? Is that all you can fucking say is, oh? Jesus Christ, you almost got us caught again. I swear you're dead from the neck up sometimes."

While Kevin sat in silence taking the verbal abuse, he seethed in anger and frustration. He did not think he did anything that bad or wrong.

As Jeff pulled back onto I-75, they could see the state police vehicles' lights flashing.

"You had better gun it," Eddie suggested.

Jeff sped up as fast as he could under the conditions. "I'll try to lose them in this fog."

"If we can't shake them, find the next rest area and we'll steal another vehicle if we have to," Eddie said.

"Sounds like a plan," Jeff replied.

Jeff looked at Eddie. He knew that Eddie was not only going to steal another vehicle, but also deal with Kevin…

***

As Matt Torrey hobbled into his home, he still felt like he'd been beaten up. His body ached and throbbed from head to toe. He was more injured than he initially thought and cared to admit.

His sons, Mathew, Mark and John all helped him from the hospital and into his house. Mathew unlocked the house, while Mark and John walked with him and assisted him inside. From there it was all a matter of guiding him to his big easy chair in the family room.

"You alright, Dad?" Mathew asked as his dad winced and sat down.

Matt quietly nodded affirmatively. His head and body ached too badly to really answer verbally.

"Well, at least your home now," Mark said. "You just rest and relax while we handle things."

"Thanks, I appreciate that," Matt said.

"No problem," John said. "So, what would you like to do for dinner tonight?"

"I don't know," Matt replied. "Isn't it a little early to worry about that?"

"Yeah, well with the weather being as bad as it is, we had better decide now," John countered.

"I say pizza," Mark suggested. "It has all of the food groups and everybody likes it. It's just a question of where."

Matt snickered at Mark's logic.

"Yeah, we can hang out with the old man drinking beer and eating pizza until Mom gets back," Mathew laughed. "Just like hunting season."

"Oh brother," Matt said. "Don't you guys have college and jobs?"

"Nope," Mathew replied. "First off it's the weekend. Next, we all made contingency plans. We brought homework. Also, any girls we know are not around, so we can't even go out with them."

"Yeah, it is the weekend, Dad," John announced.

"Oh, yeah, I forgot," Matt admitted. "I lost track of time."

"Besides, the way you're moving, I think you're going to need us for a while," Mark said. "You definitely aren't snowblowing or shoveling the driveway any time soon."

Matt shifted in his chair and seethed in pain. "Yeah, you may be right there," he grimaced.

"That whiplash effect is the worst," John observed. "You get shaken up and jerked around after getting hit. I remember my fender bender and I ached for a few days. And you had it much worse."

"Yeah, we'll take good care of you, Dad," Mathew said. "So don't worry. We won't even be slobs."

"Thanks," Matt said. "I appreciate it. You're good sons."

"So, is everybody okay with Calabrese's for the pizza?" John asked.

"Yeah," Mark and Matt said, almost in unison.

Matt quietly nodded in agreement. As he closed his eyes to relax, he thought about Rachel, how much he missed her, and hoped she was alright.

***

In spite of the horrible road and weather conditions, Rachel could not stop thinking about Matt and hoped he was alright. Melanie had helped her put everything that was important to her back in perspective. She felt terrible not doing that herself.

The fact that Matt was in a car accident brought it all home to her.

Through thick and thin and better or worse, they had weathered the storms together that life had thrown at them. The mountains had been easy, it was the small grains of sand in their shoes that had driven them nuts.

But, like most other couples, they'd made it through those things as well.

At least until recently.

The guilt was almost overwhelming and eating away at her. Tears welled up in her eyes as she thought about Matt and all they had been through. She thought about how they made love before leaving for her sister's and how nice it had been.

He was the love of her life and she needed him.

She wanted to call him so badly, but decided against it because she was driving in some terrible conditions. The first chance she got, she'd call him. Rachel wanted Matt to know that he had been on her mind since she left.

As she continued southward, her speed was gradually decreasing as the visibility worsened.

***

By the time Cassandra Stern pulled onto the exit she could barely see a thing. She was already tired, hungry, and stressed to the max from all of the tough driving.

Once off the exit she could make out some tall hazy lights a short distance away that she assumed was some gas station/convenience store combination. She didn't care which one it was, as long as she could get gas, go to the bathroom and get some food and drink.

She slowly pulled alongside a pump. Once parked, she took a deep breath and exhaled. Cassandra knew she had well over a hundred miles to go. While it may have been a little less, it was still over a hundred.

The blizzard and the dangerous road conditions only seemed to add to the distance.

Cassandra climbed out of her vehicle. She swiped her credit card on the pump and began filling her tank. Then she headed inside. She quickly went for the bathroom.

Ten minutes later, she was searching the aisles for something halfway decent to eat and drink. Cassandra ended up grabbing a shitty-tasting Cappuccino and a couple of doughnuts. It wasn't the greatest selection for a snack or a meal, but it would do for now.

As she made her way back to her vehicle, her phone's ringtone went off. She'd just received a text message.

It was *Max*.

He hardly ever texted.

Cassandra's heart sank. She was filled with a sense of dread.

Once back inside her car, Cassandra worked up the courage to check the message.

It read: *Flight delayed. Snowstorm.*

Cassandra was filled with a sense of relief. Not a great sense, but enough to make her feel a little better and a little less stressed.

The great unknown factor that crossed her mind was, how long was Max's flight delayed and how long would it take her to get back home?

The sense of relief she had quickly subsided as she drove back on the freeway.

That earlier sense of dread had returned.

Snow and Ice

Even though it was getting colder inside the vehicle, Stephen and Gordon Case dreaded the thought of going outside. Both dreaded what they thought was still out there. They bundled up as best they could to stave off the cold. Aside from being afraid to go outside, both were not in the best shape to do so either.

"Dad's been gone for quite a while," Gordon observed, trying to make idle conversation.

"Yeah," Stephen acknowledged.

"Well, how soon do you think he'll be back?" Gordon asked. "Do you think he got to town yet?"

Stephen gave Gordon a look that answered the question without saying a word. Gordon knew by that look, Stephen thought their dad was dead, or at least dying. A victim of the horror lurking out in the snowstorm.

"Do you think he's…?" Gordon started to ask.

"Yes," Stephen snapped, cutting him off.

"What do you think we should do then?" Gordon asked. "It's getting colder and we can't stay here forever."

"We can't go out there either," Stephen replied. "At least not now. That thing is still out there somewhere."

"I don't smell it as badly," Gordon argued. "Maybe it's not as close. It might be further away."

Stephen just shook his head no. "It's close enough," he said. "That's what it wants, to trick us into leaving. We're at least safe here. It wants us to leave so it can get us."

"Maybe we can outrun it and it won't catch us," Gordon suggested.

"I can't Gord," Stephen protested. "My head still aches a little and I don't feel so hot. Plus, your ankle is hurt too. There is just no way."

Gordon took a deep breath and exhaled, glumly. He knew his brother was right. "Okay, we'll stay," he said as Stephen nodded *yes*. "At least for now, until it gets too cold or help arrives."

"Okay," Stephen said as he closed his eyes to rest. "Thanks."

Gordon nodded. He realized then how much he really did love his brother. While he wouldn't admit it openly, he did.

The strong stench returned. They could hear something outside that sounded like fingertips or nails touching the roof of the car as if it was feeling for a way in. Both boys knew it had returned. They looked upwards, listening intently to every sound as the nightmare outside probed for a way in.

Chills ran through them as much from fright as the cold as they sat confined inside.

"I hope it's not strong enough to open a locked door," Gordon wondered aloud.

"Me too."

Both boys, unable to move much, sat cold and frightened beyond description as the horror outside continued in vain to try and get to them.

As the snowstorm raged, the Wendigo shrieked in angry frustration as its endless hunger became more painful. It lurked around the vehicle, hoping to find a way in, or that its occupants would leave.

It desperately needed to feed.

***

As Jim Summerlee continued south on I-75 he knew the elements were not the only deadly thing out there. He sensed that he was nearing the Wendigo and where he had to be. The feeling was much stronger now as he passed through Grayling with the storm at its worst. The hair standing up on his arms told him it was close. Yet somehow, Jim no longer felt fear like he had earlier. He was still afraid, but felt confident and self-assured, as if he knew how things would turn out. While not looking forward to a confrontation, he was ready.

As Jim continued driving he caught a glimpse of an SUV on the side of the road. He slowed down and began his approach.

With every fiber of his being he knew this was it.

***

"What is it?" Stephen asked, opening up his eyes, upon hearing something approaching.

"Huh?" Gordon asked, waking up from his brief slumber. "What? I don't know. What is it?"

"I thought I heard something," Stephen announced. "It's probably just that thing hanging around outside."

Gordon looked around, seeing nothing through the snow-covered windows. Suddenly the vehicle inside became bathed in lights as something drew closer.

"What the…?" Gordon asked.

"It's that thing," Stephen said, frightened. "It's trying to get in again. I know it is."

Gordon turned and tried to look out the back window, but it too was covered with snow. "Shit, I can't see a thing," he said.

"Don't let it in," Stephen pleaded. "It's just trying to trick us."

***

Jim parked his Wagoneer only a few feet away from the Ford Escape. While he was uncertain there were people inside, he knew that he had to check. As he climbed out of his vehicle, he scanned his surroundings warily. He had to be alert and ready to act in case Wendigo suddenly returned.

The lingering stench of death, decay, rot and corruption let him know that the Wendigo was somewhere in the area searching for prey. Jim knew that he had to act quickly or it might learn of his presence.

As he approached the vehicle, he noticed some reddish-black stains on the door. Immediately, he knew it was blood. He had a bad feeling about it. Jim decided to knock on the driver's side window.

"Hello?" he called out. "Is there anybody in there? Are you alright?"

Jim knocked again.

"Someone's knocking on the window," Gordon announced.

"Ignore it," Stephen said. "It's that thing again. It wants to get us."

Jim called out again. "Is there anybody in there? I'm here to help. Are you alright?"

"Maybe it really *is* someone here to help, Steve," Gordon suggested. "Maybe it's not that monster."

"It's that thing, I'm telling you," Stephen, stubbornly argued. "Don't do it!"

Jim cleared snow off the window and peered through the frosted glass. He couldn't make out much, but thought he caught a glimpse of someone in the passenger side front seat. They didn't appear to be responsive. Jim hurried over to the other side window and wiped off the snow.

"Hello," he said, startling the boy, who appeared to finally see him.

Gordon jumped back startled in the front seat. "Holy shit!" he gasped, but didn't unlock the door.

"We have to get out of here," Jim said through the window. "There is something dangerous nearby. You cannot stay in there or you will freeze. We need to leave."

Gordon looked back at Stephen.

"Don't do it," Stephen said. "It's that thing trying to trick us."

"Are you okay?" Jim said through the window. "Please unlock your door. I'm here to help you."

Gordon knew that Stephen didn't want him to unlock the door, but knew they had to do something. They couldn't stay there. He knew they needed to get out of the cold. Hesitantly, Gordon unlocked the door.

"No!" Stephen screamed.

The door opened and Jim leaned in. "Hi," he said. "Oh, there's two of you. Are you two alright? I'm Jim. Jim Summerlee. I saw your vehicle. Are you hurt? I can help you."

A wave of relief filled both boys, as fear quickly changed to happiness on their faces. They really were being rescued. It wasn't that monster trying to get them after all.

"My ankle kinda hurts a little," Gordon said. "But that thing is out there somewhere."

"Yeah, it tried to get us," Stephen added, echoing his brother's statement. "It was really horrible."

"I know," Jim replied, much to the boys' surprise. "Let me get you into my Jeep and we'll go someplace safe and warm. Anywhere away from here and to safety."

"Did you see it too? Stephen asked, wondering how the man named Jim knew about what they'd seen.

"No," Jim said. "I didn't see it. But I know of its existence. We can talk later about it where it's safe. Let me get you both out of here. Can either of you walk?"

"I'm okay," Gordon said. "My ankle hurts, but I'll make it."

"Same here," Stephen said. "I got a concussion playing hockey, but I'll be alright. My head hurts, but that's it."

"Good," Jim said. "Let's go. Grab whatever you need to bring with you."

He boys grabbed their personal belongings as Jim helped them to his vehicle. As they started to get inside, the horrid stench began to once again get stronger.

"Hurry in, boys," Jim said. "It's back."

Both boys finished climbing in and quickly closed the doors behind them. Once inside, they were greeted by comfortable warmth they had not felt in some time. Jim soon joined them inside the vehicle, immediately locking the doors.

All three knew without saying how deadly it was.

They heard the creature cry out in anger and frustration of missing out on more prey. They exchanged looks, each one knowing what was out in the snow.

"Okay boys," Jim said. "We're going to get out of here."

"Good," Gordon said.

"How do you know about that thing, if you haven't seen it?" Stephen asked.

"Of all the beings that were legends of my people, none were more terrifying than this one," Jim said, as he pulled back on I-75. "I'll tell you more about it on our way. But, it's bad, *real* bad and as terrible as it gets.

Snowbound

"This isn't just bad, it's really terrible, perhaps the worst ever," Rachel thought as she slowed down to barely a crawl.

"Jeez Mom, I've seen golf carts go faster," Danielle commented. "We're barely above a snail's pace now."

"Yeah, but I've never seen golf carts operate in this weather," Rachel replied.

"I suppose," Danielle said. "How much further?"

"I don't know, honey," Rachel said as she stayed focused on the road in front of them. "I can't even see a sign for an exit or a rest area."

"I feel like we've been in this storm forever," Danielle commented.

"Me too," Rachel admitted. "Hopefully we can find an exit soon."

Danielle let out a sigh. She then sniffed. "Do you smell something?" she asked.

Rachel quietly nodded in agreement.

"It's terrible," Danielle continued. "It smells like something died."

***

"Alright, which one of you fuckers did it?" Eddie asked, as he turned to look behind him.

Instinctively, everybody looked at Kevin who had a propensity for letting out very rancid farts.

"Hey man, it ain't me," Kevin protested. "Besides, those who smelt it dealt it."

"I don't think it's him, Eddie," Andrew said. "Otherwise I would have suffered and passed out from it before you even noticed it."

"Maybe it' a dead skunk or animal on the road," Jeff suggested.

"You think it might be the vehicle?" Eddie asked.

Jeff shook his head. "Nope." he replied. "Ain't no vehicle that smells like that. That's something rotting."

"It's probably Kevin's underwear rotting from the way he cracks them off," Eddie suggested.

Eddie, Jeff and Andrew all roared with laughter. Except Kevin who did not. He muttered a "Very funny, motherfucker," under his breath.

"I think we lost the cops," Andrew said. "You can slow it down, if you want. Aren't you driving a little fast for the conditions?"

"Probably, but we don't need the cops catching up," Jeff replied.

"What is that?" Eddie asked. "Watch out!"

"Holy shit, no!" Jeff exclaimed.

***

"No!" Rachel screamed as she saw the truck headlights quickly bearing down on them from behind.

Because she had little time to react and little traction to drive faster, Rachel and Danielle were rear-ended with a fair amount of force. The impact of the truck hitting them pushed the Chevy Trax off the road and into a ditch. In spite of wearing a safety belt, Rachel was pushed hard into the steering wheel. The pain she felt from being thrown around was so intense, she blacked out.

Danielle was whipped forward and back from the crash. While not totally unconscious, she was quite dazed and groggy as the truck that hit them continued down the road, onward down I-75.

***

"You guys alright?" Jeff asked, very concerned.

He looked over at Eddie who had a cut on the right side of his forehead.

"Jesus Christ!" Eddie said, still shook up. "What was that, another car?"

"Yeah," Jeff admitted. "I didn't see the fucker until the last second."

"Well, slow down then," Eddie said, as Jeff began to comply. "We ain't in no hurry to die."

"I'm glad you fuckers ain't any heavier," Eddie said. "You guys smashed into my seat during that."

The accident's impact also had an effect on Andrew and Kevin who were also battered and bruised from being thrown around in the backseat.

"I'm alright," Andrew managed to say.

"Me too," Kevin added. "Should we go back and see if they're okay?"

"Fuck no!" Eddie snapped. "The place will be crawling with cops later."

"Yeah, but they could be hurt," Kevin meekly protested.

"That's their problem, not ours," Eddie argued.

"And like Eddie said, there will probably be all kinds of cops and emergency vehicles around," Andrew agreed.

"Plus, we have to get as far away as possible," Jeff added. "My truck is damaged pretty badly and I don't know how long it will keep going. I think I'm losing anti-freeze."

"Oh," Kevin said, finally persuaded by the others' arguments. "So....what do we do next?"

"We call the police for help, dumbass. What do you think?" Eddie said snidely, more as a statement than a question. "We drive away as far and as fast as possible. Then we take a hike. We may have to steal another ride after that."

"I may have to stop and see how bad it is," Jeff said. "First chance I get, I'm checking the damage."

***

Still dazed from the accident, Danielle Torrey checked herself, moving her arms and legs to see if she sustained any injury or personal damage. Everything appeared to be normal and considering the circumstances.

"Mom?" she called out. "Mom?"

She looked over at her mother, who was unconscious. "Mom? Mom?" she cried as she reached over and touched her.

Danielle began to shake her mother gently on the shoulder and continued to call out to her, "Mom? Mom?"

After agonizingly long moments, Rachel began to regain her consciousness. As soon as her disorientation began to wane, she began to feel a sharp, stabbing pain in her side.

"Oh, God," she gasped.

"Are you alright, Mom?" Danielle asked.

Rachel grimaced in pain. "I don't know. I think I'm hurt inside."

"Where?"

"My side," Rachel said. "I think it's my ribs."

"Can I do anything?" Danielle asked, concerned.

"I don't think so," Rachel answered. "Just let me sit here and rest for a while."

"I could go for help," Danielle suggested.

"No!' Rachel groaned. "We're too far from anything and the storm is too bad. We're both safer here, right now. Help will come."

While Danielle did not totally agree with her mother, she thought it best not to leave right now. She listened while outside their car the wind continued to howl and shriek. It almost sounded like something alive out there….

***

Jeff's truck came to a screeching halt as the engine finally overheated and died from losing too much anti-freeze.

"Aw shit!" Jeff exclaimed. "That's it boys. It looks like we hoof it from here."

"Grab only the necessary shit we need," Eddie barked. "No non-essential crap, right Kevin?"

"Oh, yeah, man, totally," Kevin replied, almost incoherently.

Andrew and Jeff looked at each other and shook their heads.

"That's what too much dope leads to," Jeff replied softly enough for only his cousin to hear.

Andrew laughed. "To tell you the truth, he wasn't that bright before he started taking that shit."

"You're shitting?" Jeff asked.

Andrew just shook his head yes.

Soon, all four men were walking away from the truck with only the bare essentials on them.

"Goodbye old friend," Jeff said, waving farewell to his truck. "It was fun. Thanks."

All four men were trudging on the side of the road through the snow in tandem.

"Man, at this rate it will take forever," Kevin said.

"Shut up," Eddie snapped.

After they walked about a hundred yards, they once again noticed the foul stench they'd smelled earlier.

"Goddammit!" Eddie yelled. "I knew that was you in the truck. That smell proves it. What did you do, shit your pants?"

"I didn't do it," Kevin protested.

"Then who was it, asshole?" Eddie asked. "Fucking Santa Claus?"

Just then in the silence of the blizzard, they heard a low, guttural growl of something large and unseen.

"What the fuck is that?" Andrew wondered aloud.

"It's probably a bear," Jeff suggested.

The men continued to listen and they heard it again.

"That sounds too fucking large to be a bear," Andrew opined.

"Beats the shit out of me then," Jeff said.

"Man, that smell is even stronger," Andrew said looking around. "It's almost making me want to puke."

"And closer," Jeff added

They heard the growl again.

"That is definitely no goddamn bear," Andrew said. "I don't know what it is. What do you think, Jeff?"

"I uh..." Jeff began his answer, but was overtaken and pulled upward into the murky blizzard before the others could really see anything, and then suddenly he was no longer there.

"Jeff?" Andrew called out. "Jeff?"

The only answer was Jeff's scream of horror and pain, followed by ripping and loud chewing sounds. Jeff's last wail was cut off in mid-scream.

All three men looked up only to have Jeff's blood splatter down upon them, followed by the appearance of the most unimaginable horror ever.

"Holy shit!" Andrew screamed.

"Run!" Eddie yelled.

Eddie and Andrew headed off down the road in one direction while Kevin panicked and headed towards a nearby open field with a patch of woods next to it.

Kevin was driven by abject fear every step of the way as he ran with all of his might. As he reached the tree line, he stopped, huffing, puffing and wheezing badly after the exhausting run.

After he regained his breath, Kevin realized the trees were not a forest but a narrow strip in front of a small glen.

Fear ran through the pit of his stomach as he noticed that familiar stench all around him. He felt surrounded.

All Kevin could think to do was to start digging a hole, into the deep snow, and hope to try and hide in it. In no time, he managed to complete his makeshift hideaway.

As Kevin tried to catch his breath, he slowly looked up, not wanting to see what was there, then to his immediate left and right, seeing that two more horrors beyond his comprehension were there as well. Kevin shrieked at the sight, then dove into his freshly-made hole in the snow.

Unfortunately for him it was not nearly large enough for his body, and even as he pulled his legs underneath him, his ass was still exposed. A boisterous wail escaped from Kevin as he was taken by the closest creature, silenced swiftly while the three abominations selfishly fought over him and tore into him like a rag doll.

The only remnants left of Kevin Shannon were the splatters of blood on the snow-covered ground and the bag of dope he'd been carrying, which was pretty much representative and the epitaph of how he lived his life.

***

Running for their lives, Eddie and Andrew had somehow managed to cover about a mile of distance on the side of the snow-covered road. Out of breath, both had to stop, leaning over with their hands on their legs and breathing hard.

After a few minutes, Andrew finally spoke. "Did you hear that scream back there? I think it got Kevin."

Still breathing hard Eddie finally said. "Good riddance. The fucker was more trouble than he was worth."

Before either one could speak any more, they heard something large approaching.

"Oh, shit," Andrew muttered, still winded by the earlier run.

Eddie looked around, noticing a river and a large drainage pipe a few yards away. "Down there," he said, pointing. "We'll hide down there."

Andrew looked, then nodded and followed Eddie. They heard the frustrated and angry shriek of the horror that they'd earlier witnessed. As they stumbled and slid down the embankment towards the river, Eddie and Andrew both sensed the thing close behind them.

As they reached the huge drainage pipe that the river ran through, the creature's large, gray, leathery hand reached blindly for them, missing both men. Eddie screamed like a little girl.

Once inside the large drainage pipe, they felt a little safe for the moment. As they stood carefully balancing on the metal pipe as to not get wet from the waters, they were still out of breath, and breathing hard. Neither one knew what to expect next.

Suddenly the large gray hand attempted to reach inside the pipe to try and grab them. Both men moved frantically to avoid being taken as it tried to reach blindly for them.

Eddie slipped into the river, then quickly climbed out and regained his footing. The creature's hand brushed up against Andrew, causing him to slip and fall. He regained his balance just enough to keep from falling totally into the water.

Soon the hand was gone, and the creature wailed loudly in anger and frustration at once again being denied. For Eddie and Andrew, the shriek was almost as horrible as its stench.

Wet and cold, both men took deep breaths, relieved they'd escaped the creature's wrath.

Eddie reached into his coat pocket for a pack of cigarettes, but they were wet. He threw them down, pissed off. He was too tired and cold to even swear at them.

They knew the creature was close by waiting, because of the strong, horrid stench. It was waiting for them to emerge from their hiding place.

They knew it.

As they began to shiver even more, both realized that the terrible thing they'd faced was not the only thing that could kill them. The cold could be just as deadly.

Dead Calm & Zero Degrees

It was getting colder.

Rachel knew that. All she could do was run the vehicle for a few minutes at a time to keep them a little warmer.

In the quiet boredom and monotony of waiting for help, Danielle had nodded off, sleeping as comfortable as could be expected. Rachel, while still injured and a bit dazed listened, tried to keep an eye out for help. She noticed a terrible, stomach-turning stench outside. Rachel decided to cut the engine, thinking that was where the smell originated.

Once she did, Rachel still noticed the bad smell, and that it seemed worse. She knew it wasn't the engine. Whatever it was, she didn't know.

Rachel only knew that it was not good.

As Rachel listened, she could hear something tapping on the roof. It reminded her of long fingernails tapping on a desk. She knew something big was out there and made sure the doors were locked. Whatever it was, she didn't want it getting in there.

The cold was bad enough.

As Rachel dozed off again from being battered and bruised, she thought she glimpsed part of something trying to peer inside their vehicle.

It looked like it had dark deep-set eyes, grayish skin and had a gaping mouth with jagged drooling teeth. This caused Rachel to recoil in revulsion at the sight. From what she could glimpse, it was the most hideous and horrible thing she had ever seen. Rachel was thankful she could not see it clearly and wondered if she really had. Whatever she'd seen, it was as horrid as the stench that engulfed them.

As Rachel looked to her left and through the fogged-up driver's side window, she saw what looked like a large leathery gray palm. Rachel jumped, a little startled. The sudden movement made her wince and grimace in pain.

When she looked again, it was gone. Whatever it was, it was large. Large and seemingly unable to get in.

For now.

Rachel wondered if the pain was making her delirious. She closed her eyes and tried her best to relax. It was all she could really do in order to deal with her injuries.

She hoped help would arrive soon.

As Rachel quietly listened, she heard the fingernail tapping sound on the roof of their vehicle again. Whatever she thought she had seen or heard appeared to be still lurking around outside.

All they could do now was wait and hope.

Wait and hope.

***

"I hope we don't have to wait here too long," Eddie grumbled. "I'm freezing my nuts off."

"Yeah," Andrew agreed. "I'm getting colder."

"Tell me about it," Eddie said, shivering. "You ain't even as wet as I am."

"I'm wet enough and cold too," Andrew replied.

"You got a cigarette?" Eddie asked.

"Nope," he finally said. "You're out of luck."

"Shit!' Eddie muttered. "I could sure use one."

Andrew began to sniff the air. "Hey, the smell ain't as bad," he announced. "Maybe it's not out there anymore."

"So go out and check," Eddie said.

"Fuck that idea," Andrew replied. "Why don't you?"

"It wasn't my idea," Eddie countered.

"So," Andrew said.

"So, we need to get out of here," Eddie continued, as he began to shiver more. "The further from here the better."

"Yeah, that makes sense," Andrew agreed.

"So, go out and check," Eddie ordered.

"No!"

"No?" Eddie cursed. "What the fuck do you mean no? What are you? A pussy?"

"Why don't you?" Andrew argued. "You're supposed to be the leader and so brave. Then lead by example then, goddammit!"

"Fuck you!" Eddie spat. "I told you to do it!"

"I don't give a shit what you said," Andrew snapped back. "You're not exactly the bravest of the brave, either, chickenshit!"

"Go do it, or I'll kick your ass!" Eddie barked.

"Fuck you!" Andrew replied. "I don't think so! You're a big talker when you had me and Kevin backing your ass up. You ain't shit now."

"I'll shoot you in the ass!" Eddie said, reaching around for his gun to find it was no longer tucked into the back of his pants.

Andrew saw Eddie go for his pistol and grabbed his out of his coat pocket and pointed it at Eddie. "You missing something?" he asked, sarcastically. "I have mine. You must have lost yours."

"Fuck!" Eddie snapped. "I must have lost it on the way here."

"Why don't you go out and look for it, when you're checking to see if that thing is still around?" Andrew asked.

"You wouldn't," Eddie said.

Andrew quietly nodded. "Yeah, Eddie, I would," he finally said. "I really would."

"Mutherfucker!" Eddie spat, glaring at Andrew.

"Quit talking and get out there," Andrew ordered.

Eddie flipped Andrew his middle finger. "Fuck you!" he swore.

Andrew fired a shot close to Eddie. "That's a warning, asshole," he said. "I won't miss next time."

Eddie continued glaring at Andrew. "I'll get you for this, if I get the chance," he said.

Andrew smirked. "You better get going," he finally said.

Eddie knew that he was limited in what he could do. He kept a wary eye on Andrew as he slowly moved out of the drainage pipe and into the blizzard. Once outside, Eddie stood quietly for a moment. He waited for the thing to return. After a couple of minutes there was still nothing.

A wicked grin spread across his face. "So long, cocksucker!" Eddie yelled and took off into the blizzard.

A bit miffed, Andrew soon followed, to see how far Eddie was able to get. As soon as he emerged from the drainage pipe, he was hit in the face by a snowball thrown by Eddie.

"Now that's funny!" Eddie laughed hysterically.

"You fucker!" Andrew yelled, clearing the snowball's remains from his face. He then aimed and fired his pistol, hitting Eddie in the left shoulder, knocking him backwards. "No, *that's* funny, dickhead!"

Andrew glared at Eddie as he got back to his feet, holding his wounded and bleeding shoulder. While he could not be sure, he thought that Eddie had tears in his eyes. Just as Andrew was about to fire again, they heard the shriek of the creature as it approached.

Both men looked up and around. Eddie started back towards the drainage pipe, when Andrew fired his pistol at him again, missing.

Eddie took off towards the expressway, while Andrew headed back to the sanctuary of the drainage pipe.

Eddie could sense the creature nearby. He could feel it getting closer as he tried to climb up the snow-covered embankment in the raging snowstorm. As he finally headed up, he heard the creature step into the snow nearby. He turned around to see how close the creature was as he hit the side of the freeway.

Because of the white-out conditions and being distracted by the horror that was pursuing him, Eddie ran out into the freeway and was hit and pulverized by a large sanitation truck. His life ended with a sickening crunch, dragged under the tires and literally flattened by a truck that hauled human waste.

It was a kind of poetic justice and fitting end for a man like Eddie Temple, a real-life human piece of shit, being hit by a truck with the company name Edward's Excrement Eradicators that had the slogan "*We git all the shit*."

"Did you feel that?" asked the man in the passenger seat of the septic tank truck. "I think you hit something big."

"Probably just a goddamn animal," the driver replied as he continued down the road. "Maybe a deer. Hard to see and tell in this weather."

"You don't think it was a *person*, do you?"

"Nobody in their right mind would be walking around in this shit," the driver replied. "And if they are, they're dumber than the shit we're hauling."

***

"Another winter storm fatality," Cassandra Stern thought as she drove past Rachel Torrey's wrecked vehicle.

Cassandra briefly contemplated stopping to offer assistance, but almost immediately decided against it, because she had to beat Max home. Nothing else was important to her.

***

Rachel had to think of more than herself. She had Danielle and the baby to think about in this situation. She was a mom and their protector. Even if Danielle was older, there was still her unborn child.

"My God, the baby," she thought, terrified. With all that happened she'd almost forgotten. She hoped she was alright, especially after sustaining her injuries.

"Oh, God, no," she muttered softly, as she realized her baby could be hurt or worse.

Tears welled up in her eyes at the thought of losing her unborn child. She was sad and upset about her being so foolish and selfish about everything. While she hoped and prayed that everything was all right, deep down, Rachel suspected something was terribly wrong.

Rachel new that she needed medical help badly. She knew that she had to try and alert someone that they were in desperate need of help.

Danielle could tell her mother was upset and in pain and knew they needed to do something. She was growing frustrated and fed up with their situation.

"Mom, this is stupid," she announced. "I'm going for help. You're hurt and we need it badly."

"No," Rachel said. "The weather is too bad and there's something dangerous out there. I heard it. It could be a bear or something."

"I don't care what you say," Danielle snapped. "We're in trouble and I'm done listening to you. I don't care what you say. I'm going for help! I'm doing what I want!"

Rachel mustered up all her strength and slapped Danielle in the face, stunning her. "Now you listen good, you little brat!" she said. "You're not going anywhere. It is too dangerous. And you will listen to me, dammit. That is the end of the conversation."

Danielle was stunned, sat there quietly in a huff. She was shocked and angry that her mother had struck her. Rachel never hit Danielle before and this really upset her.

"I'm sorry," Rachel said. "But I will think of something. It is safer here in the car."

Rachel thought she heard a car drive by, but could not tell since she could not physically turn around to look. Even if she could have done so, the rear window was now covered in snow anyway.

Rachel began to think of her options and what she could do. She didn't know how much battery life she had left. She decided to start the car and began pumping her brakes. She hoped this would signal someone passing by that they needed help.

She decided to keep doing this until they were finally helped or the battery gave out. Rachel hoped her plan worked, and prayed that someone would soon see them.

Hope was all she had left.

***

Brandon Markway hoped that he could find a rest area or an exit with some restaurants or a gas station nearby and soon. As he continued south on I-75 he'd slowed down considerably. Several feet ahead, he thought he could see a vehicle off the side of the road.

"Boy, I sure hope that nobody was hurt too bad," Marlene commented as they approached what was Rachel's vehicle.

Brandon slowed down even more to a crawl. "Yeah," he agreed.

"Why are you stopping?" Marlene asked.

"I think there's something wrong," Brandon continued.

"What?" Marlene asked. "How so?"

"The lights," Brandon explained. "Somebody is hitting the brake lights. They're signaling us. We'd better check this out."

"Are you sure?" Marlene asked, concerned.

"Yes," Brandon continued. "Somebody's in trouble and it's my job to help."

"But, you're not on duty," Marlene pleaded. "It's not your job now."

Brandon just stared at her, coldly. "It's always my job," he replied. "It's what I do."

Marlene felt bad and looked down at her feet. She knew he was right.

Brandon pulled over as close to the other vehicle as he could. After stopping he paused for a moment, took a deep breath, and headed out into the snowstorm.

***

Rachel's battery finally died. Certain no one would come, she was suddenly greeted by a tapping at the driver's side window. It was soon followed by snow being cleared off of the window.

"Are you alright?" asked a younger gentleman through the glass. "Are you hurt? Can I help you?"

Rachel nodded. "Yes," she finally said, as she unlocked the door. "I'm hurt. I don't know how badly though. My daughter is okay."

The man opened the door. "My name is Brandon," he introduced himself. "Brandon Markway. I'm an off-duty paramedic."

"Oh, thank God," Rachel gasped. "I think I have some broken ribs. My side hurts pretty bad."

"Okay," Brandon said. "And how are you, Miss?"

"I'm fine now," Danielle replied, instantly mesmerized by his handsome looks and features.

"Can you unfasten your seatbelt?" he asked.

"Yes," Rachel said, as he unbuckled the belt.

"How is your mobility?" he asked. "Can you move very much or at all?"

Rachel grimaced in pain as she tried to turn and slide out of the car. "I'm afraid I'm kind of limited," she admitted.

"Okay," Brandon commented. "Well, I'm not trying to be fresh or anything, but I'm going to have to lift you and to do that, my left arm is going to have to go under your legs and my right may be near your rear to start."

"I understand," Rachel said.

"When I lift, it may hurt a little," he admitted. "But it's the only way I can think of to get you out of here."

"Do what you have to do," Rachel said. "Oh, by the way, I'm Rachel. Rachel Torrey and this is my daughter Danielle."

"Hi," Brandon said. "Okay, let's do this."

"Let's," Rachel said.

It was then Brandon noticed a horrid smell that seemed to be getting stronger. "Damn, that is bad," he said.

"I don't know what it is," Rachel said. "But I think there's some dangerous predator in the area or something. It's been lurking around the car."

"Then we better move," Brandon said. "I don't want to be caught out here with it around."

As Marlene watched from the vehicle, she noticed the bad smell as well, opened her door and stepped out into the snow. "Brandon?" she called out. "I think there's something terrible coming."

Brandon looked over at her and nodded. "I'll be right there," he said. "The lady is injured and she needs help."

"Oh, God," Marlene muttered, and walked over to help.

Danielle then unbuckled her safety belt, got out of the car, climbed up out of the ditch and went over to her mother's side of the car. They were soon joined by Marlene.

"Okay, Rachel, I'm going to slide my arm under your legs," Brandon instructed. "I need you to put your left arm across my back and shoulder as I do so."

"Okay," Rachel said, through clenched teeth.

"One…two...three...*go*," Brandon said, lifting Rachel up and out of the car.

Rachel cried out upon being lifted out and continued to moan as he carried her out of the ditch and over to his car.

"Mom?" Danielle called out, upset at seeing her mother in so much pain.

"She'll be alright," Marlene said, as she put her hands upon Danielle's shoulders to comfort her. "Brandon is great at what he does. Let's open the door to help them out."

Just as she opened the door, and Brandon arrived with Rachel, they heard a loud piercing shriek somewhere nearby.

"What in the hell was that?" Brandon asked, stunned at having never heard anything like that before. "Get in the vehicle, ladies. Hurry."

Marlene opened the door for Danielle as she got in and quickly closed it. Brandon gently placed Rachel inside the back seat near Danielle.

"You alright?" he asked.

"Yeah, thanks," Rachel said with tear-filled eyes.

"We'll get you some medical attention as soon as possible," he promised. He quickly shut the rear door and climbed back into the driver's seat.

"What was that?" Marlene asked, after closing her door.

"I don't know," Rachel replied. "But I noticed it after the wreck. I think it was hanging around outside our vehicle, hoping we would leave. I think it got tired of waiting and when you arrived it came back."

Something large moved around the vehicle. They couldn't really see it, but they could hear it. As they sat almost frozen in their seats, they heard something tapping, what sounded like fingers, on top of the car.

"What is that?" Marlene asked, frightened.

"I don't know," Brandon answered. "But we aren't waiting to find out. Whatever it is, we're getting out of here. So you better buckle up. You alright, honey?"

"Yes," Marlene replied, with a deep appreciation and respect for Brandon's ability and selfless attitude.

"Let's get out of here," he said, and with that, he started down the highway….

Dead of Winter

"We'll get out of here as soon as the snow lets up a bit," Jim Summerlee announced to the boys as they sat down on a bench inside the rest stop.

"Sounds good, Sir," Steve said. "I'm not in any hurry to go back out in this."

"*We're* not," Gordon said, correcting him.

Jim stifled a laugh. "I don't blame you there," he admitted. "I'm not either."

"Are you okay?" Jim asked. "Do you need to see a doctor for your concussion?"

"No, I'm okay," Steve said. "At least not now."

"Man, look at it come down," Gordon observed. "I'm sure glad we ain't still stuck out in Dad's car."

"This is a terrible storm," Jim commented.

"Because of that Wendigo thing you told us about?" Steve asked.

Jim nodded as they continued to watch the snow fall. "The storm itself is bad enough," he finally said. "The Wendigo makes it even worse and more unbelievable."

"And more deadly," Steve said.

"Yes," Jim admitted. "That too."

"Mother Nature sure is rough," Gordon opined.

"Yes," Jim agreed. "Very rough."

***

The drive was becoming much rougher for Cassandra Stern after passing the wrecked car. Not so much from the weather, but from her tires acting like they were losing air and going flat.

"Shit!" Cassandra muttered in disgust, knowing she had probably run over some accident debris. "That's all I need, and I'm sure not reaching Triple A out here."

Cassandra passed an abandoned truck off the side of the road before deciding to stop and check on her own vehicle. Slowly, she pulled off on what she thought was the side of the expressway.

Once outside her vehicle, she walked around to the passenger side of her car and saw a large broken piece of metal sticking out of the front tire. The tire was hissing loudly, indicating it was mortally wounded.

"Shit!" she exclaimed.

Cassandra wondered how far she could get before it was completely flat. She contemplated if she could make it to a gas station or an auto repair center. It didn't matter which one, she had to try and make it. If she didn't, the consequences would be unthinkable.

Time was still of the essence.

Just as she was about to get back inside her car, Cassandra noticed something sticking out of the rear tire as well.

"Dammit!" she cursed.

She then decided to check her other tires. As she approached the driver's side, she could see that they appeared to be alright. As Cassandra stood there for a moment, she heard an ungodly shriek in the distance.

"I had better get out of here," she thought.

***

"You need to get the fuck outta here," Andrew said to himself, after weighing his options about what to do next.

He knew that he couldn't stay where he was much longer, creature or no creature. There was the possibility of getting caught. There was also the much more likely scenario of freezing to death.

The smell had dissipated since he chased Eddie off. *Hell*, Andrew figured, *the creature probably got Eddie for that matter. Maybe, that was enough for it*, he hoped. Even if it wasn't, he knew that he had to leave at some point.

And if he was to leave, *now* would be the time to do it.

He figured he would have to bum a ride or steal some 'wheels' to get away. It wasn't much of a plan but it was all he could think of.

"*It's now or never,*" he thought to himself, as he headed out into worst of the blizzard and into the unknown.

***

As Cassandra started to head back to the car, she knew the only chance she had to beat Max home was for his plane to be delayed. And with how bad this storm was, she thought her chances were good. But she also knew that she could not leave that to chance.

As she got back in her car, she could see a man making his way up the embankment from the river a short distance ahead.

"What the hell is he doing out in this shit?" she muttered aloud to herself.

As he reached the side of the expressway, Cassandra became wary when he looked over towards her. She instinctively made sure her doors were locked as he came closer. Cassandra thought that she'd better get out of there.

When Andrew was greeted by the sight of a car parked nearby, he knew instantly that this was his ticket out of there. Not taking any chances by waving at her in hopes that they stopped to give him a ride, he pulled out his pistol and ran towards the vehicle.

Andrew planned on outright carjacking.

"*Carjacker!*" Cassandra thought instantly upon seeing the man approach with what looked like a handgun.

She hit the accelerator hard, but between the accumulation of snow and her two bad tires, she had trouble gaining any traction whatsoever and began to fishtail. Finally, Cassandra eased up a bit and began to move forward as he drew even nearer.

As Andrew made sure that he stood front and center to the vehicle, he aimed his handgun at it. He finally yelled "Stop!"

"Fuck you!' Cassandra screamed from inside her car, as she finally gained some speed and drove directly at him.

Andrew, while surprised, fired at the vehicle twice, hitting the windshield both times. While the shots didn't hit Cassandra the flying glass did, peppering her face, causing her to lose control and hit Andrew dead-on, completely running her vehicle over him.

As she did so, his coat latched onto something beneath the vehicle and he was dragged some distance down the icy road. After about a hundred yards, the coat ripped, freeing him upon the roadway.

Cassandra tried desperately to regain control of her car. But it was all in vain, as she went off the road and crashed into a large oak tree. The impact of the crash thrust her forward into the shattered windshield.

Once her forward momentum ceased, Cassandra lay unconscious, slumped back into her seat with bruises, cuts and lacerations across her face, with shards of glass protruding from it. The pretty face that she used with her body to get almost any man she wanted was almost a bloody pulp.

Meanwhile, Andrew lie on the ground a bloody mess of broken humanity. He was skinned-up, cut and bruised, both of his legs were mangled beyond repair and his right hand and arm were crushed with the handgun still in his grip and his fingers mangled around it.

Fortunately for him, as soon as he was hit, he blacked out and was in shock and barely semi-conscious afterward. He was in pain, but was too out of it to really notice how bad it was. The irony was not lost on him of how he was in the vehicle that hit Doris Madden earlier, and now he was *her* position now.

The other irony was, he was only a few yards away from the flattened and blood-smeared corpse of his former friend Eddie Temple, both victims of a kind of hit-and-run.

He closed his eyes and waited. Whether it was for the creature to return, the Angel of Death, or help, at this point it didn't matter to him. All he could do was wait as the snow began to cover him.

Andrew Furlong and Cassandra Stern, both cruel, self-centered and selfish people were now bloody, badly-injured shells of their former selves, victims of their own desires and excesses, as well as the snowstorm from Hell.

Karma had been almost as deadly as the storm and what wandered in with it.

Across twelve states, at least thirty people had died from weather conditions and related mishaps, whether it was auto accidents in slippery conditions, or heart attacks from shoveling snow.

….or victims of the Wendigo.

Once the storm peaked, its ravenous hunger became worse, making it more desperate and more dangerous.

It needed to feast badly. The Wendigo followed the storm. While there were animals a-plenty in the woods, it needed Man as its sustenance.

Nothing else would do.

It continued to move through the blizzard, searching for prey, without mercy. It would do whatever it had in order to try and satisfy its terribly endless appetite.

It was the kind of hunger that bordered on insanity, as it was all-consuming and grew with each meal.

There were fewer humans in the area and out in the storm, but it knew there were some close by.

Once again, the scent of Man close by filled its nostrils, making the Wendigo's mouth water.

Much like the Wendigo's appetite, the storm continued to rage.

***

Cassandra Stern slowly began to regain her consciousness. Instinctively, she reached up to touch her face, but stopped before actually doing so. She sensed how she could not see out of one eye that she was injured more than she really cared to know.

Cassandra knew it was bad, just not *how* bad.

She reached over for her purse in the seat next to her and pulled out her cell phone. Somehow, she was able to dial 911.

"Hello, my name is Cassandra Stern," she said, when she finally received an answer. "I've had an accident. A man was shooting at me and I crashed trying to get away from him. I don't know where I'm at. I think I'm ten to twenty miles south of Grayling on I-75. I'm hurt bad. I'm…"

Cassandra blacked out from the pain and shock of her injuries, dropping her phone, as the dispatcher called "Ma'am? Ma'am?"

When the dispatcher received no answer, he ordered a state police patrol car to head in the general area where the call had come from.

As she sat slumped in her seat, she was brought back to semi-consciousness by a terribly horrid scent that filled her nostrils, making her almost physically ill.

As she started to come to, she was greeted by the horror of all horrors peering through her side window.

She screamed in abject terror at the exact same time it shrieked from endlessly painful hunger.

The fright was almost too much for her as she fainted from the shock of seeing it.

***

Andrew was lying on the ground, still partially in shock. He knew he was in very bad shape, perhaps even critical condition. What he could move was almost unbearably painful and what he couldn't greatly concerned him.

He was conscious enough to know that if he didn't get help soon, he was a dead man.

Whether it was from his multiple injuries, the elements, or that creature, he knew that death was close at hand, lurking around him and ready to pounce.

Even in his current condition, he could smell the horrid stench of the creature approaching again. He could feel its presence nearby and no longer cared.

Andrew was ready to meet his fate, whatever way it was to come.

And he knew it was coming soon.

Wind Chill Warning

"We will get your mom to a hospital soon," Brandon said upon hearing Rachel moan in pain, as she nodded off. "Honey, check your I-Phone for the nearest medical facility."

"Okay," Marlene said, as she began to search on her phone. After a few moments, she found a place. "There's Mercy Hospital Grayling. Then there's Mercy Family Care of Roscommon."

Brandon began to drive his truck a little faster. "We need one with an emergency room," he said.

"Mercy Hospital Grayling then," Marlene continued.

"Program the GPS, please," Brandon said as he continued driving.

"The first service drive I see I'm turning around," he said. "We don't know how bad she is hurt, so time is of the essence."

Tears welled up in Danielle's eyes.

Marlene could see she was upset. "Are you alright, honey?" she asked.

Danielled sniffed, trying to hold back the tears. "I'm scared," she said. "I'm worried about my mom."

"Now you don't worry Danielle," Brandon said, confidently. "We'll get her to a medical facility and she'll be alright. You have to believe that. I have never lost anybody that was in stable condition as a paramedic and I'm not about to start now. So you keep believing your mom will be alright, okay?"

Danielle choked up, quietly nodded. "I will," she finally said.

"Good," Brandon said as he wheeled his truck around on a service drive. "Because we'll get her there soon."

"Okay," Danielle said while looking at her mom, sleeping.

Marlene looked at her husband in both amazement and admiration. She had only really seen him in action one time, and that was nothing like this. She realized this was even more serious than that one time. Marlene now understood that Brandon dealt with life and death scenarios every day. It finally dawned her why he sometimes had a problem with her whining and complaining over what were basically trivial things.

Marlene reached over and touched Brandon's shoulder and gave it a squeeze. He looked at her as she smiled and nodded. Somehow, they both knew it would be alright.

At least Marlene hoped it would.

***

Andrew hoped that death would be quick. Quick and painless as possible. At least his suffering would be over. The shock was finally wearing off and he was in a great deal of pain. That and the fact he was freezing too.

Every part of his body ached. His entire body felt like one huge, very painful toothache.

With the creature in the area he just wished it would hurry up and put an end to him.

"For Christ's sake please kill me now," he thought.

He knew by the stench that hung in the cold winter air that it was close. With as much pain as he was in, he welcomed it.

As Andrew began to fade out from consciousness, he sensed something nearby and approaching quickly. He knew that it was all a matter of time. As he fought to keep his eyes open, the falling snow that landed on him helped to blur them and keep him from seeing clearly.

He knew the creature coming for him. Andrew couldn't see much but he could sense and see a shadow of something large standing over him.

As the shadowy figure leaned over him, Andrew screamed and then passed out.

He lost consciousness before finding out the shadowy figure lurking over him was a Michigan State Trooper.

"Call EMS, Smitty," the state trooper yelled to his partner. "He's in pretty bad shape, but he's still alive."

***

Cassandra realized she was still alive once she came to. Her body ached terribly and her face and head were beginning to sting from the cuts and abrasions. Cassandra was filled with too much fear to look at herself in the rearview mirror. Yet, somehow she felt the need to.

She leaned forward as far as she was able to, reaching out adjusting the mirror.

She took a deep breath and summoned up the courage to look. Once she did, her heart sank and she wanted to throw up. She was horrified to see her face was badly mangled in the accident.

She tried to cry, but her injuries prevented her from doing so, and only managed a pitiful, sad gulp. The physical pain from the accident did not compare to the mental and emotional devastation she felt from seeing her battered face.

"Oh, God, no," Cassandra gasped. "Why couldn't I have just died? Why couldn't you have killed me?"

Cassandra knew her life was basically over.

Even if Max had beat her home and found the letter she could have said it was all a joke, made love to him and it would have been alright afterward. And if he didn't believe her she knew that she had the looks and body to apologize, give him a blowjob and eventually be taken back and forgiven.

Not now.

Not with her face looking like it did. The biggest irony and most painful thing of all was, she now looked like the person she actually was inside.

Hideous.

As she sat in her car hurt and depressed, Cassandra realized she had just learned the most painful lesson in her life, and it was almost unbearable.

***

The pain had been almost unbearable as Brandon carried Rachel into Mercy Hospital Grayling. To the objection of some staff, he placed her on a gurney and informed the nurses of Rachel's condition.

Marlene and Danielle stood in the background, watching almost in awe of his proficiency and knowledge of what to do in this situation. Brandon then had Danielle approach the desk to give them her mother's information, while they began to take care of her.

Afterwards, Danielle sat down in the waiting room, almost in tears, after they had taken her mother back into the treatment area.

Brandon sat down next to her, while Marlene sat on the other side of her. "We'll wait with you, if you want," he said.

Danielle, who had been looking down at the floor, looked up at him. "Thanks, I really appreciate it," she said. "But you really don't have to."

"True," Brandon said. "But I think we had better. You're all by yourself and probably could use the company."

"I really need to call my dad," Danielle said. "He had an accident. That's why we're coming home when we did from my aunt and uncle's. My older brothers are with him. He ain't hurt bad, but I know he'd want to know."

"Here," Brandon said, handing her his cell phone. "Call your dad. We'll stay here until they manage to get up here. We'll help you keep watch on your mom."

"Thank you so much," Danielle said, crying.

"Call your dad," Brandon ordered. "He might be worried about you too."

"Thanks," Danielle sniffed, as she got up and hugged Brandon, then started to dial her home number.

Brandon looked over at Marlene. "I'm sorry," he said. "But she needs someone with her until her family gets here. She's a kid and we just couldn't leave her."

"I know," Marlene said, smiling. "You are a good man. I'm so sorry about everything."

Brandon took a deep breath. "Thanks," he said. "It comes with the territory. It's already been a long day for us. Especially for her and her mom. We don't need to make it any longer."

Marlene quietly nodded in agreement. It had already been a very long day.

***

It had already been a long couple of days for Jim Summerlee and fatigue was beginning to set in. Still, he knew that he had to be ready and alert for anything. He also had to appear storng and brave for his two young passengers.

So far, they hadn't been any trouble. Both boys had listened to him and been well-behaved so far. Considering what they had been through themselves, they had been as brave and courageous as any adult could have been.

They knew the creature was very close, by the faint aroma that had made its way inside of the rest area building. They knew it was angry and frustrated by its loud, horrifying shriek, which startled the boys, making them jump.

"It's still out there trying to get us," Steve announced.

Jim nodded. "The storm is waning and it's getting more desperate," he said. "And more hungry."

"How much longer do you think it will be out there?" Gordon asked.

"Probably as long as this storm is going," Steve surmised, before Jim could answer.

It was then Jim sensed something was wrong. He knew that grave danger was coming. Before he could say anything, the creature's hand crashed through the glass door and the adjoining windows they'd only moments ago been looking through.

"Holy shit!" Steve exclaimed, loudly.

"Jesus, look out," Gordon shouted, fearfully.

Jim instinctively pushed the boys aside and out of harm's way as the Wendigo's hand reached furiously for them.

"Head to the bathrooms, boys!" Jim ordered. "It can't reach you there!"

Both boys rushed to the nearest bathroom, but Gordon stopped at the door.

"Wait!" Gordon said loudly as he stopped. "That's the girls' bathroom!"

"Who gives a shit?" Steve asked. "Nobody's going to see us."

Once inside, both boys stood in the doorway, looking out to see what exactly was going on.

Meanwhile, Jim reached into his pouch and pulled out his sharp, silver-bladed knife and a jar of the consecrated earth as the Wendigo blindly felt around for its would-be prey. Jim stuck the blade of his knife into the earth and moved it around in hopes of the knife keeping some of the dirt on it.

Jim waited for his opportunity to strike. When the Wendigo's hand came close to him, he used this chance to thrust the knife deeply into its hand. Once in, he twisted the knife after driving it in. As the Wendigo recoiled in pain, it knocked Jim backwards onto the floor.

Jim fell back hard and was a bit dazed, as the Wendigo pulled its hand out of the building. Gordon and Steve rushed out of the bathroom to help Jim.

"Are you alright?" Gordon asked.

"You okay?" Steve asked.

"Yeah," Jim muttered as they both helped him up.

They could hear the Wendigo out in the snowstorm shrieking in great pain and anguish. Soon, the shrieks grew very faint and less frequent. Its horrid smell had also great dissipated.

"Is it gone?" Gordon asked.

"For now," Jim replied. "We'll be safe for quite a while."

"Until the next bad storm, right?" Steve asked, but as more of statement than a question.

"Yes," Jim admitted. "That could be next month, or next year, or even ten or twenty years from now."

"So someday in the future it will be back," Gordon concluded.

"Yes," Jim answered as he fumbled through his coat pocket. "You boys should call your mom now. Here…use my cell phone."

Wind Chill Advisory

When John Torrey answered the phone and heard his sister, Danielle, crying on the other end, he knew it was serious. He quickly handed the phone to his dad.

"Here, Dad, you better take this." John exclaimed. "It's Dani."

"Hello?" Matt said. "What is it?"

"We were in an accident," Danielle said. "We were coming home to see you and we were rear-ended just south of Grayling. Mom's been hurt. Right now we're at Mercy Hospital in Grayling."

"Oh, shit," Matt muttered.

"What is it?" John asked.

Matt waved his hand for John to be quiet for a moment, then repeated what Danielle had told him. "Your mother's been hurt in an accident."

"Oh, shit," John said. "Is she hurt real bad?"

"Who's hurt?" Mark asked, just entering the room.

"Mom," John answered. "Go get Mathew."

"Oh, shit," Mark exclaimed, before going to get Mathew.

"How bad is she hurt?" Mathew asked, running into the room.

"Mom thinks she broke her ribs," Danielle replied to Dad's question. "But, we don't know for sure. Some nice people brought us here. The Markways. He's a paramedic. Our cell phones were dead and we couldn't call and they brought us to the hospital."

"Thank God," Matt said. "How did it happen, again?"

"Somebody rear-ended us at a high speed," Danielle explained. "They hit us so hard it pushed us off the road and partly into a ditch. They didn't even stop."

"You said, Mercy Hospital of Gaylord?" Matt asked.

"No, Grayling, Dad," Danielle said, correcting him.

"Are you okay?" Matt asked.

"Yeah," Danielle said. "The Markways, they're the people who brought us here, are staying with me, until you guys get here."

"Okay, good," Matt said. "Thank them for me. They do not know how much I appreciate this. Give us some time and we'll be up there as soon as possible. Love you. Goodbye."

Matt hung up the phone.

"What is it?" Mathew asked. "How bad is mom hurt?"

"Dani said she thought she had some broken ribs," Matt explained. "She said some people came by and took her to the hospital in Grayling. Apparently, he's a paramedic. Can you drive us up in your Tahoe, Mathew?"

"Sure, Dad," Mathew said. "I was going to offer to."

"Good," Matt said. "We'll fill up before we get on I-75."

"Thank God for guardian angels," John said.

"Amen to that," Mark agreed.

"Okay guys, let's go," Matt said.

Within five minutes, they were loaded up into the Chevy Tahoe and heading towards Mercy Hospital in Grayling.

As they headed on their way, Matt hoped and prayed that Rachel was alright.

***

"Are you alright?" the state police trooper asked Cassandra through the driver's side window.

"Are you shitting me?" she thought. *"Hell no, I'm not alright, I'm goddamn disfigured."* All she could muster was an affirmative nod.

"Is your door locked?" the state trooper asked.

Cassandra unlocked the door, and the state trooper then opened it.

"Are you badly hurt?" he asked. "Can you move at all?"

Cassandra could only nod. She saw and heard the reflection of the ambulance siren nearby.

"Okay, what do we have?" asked the paramedic as he approached the scene.

"A woman, age unknown, with some head trauma," the state trooper replied.

"Okay," the paramedic replied, who then reached over and unfastened her safety belt.

The two men then helped her over to the ambulance. As she was helped inside and onto the gurney, she could not help but notice someone already in the ambulance and heavily sedated. Cassandra knew it was the man that she hit, but was too caught up in her own personal misery and devastation to care or pay him much attention.

Her world had already come crashing down before the accident and was now totally shattered and in ruins. As Cassandra Stern was being rushed to the nearest hospital, she was hurt, devastated and angry.

Very angry.

***

By the time Max Stern arrived home, he was damn near livid. He was irate over the trip to Houston actually being unnecessary. He was pissed over the number of delays that he had to endure because of the storm. He was irritated over Cassandra not answering her phone, since he needed her to pick him up from the airport.

The "next-to-last" straw was being put in a position of being forced to "bum" a ride from a colleague who lived nearby. Max hated to inconvenience anybody.

So, by the time Max arrived home, then found and read Cassandra's letter, he suddenly became too calm and eerily cool, even as he was filled with great anger.

He took a deep breath as if meditating and began to get methodical in his anger and retribution.

Max went into Cassandra's business account that had his name on it and drained it of the amount he gave her to start her business, leaving her with half of what she had.

Then he began to go through her clothes and belongings that she left behind, gathering them up for donation to charity.

He then called his lawyer for legal advice and protection. Max would start divorce proceedings and make sure she did not get one red cent from him. Just to make sure, he began removing her name from his accounts that she had her name on. He did this to the ones that he actually could.

Max Stern was going to get his pound of flesh. He would see to that. And it would be very painful.

He didn't appreciate being made a fool of. So, while the urge to kill Cassandra was great, he knew the best way to hurt was where she was most vulnerable.

Financially and economically.

Max had truly loved her. So much in fact that he overlooked many of her shortcomings, such as her lack of humanity and her selfishness. If Max was going to get hurt, then he would see to it that she did too.

One thing he was sure of was that Cassandra was going to feel a great deal of pain for a very long time.

***

Rachel wasn't sure how much time had passed since arriving at Mercy Hospital, but she knew that she was in a room and her pain had greatly subsided. It seemed like it'd been hours that had passed.

Danielle was seated in a chair. She was accompanied by Brandon and Marlene Markway.

"Hi," Rachel muttered.

"Hi, Mom," Danielle said. "I asked the Markways to stay with me. How are you doing?"

"Okay, I guess," Rachel replied, hoarsely. "So, what's the prognosis? Did the doctor say anything?"

"I'll go get him," Brandon offered, and he then left the room.

Within moments, a doctor in his mid-forties walked in. "How are you feeling?" he asked. "Better, I hope. I'm Dr. Franklin."

"I'm feeling a little better," Rachel answered.

"Well, you were in some rough shape when you arrived," Dr. Franklin continued. "You had two broken ribs and a ruptured spleen. We took care of those injuries with some surgery. Unfortunately, because of those injuries we couldn't save the baby. There was too much damage to the fetus. I am truly sorry."

Tears welled up in Rachel's eyes. "No," she muttered, still hoarse after the surgery.

"I'm sorry," Dr. Franklin said. "We did everything we could, but there was no heartbeat. I'm sorry for your loss. If there is anything I can do, please do not hesitate to ask."

Dr. Franklin nodded, then quietly left the room.

Rachel began sobbing, "No, no, no," she gasped.

"I'm sorry, Mom," Danielle said, as she leaned over and hugged Rachel as best as she could. "Dad and the boys are on their way. Hopefully they'll be here soon."

Rachel could only cry and shake her head in disbelief. The news of losing her baby left her devastated.

"Look, I'll take Danielle to get something to eat," Brandon announced. "I know she's probably getting hungry, because I know I am. You want to come too, honey?"

"I'll stay," Marlene offered.

"Are you sure?" Brandon asked.

"Yes," Marlene said. "I can relate to her on this."

"Okay," Brandon said, with some hesitation as he and Danielle left for the cafeteria.

"Thank you," Rachel said.

"I know what you're going through," Marlene admitted. "I've had two miscarriages recently."

Rachel nodded. "I had one some years ago," she said. "I just feel so bad about it all. I feel just awful."

"It wasn't your fault," Marlene said, trying to console Rachel. "You were in a car accident."

Rachel shook her head. "I feel like it is, though," she said. "When I first found out, I blamed Matt for it. We had three sons in their twenties and Danielle. I had my personal training business that was doing well and I did not want any more kids. I was so mad at him. I even thought about getting an abortion. I was absolutely terrible. I shouldn't have come home when I did."

Marlene wasn't sure what to say or do at first. "But you didn't have an abortion," she said. "Maybe by not going through with it, you really wanted to have this baby."

"But, I was so terrible," Rachel continued. "I hurt Matt because of something I did not want at first. I hurt him because of my own selfishness. I feel like I caused so much damage."

Marlene's eyes began to well up with tears also. "I know what that is like too," she sobbed. "Only mine was wanting to have children. I've been too sensitive or made it so he had to walk on eggshells. I put what I wanted before ourselves. We had a fight while on a ski weekend with friends and that's why we were coming home. I blew up at him over a joke he made about motherhood. I made a big deal over nothing and he had enough."

Rachel reached over and squeezed her hand. "That makes two of us," she said. "It's amazing how stupid we can be. We want good men, but when we get them, we treat them like shit, when we're angry about something else."

"Yeah, but I pissed off our friends and even my brother," Marlene confessed. "I think I caused a great deal of damage myself. I just don't know."

"Thanks for being here with me," Rachel said. "I have somebody to commiserate with."

Marlene squeezed Rachel's hand in return. "Yeah," she sobbed.

After a long pause of silence, Rachel finally spoke, just as a different nurse entered the room. "Not to change the subject, but what do you think that thing was we heard out in the storm?" she asked.

"I have no idea," Marlene said, while nodding. "But it sounded godawful. Especially that smell. Maybe it was Bigfoot or something."

"It sounded much bigger," Rachel said. "And you're right, that smell was terrible. It reminded me of something rotting. I just wonder what it was."

"The Wendigo," the nurse said, momentarily forgetting where she was and injecting herself into the conversation.

"The what?" Marlene asked.

"The Wendigo," the nurse repeated. "It sounds like you're describing a legend of my people. I'm sorry, I didn't mean to eavesdrop, I'm your nurse, Mrs. Torrey.

My given name is Fawn. Fawn Summerlee. I am Ojibway. I was reassigned and pulling double duty from us being short due to the storm. I know I probably shouldn't have said anything, and it was very unprofessional of me, but I think I know what you thought you heard."

"So what we heard was supposed to have been a Native American legend?" Marlene asked.

"It sounds like it," Fawn continued. "My husband Jim is Ojibway and his grandfather is a medicine man, so we know about our heritage and our legends. It sure sounds like you had an encounter with one by what you described."

"So this is real and not a myth?" Marlene asked.

"Apparently," Rachel said. "We heard it, smelled it and before you and your husband arrived and right after the accident, I thought I caught a glimpse of it."

"You were very lucky, then" Fawn said. "Let me get your vitals first and I'll tell you about it."

"Please do," Rachel said.

"Yes," Marlene agreed "We'd like to know more about it."

***

"Hello, Mr. Stern," said a voice on the phone. "We thought you should know that your wife was badly injured in an accident. This is Mercy Hospital Grayling. I'm Head Nurse Dawn Kravitz."

"Really?" Max asked. "How bad is she?"

"She's had some head and face trauma," the nurse replied. "But she is stable and going to be alright."

"Really?" Max asked again. "Face trauma?"

"Unfortunately, due to the cuts and abrasions, she may need some more surgery down the road," the nurse continued. "But plastic surgeons can do wonders these days. We were supposed to contact you, being her spouse and all. Is there anything else we can do?"

"Yeah, fuck her!" Max snapped. "It serves the bitch right for leaving me in the first place for her lover, goddammit. Goodbye."

The nurse was stunned and quietly hung up the phone. This would be fodder for future gossip outside of work.

Max took another drink from his bottle of Vat69 as he both celebrated and mourned the end of his marriage. At this point, he no longer cared if she lived or died. She had made her choice. Now she had to live with it. No matter how horrible the choices and their consequences were.

Digging Out

"Boy, that thing sounds horrible," Marlene commented on what Fawn Summerlee had just told them about the Wendigo.

"Like I said, of all the evil beings in our legends, the Wendigo is the most terrifying," Fawn said. "It is the worst. It is a manifestation of mankind's worst traits, like greed, selfishness, and other bad behaviors."

"Kind of like our own personal demons come to hunt us down and eat us," Marlene suggested.

"Yes, in a way," Fawn said. "If you have any more questions, I'll be around. Now if you'll excuse me, I need to check on other patients."

"Thank you, Fawn," Rachel said. "For everything."

"You're welcome," Fawn said. "Please don't tell anybody I told you. I hope I didn't scare you too much."

"You did, but it helped us," Marlene said. "We appreciate it."

Fawn nodded, smiled and left the room.

"What do you think?" Marlene asked. "Do you believe her?"

"I don't know," Rachel said. "I sure can't explain what we heard and smelled. What I found most interesting was that she told us it represented the worst a human can do to another human, and ultimately oneself. She also said as long as we put our families first instead of ourselves we would have nothing to fear from it. That it would starve and die out. Maybe it was some kind of parable."

"Like Bible stories," Marlene said. "So, we kind of brought this on ourselves by the way we acted."

"Yes," Rachel said. "Maybe, by realizing how bad we both were, it saved us from a different fate."

"God, I hope so," Marlene said. "I'm more afraid of losing Brandon than being out there with any legend or monster."

"Same here with Matt," Rachel admitted. "Apparently, we both have some making up to do. But at least we have that chance to do so."

"I guess we both passed a test," Marlene said. "Hopefully we can work it out with our husbands."

"Why don't you go catch up with Brandon?" Rachel suggested. "I appreciate your company, but I'm getting very tired and need to get some rest."

***

After hours of surgeries and procedures, Cassandra Stern was sedated and resting comfortably. She was too tired and medicated to really care about her looks or even her future with Max.

At this point she was still clinging to the hope she would be able to work something out with him.

Occasionally, her peaceful slumber would be interrupted by the nightmare of something she saw while she was still in her car. In her sedative induced mind, she wondered if it had been real. It seemed too real and awful for it to be the result of a hallucination from a bump on the head.

It had a horrid smell and terrifying shriek that she could not forget.

Soon the nightmare passed and she slid back into a gentle peaceful sleep. The first one she had in quite some time.

It would also probably be her last one for quite a while.

***

Andrew knew that he'd been unconscious for quite a while. He didn't know how long exactly, but he sensed that it had been for hours. He was still very groggy and out of it. He figured he was heavily sedated because he didn't feel much of anything.

He could barely open his eyes. What he could see was very blurred, because of his heavy eyelids. In spite of this, he knew that some medical staff were all around him. He could hear muffled voices and sounds. Andrew wanted to talk, but couldn't.

For all intents and purposes, Andrew was a prisoner in his own body, held captive by his own injuries and the painkilling drugs.

Even though he was semi-conscious and unable to move or think clearly, he could not shake the horrific vision of the creature he'd witnessed. The image of it was seared into his memory.

It was part of the nightmare that had awakened him to this state of semi-consciousness.

For him, it had been terrifying enough when he was awake, so he did not want to dream about it.

As hard as Andrew tried to wake up, he was too battered, weak and medicated. He wished that he could move both in reality and his dreams.

Once again, sleep overtook him and the nightmares of the Wendigo returned.

And as bad as that was, it would pale in comparison to what the future had in store for him.

That would be much worse.

***

"Well, it looks like the worst of the storm has passed," Jim Summerlee announced to his two young companions.

"It feels like it's been snowing forever," Steve complained.

"Not forever, but long enough," Gordon said.

"Well, are you two ready?" Jim asked.

"Are we still meeting our mom in Midland?" Steve asked.

"Yes, I told her that we would meet her at Culver's," Jim replied. "It's a restaurant."

"Okay?" Gordon said.

"Are you sure it's safe to go out there now?" Steve asked. "Is it really safe to leave now?"

"Yes," Jim said. "I think it's safe, now. Let's go."

All three headed to Jim's Jeep Wagoneer and climbed in. He then started his vehicle.

"It will be good to see Mom," Gordon said as Jim wheeled his Jeep towards the expressway.

"Hopefully she's not pissed anymore," Steve said.

Jim laughed. "I wouldn't worry too much," he offered. "By the time we meet up with her, I think she'll be over being mad."

***

Marlene hoped that Brandon was through being angry with her. As she entered the cafeteria, she quickly located the table where Brandon and Danielle were sitting. When Brandon saw Marlene, he waved for her to come over and join them. Marlene walked over and sat down next to Brandon.

"How's my mom?" Danielle asked.

"She told me to come down here, because she was tired and needed some rest," Marlene replied.

"Okay," Danielle said. "Well, I'm done. I think I'll go back and wait in her room then."

"Alright," Brandon said. "We'll be back in a little bit."

"Okay," Danielle said. "See you in a little while."

They watched as Danielle dropped her tray off and left the cafeteria.

"So, how are you doing?" Brandon asked.

Marlene took a deep breath and exhaled. "Well," she said. "You're either going to think I'm nuts or laugh at me, but something about all of this put things in perspective."

"Really?" Brandon asked, surprised.

"Yes," Marlene answered softly. "First off, let me sincerely apologize to you for everything. I've been such a bitch to you and for that I am truly sorry. You are a very good man who deserves to be treated better. A lot better. I feel like I have failed in treating you right."

Brandon didn't know what to say and was speechless.

"Please forgive me," Marlene said as tears welled up in her eyes. "I do not want to lose you. You are the best thing that ever happened to me."

Brandon was only able to blurt out a "Really?"

"I would never have realized it, if all this hadn't happened," Marlene admitted.

"You think this was some kind of fate?" Brandon asked.

"Yes, maybe," Marlene continued. "If we hadn't left when we did, we, or rather you, wouldn't have rescued Rachel and Danielle. I think all this happened for a reason. It had to."

"Maybe," Brandon agreed. "I don't know. I've been sitting here wondering that myself. Maybe this was some kind of catalyst for us working things out."

Marlene smiled. "I sure hope so," she said. "Come on, let's go."

"Okay," Brandon said as he stood up and put his tray away.

After leaving the cafeteria, they headed down the hallway. As they approached a small bathroom for an individual, Marlene grabbed Brandon's hand and led him inside.

Once inside and the door was closed, they were both soon partially undressed and going at it. Brandon lifted her up, with her back braced against the wall as he began to bore into her with great intensity. For being what Marlene referred to as *fast and furious,* it was the best spontaneous sex they had in quite some time.

When they finished, both knew everything was going to be alright.

***

"You alright?" Matt asked, as Rachel woke up to see him sitting next to her bed.

"Yes, I'm fine now," Rachel replied, hoarsely. "When did you get here? How long have you been waiting?"

"Not too long," Matt replied.

Rachel then noticed her sons and Danielle near the foot of her hospital bed. Tears welled up in her eyes. "It's so good to see you all," she said.

"How are you doing, Mom?" Mathew asked.

"Better now," Rachel answered. "Where are the Markways? Did they leave?"

"They're out in the waiting room," Danielle said. "They thought it was a little too crowded."

"Please go get them," Rachel requested. "They saved my life. Please have them come back before they leave."

"Okay," Danielle said, before going out to retrieve the Markways.

"Did you meet them?" Rachel asked.

"Yes, we did," Matt answered. "We thanked them. I told them that you would insist that we take them to dinner when you recovered, as an expression of our gratitude. They said it wasn't necessary, but we insisted."

Soon, the Markways were back in the crowded room, standing next to Rachel's bed.

"How are you doing?" Brandon asked.

"Better, much better," Rachel said as she reached out and touched Brandon's hand. "Thank you so much for everything."

"You're welcome," Brandon said. "But I really didn't do much."

"You rescued me and my daughter," Rachel said, as she then reached over and squeezed Marlene's hand. "That was a lot. And thanks for all you did too. I appreciate it. You helped me a great deal."

Marlene squeezed Rachel's hand back "I think we helped each other," she said. "I think I made a new friend too."

Rachel smiled. "That goes for me as well," she said. "I am grateful for both of you. We owe you both, so much."

"I don't know about that," Brandon commented. "Your family insisted that we be treated to dinner when you are recovered. But you really don't have to do that."

"I'm afraid you're outvoted Brandon," Matt said. "I know Rachel would insist too."

"You betcha," Rachel agreed.

"Okay, I know when I'm licked," Brandon said.

Rachel leaned her head back and yawned.

"You okay, Mom?" John asked.

"Yes," Rachel answered. "I'm still a little tired."

"Well, I think that's our queue to leave," Brandon announced. "You need your rest and family time and we need to hit the road. We'll be in touch."

"Again, thank you so much for all that you both did," Rachel said. "We greatly appreciate it."

"Yes, thanks," Matt said as he got up and shook Brandon's hand.

Before leaving, Brandon and Marlene shook hands with Mathew, Mark and John. "And you stay out of trouble," he said as he hugged Danielle.

"I'll try," Danielle said, as she then hugged Marlene.

Marlene went back and squeezed Rachel's hand. "You have a speedy recovery," she said. "We'll see you in a few weeks."

"Okay," Rachel said. "Kids, why don't you see the Markways off so I can talk to your dad?"

"Okay," Mathew said. "Come on guys."

The Markways and the four Torrey children then shuffled out of the room.

"You alright?" Matt asked.

Tears welled up in Rachel's eyes and she shook her head. "No," she managed to gulp. "I lost our baby Matt, and it's all my fault."

"I know," Matt said. "The doctor told me while you were sleeping."

"I'm so sorry," Rachel continued. "I screwed up. Worst of all, I blamed you for everything. I was so terrible. I'm so sorry for treating you like that. I love you so much."

"It's alright, Rachel," Matt responded, reaching over and holding her hand. "You have nothing to apologize for. All is forgiven and it's in the past."

"I'm just so sorry," Rachel said, crying.

"We'll get through this, Rachel," Matt said "I'm just glad you're still here. The thought of losing you would be unbearable. You're my soul mate, after all."

"Come here," Rachel said holding her arms out. "I need a kiss."

Matt stood up and leaned over as Rachel kissed him passionately.

"I'll do my best to make it up to you," she said, when they finished.

“I’ll hold you to that,” Matt said. “Let’s get better first.”

“Definitely,” Rachel agreed. “Right now, I wish I could go home.”

***

Instead of heading for home, Brandon Markway decided to stop at a Holiday Inn Express.

“Why are we stopping here?” Marlene asked, a little surprised.

“Because a hotel room is a hell of lot more comfortable than a small bathroom,” he replied. “And we need to make up for some lost time,”

“We’re going to spend most of the rest of our weekend in bed?” she asked.

“That’s the plan,” he said. “It sounds better every time I think about it.”

Marlene shook her head. “Okay, I’m game. You had better be ready to perform like on our honeymoon.”

“You can count on that,” Brandon said. “I’m up for the challenge. Pun fully intended.”

“I’d better be able to,” Marlene joked, as she knew this was another chance.

***

“Not a chance!” Max Stern snapped at Cassandra’s asking forgiveness and an offer of reconciliation. “You made your fucking choice. Live with it. Fuck you! Goodbye!”

Max slammed the phone down.

Even though Cassandra expected it, she was taken aback and surprised by his anger. She knew that he had a temper, but he’d never really directed it towards her. At least not like that, until now.

Even more upsetting to her was that after three days in the hospital, nobody called or visited her. Not a single solitary family member, so-called friend, business associate or acquaintance bothered to call. Then again, she didn't really have any close friends or relatives that she talked to regularly. She had burned too many bridges in her life.

Now it was coming back to her in spades.

Cassandra Stern never felt so alone in all her life.

A now-solitary life that was well on its way to becoming to her a living hell.

As the snowstorm from Hell continued eastward, the Wendigo continued along with it, claiming victims and devouring them voraciously or giving them heart attacks before they could claim them, inadvertently teaching lessons to some and bringing families together while literally consuming others' lives, here in the wretched, deep bitter snow blizzards. It had preyed on people in Saginaw, Bay City, Port Huron and Sarnia, Canada. It was one and yet many. Its endless hunger still driving its rage and pain.

***

Andrew Furlong was filled with great anger and pain. Internally, he was filled with a lot of rage. But he was too weak and sedated to be demonstrative of it.

Because of his injuries, the doctors had to amputate both legs above the knees, as well as his right arm above the elbow. They said it was the only way they could save his life.

He thought it was ironic that he lost about a third of his body in order to remain alive. In his mind, he was just, simply…..*existing.*

On top of that, the authorities placed a guard outside his door. This was due to the fact that they had matched his handgun with ballistics to the Gilmoe brother's deaths, Eddie's pulverized corpse having a bullet in his shoulder, and Cassandra Stern's windshield.

Andrew knew that he was in deep shit without any way to keep his head above it. He was now a cripple who in all likelihood was going to jail for a very long time.

He wished that he was dead.

Anything would have been better than the life he was going to live.

Storm Aftermath

By the time, what many called the "Storm from Hell" had passed through the state of New York and out to sea. 57 lives across the country had been lost because of it.

Lost amidst all of this was the unknown amount of people that had somehow come up missing. While some would be attributed to human foul play, the majority were victims to something much more horrible and sinister.

By the time the snowstorm had passed, the Wendigo had claimed many victims. Even so, its hunger remained endless and unsated as it wandered on the peripheries of Man's world.

Those it had not managed to kill had their lives changed by it. Some would never be the same or they had been changed by the experience….

***

Matt and Rachel Torrey, along with their kids, celebrated the end of winter with Brandon and Marlene Markway over dinner at Maggiano's Little Italy in Troy.

"I'd like to propose a toast on behalf of our family, to Brandon and Marlene Markway," Matt announced. "We thank you for rescuing my wife and daughter. We thank you. Also for going above and beyond that and staying with them until we arrived. For all that we thank you and are forever appreciative. We'd like to think somewhere along the way we made some new friends"

"Here, here," echoed Mathew, Mark and John, while Rachel and Danielle applauded.

"Raise your glasses," Matt commanded. "To the Markways' much peace, love, joy and happiness."

"Amen," Rachel said.

Everybody clinked their glasses together and toasted.

"You didn't drink your wine," Matt observed, Marlene not drinking. "Is everything alright?"

"Oh, yeah," Marlene said, smiling. "I have an announcement myself to make. Well, actually we both do. I didn't drink because I'm two month's pregnant."

"Oh, wow!" Rachel said. "I am so happy for you!"

"Wait, that's not all," Marlene continued. "We're having twins! They're boys."

"Wow!" Mathew joked. "Two in one shot! Way to go, Brandon!"

"Well, it was a cold winter after all," Brandon replied. "We had to keep warm somehow."

Everybody roared with laughter.

As everyone was talking and congratulating Brandon, Marlene pulled Rachel aside. "So, how are you doing?" she asked. "Is everything alright between you two?"

"They're a lot better now," Rachel replied. "I had to do some deep soul-searching and we had some very long and heartfelt conversations but we, or should I say I, have made amends. I guess the thought of losing him made me realize a few things. That was our mid-life marriage test, I guess. Thank God I am fully recovered now and things have been great between Matt and I. Actually, they couldn't be better. It almost feels like a second honeymoon in a way.

"That's really good," Marlene said. "Glad to hear it all worked out."

"Yes," Rachel said. "Thank God. Other than that, I am going up north for a while to help out my sister. She has cancer and is undergoing more chemo. She could really use my help and the company. Matt suggested it and I agreed. He'll come up on the weekends with Danielle."

"That's good," Marlene said. "Will she be alright?"

"Hopefully," Rachel replied. "She's gotten through the worst of it, but is very tired and weak. As for me and Matt, it's much better now. I may have forgotten and it might have taken me a while to remember, but I finally realized what my priorities should be and that I am married to the best. Sad that it took me almost losing him to realize it. I am lucky. Very lucky."

"Yes, we are," Marlene said, as both women's eyes welled up with tears and they hugged. "We have the best and actually know it. Life is good, even with trying and bad times. Life is good."

***

"Wow, they're playing pretty good," Jim Summerlee said as he watched Gordon and Steve Case play their last game of the season, their league all-star game.

"Yes, they are," Marianne Case agreed, while sitting next to him. "Thanks for coming. I know the boys will be glad to see you."

"Hey, I'm glad too," Jim replied. "They were pretty brave during everything. I am truly sorry about your husband, though."

Marianne Case took a deep breath. "Thank you," she finally said. "The boys told me all about it. Thanks for rescuing them."

"You're welcome," Jim said,

"They had nightmares for awhile afterwards," Marianne said. "Thanks for calling to check on them and setting their minds at ease."

"I thought I had better," Jim said. "They weren't alone there."

They watched Steve score a goal on a pass from Gordon. Both Marianne and Jim stood on their feet and exclaimed, "Yeah!" After a brief celebration, they finally both sat back down.

"The real irony of all this is, the boys are playing better and enjoying hockey more without Richard always harping on them," Marianne confessed. "I hate to say, only knowing you for a short time but, my husband, he could be a real overbearing asshole."

"I know the type," Jim said.

"I would have left him and taken the boys, if he didn't get killed," Marianne confessed. "Especially after he hit Gordon over hockey. That would have been the last straw. I guess I hadn't before because he'd always been involved and around."

Jim nodded. "I understand," he said.

Soon the horn sounded, marking the end of the game.

Both headed to wait near the locker room for the boys to come out after changing and taking their showers. Soon, Steve and Gordon exited with the other hockey players, still a bit wet from the showers.

"Hi boys," Jim said, with a big smile.

"Jim!" Steve exclaimed excitedly. "…er, I mean, Mr. Summerlee! Holy cow!"

"Wow!" Gordon said. "It's great to see you, Sir! Thanks for coming!"

"I wouldn't have missed it, boys," Jim said.

Both boys high-fived Jim, enthusiastically.

"So, how have you been?" Steve asked.

"Oh, pretty good," Jim replied. "How are you two doing?"

"Good," Steve replied.

"Pretty good," Gordon agreed.

"So, what's next?" Jim asked.

Gordon and Steve looked at each other and answered together, "Baseball season."

***

Since the accident, Cassandra Stern's circumstances had changed greatly. Max quickly divorced her. He had even filed while she was still recovering in the hospital. It quickly went from bad to worse.

Since she was the one who cheated and Max was not abusive or cruel, Cassandra received no settlement or alimony.

On top of that, she had to sell her business at way less than what she thought it was worth to pay for lawyers and surgical procedures. Instead of living in a nice house, in a very nice neighborhood like she had grown accustomed to all her life, she had to settle for a meager one-bedroom apartment.

Cassandra no longer had an expensive and fancy wardrobe or nice extras that she had when she was married to Max; it was practically bargain-basement for her. Now that she worked at a job that she once considered beneath her, she had to look for what was on sale when it came to the necessities of life.

She was also still alone. Most men were not interested in her, mainly due to her scars.

She was bitter and alone.

Cassandra's life was now a kind of solitary confinement, only without the jail cell factor.

***

Andrew "Belch" Furlong would be spending at least 25 years-to-life in a mental facility. As bad as *that* was, it was still better than Jackson Prison. It was bad enough being called the "*One-Armed Bandit.*"

Andrew was charged and found guilty in the death of Odell Gilmoe and was charged as an accomplice in the deaths of Jearvis and Marvell Gilmoe. He also had manslaughter charges in Eddie Temple's death and Kevin Shannon and Jeff Sanderson's disappearances. On top of that, he had a multitude of charges for carjacking, drug dealing, attempted murder, numerous firearms charges, and robbery.

The only circumstances keeping him out of a prison were that he was a triple amputee where he would not stand a chance there, and the fact that he told a story of how some kind of monster chased Eddie to his death, killed Jeff and probably Kevin too.

This helped the prosecutor decide that he needed to be incarcerated to a mental facility. The prosecutor assumed that no sane, rational person would tell such a far-out fanciful tale.

The worst punishment of all for him, and the one he found the most horrific and tortuous, was that every night, Andrew had terrifying nightmares of something mysterious and deadly and forever branded into his darkest memories, memories he could never possibly escape from, and they would eventually escort his own soul into an abyss far colder and more desolate than any white-out winter storm: the *Wendigo.*

About the Author

Tom Sawyer is a Michigan writer. Since starting out as a 17-year-old with a weekly newspaper, he has authored the novels *The Lighthouse, Fire Sale, The Sisigwad Papers, the Last Big Hit*, the *Dracula* sequel *Shadows in the Dark*, the acclaimed collection *Dark Harbors,* and *From Paradise to Hell*. He has also written a number of short stories that have been featured in various publications. A lifelong Waterford resident, he and his wife Colleen have three children.

www.downwarden.com/blackbedsheet

www.downwarden.com/blackbedsheet
A mummy of ancient legend vs. a vicious Mexican mafia.
From the author of Nightcrawler
John Reinhard
DIZON
LA
MOMIA
(The Mummy)
Ask for it
wherever
books are sold!
ISBN: 978-0-69231456-2
www.downwarden.com/blackbedsheet
FRED WIEHE
"Dangerously entertaining!"
--Jonathan Maberry,
NY Times bestselling author,
DEAD OF NIGHT
ALERIC:
MONSTER
HUNTER
978-0-9886590-7-0
www.downwarden.com/blackbedsheetstore
"A bullet train tale..of killer creativity
and a thrill worth reading ten times more!"
--S.D. Hintz
Blood Orchard
JASON GEHLERT
-with- Joe Rutigliano
JEREMIAH BLACK
978-0-9858829-9-0
www.downwarden.com/blackbedsheet

Extreme Science Fiction
Read the sensational debut novel!
GENESIS
Book One of the Kingdom Come Series
WADE GARRET
BLACK BED SHEET
www.downwarden.com/blackbedsheetstore
GENESIS
WADE GARRET
NICOLE VLACHOS
NICOLE VLACHOS
BECAUSE THE NIGHT
Vlachos writes "...exactly the kind of book that seeks to join many of today's top writers in revitalizing the genre."
—DarkMedia Online
BECAUSE THE NIGHT
FROM THE AUTHOR OF IN THE ABSENCE OF SUN
AVAILABLE WHERE BOOKS ARE SOLD
www.downwarden.com/blackbedsheetstore
IN EBOOK EVERYWHERE
Bone Sai
A short tale of wicked horror by RUSCHELLE DILLON
WWW.DOWNWARDEN.COM/BLACKBEDSHEET

<u>Wherewolf by Franchisca Weatherman. 978-0-9833773-7-5</u>

When a pack of werewolves hits a small southern town, the local Sheriff realizes this is one case he can not solve alone. He calls in the F.B.I. to help him take down the killers that are taking the lives of the local teens. When the wolves abandon the town for the streets of New Orleans during Mardi-Gras celebrations, the hunters become the hunted in an all-out war where no one may survive....

Morningstars by Nick Kisella

While at his dying wife's bedside, Detective Louis Darque is offered a chance to save her by his biological father, the demon B'lial, but at what price?

Whispers in the Cries

by Matthew Ewald

978-0-9833773-6-8

Hunted by the shadowed entity of his grandfather's past and its brethren of demonic beasts, Randy Conroy must survive the nightmare his grandfather could not. A thrilling ghost tale of the Queen Mary and haunted souls.

Meat City & Other Stories by Jason M. Tucker 978-0-9842136-9-6

Take a trip along the arterial highway, and make a left at the last exit to enter Meat City, where all manner of nasty things are clamoring to greet you. Granger knows what it's like to kill a man. When the corpse of Granger's latest victim staggers to his feet though, all bets are off. These and other slices of horror await you on the raw and bloodied streets. Enjoy your visit . . . .

Nevermore by Nik Kerry

. When Raven's world comes crashing down around her and her thoughts turn to suicide, this is exactly what she does. As she swings the last swing of her life, she jumps off, sprouts wings, and flies away to another world where she finds a group of teenagers just her age who accept her into their lives.

The Return of
SPRING-HEELED
Jack
Jennifer Caress
"Reminds me of
early Stephen King.."
--Multiverse Reviews
www.downwarden.com/blackbedsheet
Jennifer Caress
The Return of
SPRING-HEELED
Jack
978-0-9858829-7-6

27 THRILLING TALES & VERSES OF HORROR,
SUSPENSE AND IRONY TO JOSTLE AND
SHOCK THE IMAGINATION
Blood
Verse
PATRICK JAMES RYAN
"AN EXCITING AND ORIGINAL COLLECTION
FROM A VOICE IN HORROR WE'LL SOON ALL BE READING!"
-- Black Hamster TV
www.downwarden.com/blackbedsheetstore
Blood
Verse
PATRICK JAMES RYAN
ISBN: 978-0-9886590-3-2

"Outstanding, terrifying and inspiring!"
--Francy Weatherman, radio show host Francy & Friends
A diverse anthology
by over 30 rising authors
in tribute to writer Yvonne Mason
Compiled & edited by
Kelly J. Koch
Blessings
from the
DARKNESS
downwarden.com/blackbedsheetstore or wherever books are sold
978-0-6159489-3-5

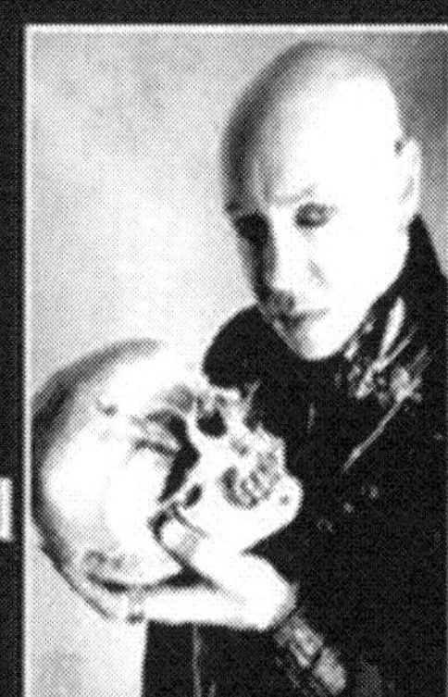

NOCTURNAL OFFERINGS

Alan Draven

www.downwarden.com/blackbedsheet

www.downwarden.com/blackbedsheet

Sponsored by Black Bed Sheet

Watch BLACK HAMSTER TV on Veetle.com

Listen to Francy & Friends radio show

A vicious satanic cult. Jim DiMario's daughter.
She must be saved.
Inspired by true events
OUTER DARKNESS
BART BREVIK
OUTER DARKNESS
BART BREVIK
www.downwarden.com/BLACKBEDSHEET
978-0-9833773-0-6
OUR TRUE NATURE LIES WITHIN A STRAIN... ...OF INHUMAN DESIGN.
HUMAN NATURE
A NOVEL OF INHUMAN TERROR
MATTHEW EWALD
www.downwarden.com
blackbedsheet
BLACK BED SHEET
978-0-9842136-6-5
"Mommy Dearest meets The Exorcist, thrilling & deeply disturbing"
–Francy Weatherman, internet radio show host
A mother.
A daughter.
A demon...
Read the novel
Charla
ALEXANDER BERESFORD
ISBN: 978-0-1475085966
www.downwarden.com/blackbedsheet

We employ and recommend:

Foreign Translations

Cinta García de la Rosa
(Spanish Translation)
Writer, Editor, Proofreader, Translator
cintagarciadelarosa@gmail.com
http://www.cintagarciadelarosa.com
http://cintascorner.com

Bianca Johnson
(Italian Translation)
Writer, Editor, Proofreader, Translator
http://facebook.com/bianca.cicciarelli

EDITOR STAFF

Felicia Aman
http://www.abttoday.com
http://facebook.com/felicia.aman

Kelly J. Koch
http://dressingyourbook.com

Tyson Mauermann
http://speculativebookreview.blogspot.com

Kareema S. Griest
http://facebook.com/kareema.griest

Mary Genevieve Fortier
https://www.facebook.com/MaryGenevieveFortierWriter
http://www.stayingscared.com/Nighty%20Nightmare.html

Shawna Platt
www.angelshadowauthor.webs.com/

Adrienne Dellwo
http://facebook.com/adriennedellwo
http://chronicfatigue.about.com/

William Cook
http://lnkd.in/bnC-yMd
http://www.amazon.com/Blood-Related

and HORNS